Donut Disturb

Ellie Alexander

St. Martin's Paperbacks

First published in the United States by St. Martin's Paperbacks, an imprint of St. Martin's Publishing Group.

DONUT DISTURB

Copyright © 2022 by Katherine Dyer-Seeley.
Excerpt from *Muffin but the Truth* copyright © 2022 by Katherine Dyer-Seeley.

All rights reserved.

For information, address St. Martin's Publishing Group, 120 Broadway, New York, NY 10271.

www.stmartins.com

ISBN: 978-1-250-78946-4

Our books may be purchased in bulk for promotional, educational, or business use. Please contact your local bookseller or the Macmillan Corporate and Premium Sales Department at 1-800-221-7945, ext. 5442, or by email at MacmillanSpecialMarkets@macmillan.com.

Printed in the United States of America

St. Martin's Paperbacks edition / July 2022

10 9 8 7 6 5 4 3 2 1

To Rochelle and John,
A real Ashland love story

Chapter One

They say that love runs deep. After a particularly cold and snowy winter, spring had made its return to our little hamlet, Ashland, Oregon, where the first blooms were pushing up through the ground, reminding us that even in the midst of winter's deep slumber, magic was bubbling beneath the surface. Just like love. Sometimes you couldn't see it, but it was always there, pulsing through our veins, underneath the top layer of our skin. The depth of my love for my hometown had only grown since my once estranged husband, Carlos, had decided to plant roots in Ashland with me. We had spent the last blissful months creating new routines together: leisurely Sunday mornings savoring French press on our back deck while being serenaded by cooing doves and flittering finches; Carlos tending to the vines and our ever-growing clientele at our organic winery, Uva; and more than anything else, curling up in his arms every night knowing that we were a team—we were in this together. I couldn't believe how seamlessly he had adapted to life on land.

Our first years of marriage had taken us far from Ashland's shores, from one exotic port to the next. We had traversed the globe, visiting crowded cities and vacant gold sand beaches. That life had been filled with adventure and a sense of wanderlust, but it had also been lonely. Despite being constantly surrounded by groups of happy passengers on the *Amour of the Seas,* where we both worked as chefs, my time at sea had been solitary. It wasn't until I had come home to Ashland that I realized quite how isolated my lifestyle had been on the boutique cruise ship. That had changed dramatically since immersing myself in the day-to-day operations of running our family bakeshop, Torte.

Ashland might be small in size, but it was mighty in its ability to draw everyone in and capture us under her spell. That could be due to the fact that the Oregon Shakespeare Festival's theater campus was in the middle of town. The artistic community was the lifeblood of Ashland, attracting actors, musicians, playwrights, and artists who worked in every medium to our remote corner of southern Oregon. Some of Ashland's charm could also be attributed to the stunning landscapes that swept out in every direction through the surrounding valley. Flaxen rolling hills, dense old-growth forests, and a bevy of wildlife hedged in the plaza, which resembled an Elizabethan village. Visitors often commented that it looked as if every shop and storefront had been plucked straight from the pages of a Shakespearean manuscript.

I couldn't argue with that analogy. After traveling the world, I knew without a doubt that I was incredibly lucky to live in this place that had become such a part of me. It was hard to imagine my old life, and I didn't let a day go by without pausing in gratitude for the abundance of good things that had come with deciding to make Ashland my permanent home again.

That thought ran through my mind as I assembled ingredients for my first bake of the morning. I had arrived early at Torte, our family bakeshop, before the rest of my staff. Having the commercial kitchen to myself for an hour was my favorite way to start the day. It gave me time to center myself before the rush of customers, the whirl of mixers, the pulse of coffee beans in the grinder, and being pulled a thousand different directions throughout the day as my team whipped up the most delectable sweet and savory pastries in the Rogue Valley. Not that I was biased or anything.

I'm sure every small business owner can relate to the inordinate amount of work it took to keep our shops thriving. I never minded having a lengthy task list. I preferred having multiple projects on the docket and enjoyed that I never knew what the day might bring. One day we might be baking dozens upon dozens of buttercream-and-jam-filled macarons. The next we might be piping elaborate Swiss buttercream roses on a tiered wedding cake. It wasn't just the bakeshop that kept me on my toes either. I also helped Carlos manage Uva, our small vineyard outside of town. Mainly I focused on vendor relationships and staffing for the tasting room. As if that wasn't enough on our plate, we had recently expanded with a seasonal ice cream shop, Scoops, that we were in the process of prepping to reopen with the return of spring weather.

This morning my first project was recipe testing for a special client. I tied on a cheery red Torte apron with our teal blue filigree logo—a single-layer torte. My parents had opened the bakeshop when I was young. They had picked our signature royal colors as an homage to the

Bard. Touches of Shakespeare were evident throughout the two-story space. Upstairs we kept a rotating quote on our chalkboard menu, usually something by William Shakes himself, but we also liked to toss in modern poetry and the occasional meme. This week's quote was a nod to love: "Love alters not with his brief hours and weeks, but bears it out even to the edge of doom."

The first floor of the bakeshop housed our espresso and pastry counter and a collection of cozy seating in front of large windows that offered our guests a firsthand view of the bustling plaza. The red and teal theme continued in the corrugated metal wainscoting. There were stacks of books, games, and buckets of chalk for our vanilla steamer customers, who happily entertained themselves coloring on the base of the chalkboard menu while their parents and grandparents sipped cappuccinos and noshed on lemon tarts.

An expansion a few years ago had allowed us to take over the basement space as well. We had moved our baking operations downstairs, which had dramatically improved our kitchen square footage. The new kitchen was bright and light, with marble countertops, a distressed bar, wood laminate flooring, and baking zones. The open-concept kitchen had been a labor of love for Mom and me. We had made every decision, down to where to position light switches and outlets. Our goal was to create a kitchen that had good, natural flow. I think we had achieved that with a mixing zone featuring neat rows of our workhorse mixers and a decorating zone with bright overhead lighting and pull-out drawers for tools, sparkling sugars, and sprinkles.

The pièce de résistance, though, was the massive built-in wood-fired oven that we had unearthed in the construction process. The fireplace took up nearly half of the far brick wall. That area was deemed the bread zone. Huge stainless steel rolling carts flanked the fireplace. Soon loaves of rising bread would wait on the carts for their turn in the oven. We could feed two birds with one scone, since there was no need to proof the bread in a traditional oven. The heat radiating off the bricks did the work for us.

The unique wood oven was always a conversation starter with our guests. Customers who enjoyed their coffee and breakfast downstairs on the couches and chairs adjacent to the kitchen loved the earthy vibe and heavenly aroma of applewood burning in the oven. My team and I loved it for that and also because baking rustic breads and hand pies in the pizza oven elevated flavor profiles and added a nice touch of char to our products.

I had already added a fresh bundle of applewood to the oven and made a pot of strong coffee, so I turned my attention to my notes for our special client, who happened to be a very dear old friend—Thomas Adams.

Thomas and I had known each other since childhood. We dated in high school but then went our separate ways. He had stayed in Ashland to attend Southern Oregon University and train to be a police officer, while I ventured to New York for culinary school. Our paths had crossed again when I returned home. At first there had been a few awkward moments while we tried to figure out where we stood with each other. Fortunately we had landed on friendship. As proof that things always work out the way they're meant to, Thomas had gotten engaged to a fellow detective, Kerry, and Torte was catering the wedding.

Detective Kerry was much more private than Thomas. In fact, even after I'd known her for a few years, she had rarely divulged anything about her personal life or past. Maybe that was why they were a good match. Their personalities were in balance. Thomas was gregarious and outgoing with a low-key personality. Having grown up in Ashland, he knew everyone in town by name. His mom owned A Rose by Any Other Name, the flower shop next door. Kerry kept things close to her chest, but lately I felt like I was starting to see through some of the tiny cracks in her external armor. We had been spending quite a bit of time together with wedding preparations, and one thing that I had come to appreciate about her was her ability to hold space for people when they were in the throes of crisis.

I couldn't imagine the things she must have seen in her line of work. I had come to realize that she used her firm boundaries as a coping mechanism the same way Thomas used his lighthearted approach when it came to serving the community.

Kerry had wanted a simple courthouse wedding, but Thomas was a big dreamer with visions of inviting the entire town to their nuptials. It left to his own devices, he might have sent out invitations to everyone in the Rogue Valley. But after some negotiating (a skill every married couple needed to learn to master—myself included), they had landed on a picnic wedding in Ashland's crown jewel, Lithia Park. Janet, Thomas's mom, and my mom had been sewing pretty patchwork-quilt picnic blankets for each of the guests. The invitations had requested that everyone dress in spring pastels. Thomas and Kerry were to be married by local judge Mimi Barbarelli at the outdoor band shell the last weekend in May. The park would already be a symphony of spring blooms, yet in addition to nature's bounty, Janet was arranging rows and rows of flower garlands to drape across the band shell. We would hang pale pink, yellow, and blue paper globes from waxy oak trees. Torte was catering picnic boxes for each of the guests, along with the wedding cake, a groom's cake, and an assortment of Thomas and Kerry's favorite donuts.

Instead of a traditional ceremony and reception, they intended to exchange vows and then hand the entertainment over to my bestie, Lance, the artistic director at the Oregon Shakespeare Festival, who had sketched out grand visions of romantic sonnets and select pieces of Shakespeare's works to be performed by actors from the company, followed by an aerial spectacular with Curtain Climbers Dance Company. The ethereal dance in motion would include silks, hammocks, and a trapeze, and combine elements of yoga, gymnastics, and dance. He had wanted to cap the night with a full orchestra.

"Dearest," Lance had said to Kerry at our last meeting, when she had rebutted the idea of hiring the Rogue Symphony in addition to everything else. "Why have a beautiful band shell without actually utilizing it? Trust me, weddings require dancing. After your love and Torte's delectable picnic spreads have satiated everyone, Mother Nature will dim the lights, and we'll ask everyone to roll up their blankets and get to their feet to spend an evening under the stars tripping the light fantastic."

"Tripping the light fantastic?" Thomas had scrunched his face. "Who says that?"

"Uh, moi." Lance had tapped his chest and continued on with his grandiose plans for their wedding.

We had all chuckled. Everyone in the room knew that Lance meant well, and that there was no arguing with him once he set his sights on a "vision." In truth, I think Kerry appreciated not having to sweat any of the details. Torte was taking care of the food, Janet was overseeing decorations, and Lance would ensure that this wedding was the talk of town for years to come, so Thomas and Kerry simply needed to show up and enjoy themselves. Although Kerry did win the battle of the bands, putting her foot down on hiring the Rogue Symphony and opting for a local jazz trio instead.

Coming up with the perfect wedding menu had proved more challenging than I expected. I thumbed through my notebook until I landed on the list of potential recipes for the picnic boxes and forced myself to concentrate.

I wanted to make sure the menu was delicious and reflective of the celebratory nature of a wedding but also included food that guests could actually eat while sitting on blankets in the park. Anything that required cutting was out. As was anything that needed to be kept warm. Nor did we want to serve the wedding guests food that was messy or drippy and risk spills down the front of cocktail dresses and expensive suits.

We had been experimenting with layered sandwiches and a variety of pastas and green salads. The last few weeks we had taken to crowdsourcing the potential wedding menu. Everything we tested got shared with Torte customers upstairs, and I had been keeping copious notes on customers' feedback.

Today I wanted to try a new combination for a club sandwich made on our rustic bread, along with Mom's famous potato salad. But first, I was going to focus on something sweet—a fruit salsa with cinnamon crisps for dipping. They might work nicely as an appetizer in the picnic boxes, and even if they were too messy for the reception, we could feature them on the specials board at Torte.

To start, I brushed hand-rolled tortillas with melted butter infused with fresh orange and lemon zest. Then I sprinkled them liberally with a mixture of cinnamon and vanilla sugar with the faintest hint of cardamom. Once I dusted them completely with the sugary spice, I slid them into the wood-fired oven to crisp. While they toasted, I gathered all of the fresh fruit included in our weekly deliveries and began chopping apples and pears. I tossed them in a large bowl with fresh lime and more lemon and orange juice. Next I added raspberries, halved cherries and grapes, strawberries, pineapple chunks, and kiwi slices. The colorful fruit certainly looked appetizing. I mixed in a jar of our homemade marmalade and a splash of coconut extract. Soon the kitchen smelled of citrus and cinnamon, one of my favorite combinations. I removed the crisped tortillas from the oven and broke them into large chip-like pieces. I dipped one into the fruit salsa. My taste buds sang with delight at the melody of fruit flavors, which mingled with the sweet and spicy chips.

This was a winner in my book. I couldn't wait to share it with the team and get their thoughts. With one potential picnic recipe down, I turned my attention to a new spin on a club sandwich. I began by cutting our rustic seven-grain bread into thick slices. I arranged the bread on an oven-safe tray and brushed each slice with olive oil infused with rosemary. The bread would toast just long enough to crisp up. The club sandwich was a classic and something that pleased most palates. For the wedding boxes, I wanted to elevate it with additions of avocado mayo, basil pesto, and sun-dried tomato jam smothered between layers of shaved ham, herbed turkey, bacon, Swiss, heirloom tomatoes, and crisp romaine lettuce. The key would be using the ingredients to hold the sandwiches together.

I found my rhythm spreading creamy mayo and pesto on the toasted bread and building each layer. Once my sandwiches were complete, I used a sharp knife to cut them into four triangles and secured them with fancy toothpicks. If nothing else, the sandwiches certainly looked festive and party-worthy.

To complete the tasting meal, I grabbed chilled boiled eggs and Yukon gold potatoes from the walk-in for Mom's picnic potato salad. The running joke in our family had been that Mom got invited to events and gatherings not for her winning personality but for this dish. For years she had stayed tight-lipped about the secret ingredient in her summer salad, but since she had begun to scale back, she had passed it on to me in order to continue the tradition.

I cut the soft potatoes into small squares, keeping the skins on. Then I chopped the hard-boiled eggs and tossed them together in a large mixing bowl. I added a generous amount of mayo, pepper, salt, celery seed, and a touch of powdered mustard. Next came bread-and-butter pickles, and finally the super-secret ingredient—pickle juice. My mouth watered as I mixed everything and plated my sample meal with a scoop of the potato salad, a slice of club sandwich, a handful of cinnamon chips, and a ramekin of fruit salsa.

This just might be the winner, I thought as I appraised my work. Now I needed taste testers.

As if on cue, the basement door opened and Andy, Torte's resident barista, walked in.

"Morning, boss. What's cooking?" Andy waved his hand under his nose. "I smell cinnamon."

"Good nose." I waited for him to take off his coat and come into the kitchen.

Andy was in his early twenties with a muscular build, boyish face, and a most affable personality that endeared him to everyone. He had dropped out of college to pursue his dream of becoming a coffee roaster, and he was well on his way to succeeding. Last summer he had taken first place at the West Coast Barista Cup, which had given him serious credibility amongst coffee aficionados and had garnered him an adoring fan club (headed by Bethany, one of our pastry designers). Instead of using his winnings from the competition to take off on a ski trip, Andy had invested it in a small roasting machine that he had set up in his grandmother's garage. Torte was the beneficiary of

Andy's foray into coffee roasting. He had been bringing in his small-batch organic roasts to share with staff and our customers. They had become wildly popular. So much so that I had told Andy last week he was going to have to upgrade his roasting equipment to keep up with demand.

"What do you have for us today?" I asked as he approached the island carrying a stack of containers. Every container was labeled with masking tape with notes on the roast's flavor profile.

"Get ready to be blown away by my newest roast." He lifted the lid on the top container and held the beans just under my nose so that I could get a whiff of the aroma.

I breathed in the scent of caramelized honey and brown sugar with a finish of coconut and blackberries. "That smells amazing. I'm blown away."

Andy flipped his head to the side. His freckled cheeks were lined with marks from his sunglasses from spring skiing on Mount Ashland. "I hate to say it, but I told you so."

"You're not getting a big head, are you?" I teased.

"Well, when the beans come out this good, what can I say?" He winked and pressed the lid onto the plastic container. "Don't worry, Jules. You know that there is no way my grandma would let me develop an ego, but I am pretty psyched about this batch. I've got an idea for an iced latte in mind. I'll bring you a sample in a few."

"Before you go, can you do me a favor and taste this?" I pointed to the picnic plate.

Andy's eyebrows pulled to the top of his forehead. "Are you kidding me? Like you have to ask." He went right in for a chip and plunged it in the salsa. "Yep. That's a yes for me."

"You haven't even tried the rest of the plate."

"You're the one who taught us that we eat with our eyes first, and my eyes are saying 'yes please.'" He grinned and took the plate upstairs with him to prep the espresso bar as Steph and Sterling arrived. The two of them had moved in together while Stephanie finished her last year of college at SOU. Sterling was our sous chef with the heart of a poet and a desire to feed souls with his food. It was a quality that we shared, and something that had immediately endeared him to Carlos. They had become inseparable in the kitchen. One might even say insufferable when they pulled our head bread maker, Marty, into the mix to team up on pranks and bad jokes. Sterling's striking features and lustrous blue eyes also made him a favorite amongst teen girls. Whenever he happened to be upstairs at the pastry counter, a line would quickly form around the block. Everyone would tease Sterling that his sultry look was sure to cause a stir.

"Whenever business is slow, all we need to do is send Sterling upstairs," Marty would say with a grin.

Sterling took his adoring fans in stride. "Nah, it's your sourdough they come in for, man."

Steph had transformed both physically and emotionally in the time that I had known her. Slowly she had begun to shed her aloofness and the thick black eyeliner she used to apply with a heavy hand. Her creativity and talent came out in her baking and design ability. Thanks to her superior skills in the latest trends in cake artistry, our daily custom cake order board was always full. Since cohabiting with Sterling, she had a new lightness about her. She had chopped her hair into a chin-length bob streaked with lilac highlights and forgone her old makeup routine.

"That looks festive," Sterling noted, tying an apron around his waist and sweeping a strand of dark hair from his eye.

"Fruit salsa with cinnamon pita chips, paired with wedding clubs and Mom's potato salad. Have a taste and let me know what you guys think. I think we might be closing in on a final menu for the wedding picnic boxes."

Sterling dipped a chip into the fruit and gave me an appreciative grin. "Fresh. I like it."

Steph tucked her violet hair behind her ears and leaned in for a bite. "It's a nice color and texture."

"Good. That's what I was going for, and something light for guests to start with, right? It doesn't seem too messy, does it?"

"No, I think it's fine." Sterling heaped salsa onto another chip. "Speaking of the wedding boxes, we just saw Detective Kerry on our way in. She was asking if you were around."

"Really?" I glanced at the clock. It wasn't even six yet.

"She seemed pretty on edge," Steph added as she removed the day's stack of custom cake orders from the whiteboard. "We told her you were probably here. The lights were on in the basement, but she saw some guy near the fountains and took off after him."

"Some guy?" I asked.

Steph shrugged. She spread the order forms on the island. "I didn't recognize the guy, but Kerry kind of freaked out."

"Freaked out?" I repeated. That didn't sound like her.

Sterling helped himself to another chip. "Yeah, she told him to get away from the fountains. He didn't seem to be doing anything wrong, but she chased him down."

I wondered if it was wedding nerves. Even with a casual park wedding, it was normal for the bride to have a moment of panic or two.

I didn't have time to dwell on it because the rest of the team arrived, and soon the kitchen was brimming with the smell of German chocolate cakes and sweet bread, and

Andy's special roast was wafting down the stairs. Before it was time to open the front doors for the morning rush, I went up to check on the pastry case and make sure everyone had what they needed for the onslaught of hungry customers.

Seeing Torte in its morning splendor never failed to bring a smile to my face. The warm dining room looked inviting with pretty vases of apricot- and fig-colored tulips on each table and the soft glow of the pinkish sunrise filtering in through the front windows. Our current window display paid homage to May flowers. Tissue paper flowers in pastel shades hung from silky ribbons. Cupcakes fashioned from succulents and roses were positioned on cake stands of varying heights, and candy-striped bunting stretched from one side of the window to the other with a popular lyric by John Lennon about allowing love, like a flower, to grow.

I paused and took in a slow, deep breath, knowing the dining area would soon be bustling with people. A simple stolen moment of bakeshop Zen was all I needed, but a loud banging on the door made me startle. I looked up to see Kerry waving frantically. My stomach dropped.

I made a beeline for the door.

Something had to be wrong. Kerry was usually unflappable.

"Hey, what's up?" I asked with concern as I unlocked the door.

Kerry's cheeks were flushed with color. Her words tumbled out in a jumble. "Jules, I need to talk to you . . ." She paused and darted her eyes from side to side. "Alone."

"Sure. One sec." I motioned to Andy that I would be right back and stepped outside into the candy-colored early light. The air was brisk and scented with pine and jasmine. Aside from a couple of delivery trucks, the plaza was silent. The only sound came from the bubbling fountains and birds squawking nearby in the park.

"Is something wrong?" I studied Kerry. "Is it Thomas? The wedding?"

Kerry wrung her fingers together. Her auburn hair spilled from her ponytail, which had come loose. She kept shaking her head like she couldn't believe what she was about to say. "You have to promise me you won't repeat this, okay?"

"Of course."

"I have to talk to somebody about this, and I don't know who else to go to. Thomas will lose it if I tell him. He'll probably cancel the wedding. And I can't tell the Professor."

Her voice was shaky. So were her hands. I'd never seen her like this.

I pointed across the street to an empty bench next to the Lithia bubblers. "Let's go sit down. You can talk to me, and I promise I won't repeat anything you say."

She glanced around us as we crossed the street like we were being watched.

Once we sat down, I placed my hand on her arm. "Kerry, I promise whatever you need to tell me, I'll keep in confidence."

"I know. That's why I came to you." She tapped her forehead with the tips of her fingers.

I couldn't fathom what she wanted to tell me that she couldn't tell Thomas or the Professor.

"It's my dad," she managed to whisper. "He's here. He's in Ashland."

"Okay." I paused for a minute, unsure of how to respond. "I'm guessing that's a bad thing?"

"The worst." She swallowed hard and twisted her shiny engagement ring. "It's the worst possible thing I can imagine."

Kerry hadn't offered much detail about her past. In my experience, when people were tight-lipped about their history, there was usually a reason. I hadn't seen it as my place to press her. Mom had been of the same mindset. She and the Professor had taken on the role of Kerry's surrogate parents when it had come to wedding planning. Kerry had mentioned that she wasn't intending to invite her family, so it wasn't exactly a shock that news of her dad's arrival in Ashland wasn't met with delight.

"You have to help me, Jules. We've got to get him out of here before Thomas finds out."

"I'll help however I can, but don't you think Thomas would want to be looped in?"

She shook her head with such force it made my temples ache. "No. He can't know. You don't understand. It's not that I don't want my dad here—I mean, I don't—but it's that he *shouldn't* be here."

Whatever she meant, I wasn't getting it. I waited for her to say more.

"Jules, he's supposed to be in jail. I have no idea how he got out. He should be behind bars, and now he's here to ruin my wedding."

Chapter Two

"Jail?" I clasped my hand over my mouth, saying the word louder than I had intended.

She nodded in disgust. "He's eight years into serving a ten-year sentence. I don't know what he's done. I don't want to know. The only thing I care about is making sure he has no contact with Thomas or the Professor."

"Kerry, I'm so sorry." I reached my hand toward her again. "This must be stressful for you, but I'm still unclear on why you don't want Thomas or the Professor to know. They can help. They would want to help."

"No, they don't know. They can't know that he's here." She shook her head vehemently. "I've worked so hard to make sure that my past stays far, far in the past. My parents are the entire reason I entered the police academy. They both were in and out of jail the whole time I was growing up. Do you know how embarrassing that is? I was the kid in class who never had a parent show up for career day. What would I say? My dad is an armed felon." She sighed and tugged her engagement ring all the way off her hand.

She stared at it and then shoved it back on her finger. "My aunts and grandparents stepped in to help raise me, and then in high school, I stayed at friends' houses until I was old enough to get out for good. I can't believe he's doing this to me now. He's going to ruin the wedding."

"You haven't told Thomas any of this?" That was a surprise to me. Thomas was one of the kindest people on the planet. I knew how much he adored Kerry and that he would do anything for her. Having challenging relationships with her parents wouldn't change that.

"Yes, I mean, I've told him pieces over the years. He knows the big picture, but he has no idea that I've been in contact with my dad. He's protective of me, you know?" Her eyes drifted to the diamond ring.

I nodded, waiting for a delivery guy carting cases of soda and juices to the Green Goblin to pass us.

Kerry was quiet until his cart rumbled around to the other side of the fountain. "Thomas doesn't want to see me hurt. He's the one who suggested I sever ties when my dad started hitting me up for money last year. I should have listened to his advice. Trust me, I've done everything I can to make it clear that the only contact anyone in my family has with me is on my own terms, but I shouldn't have even emailed him. It's my mistake. I told him about the wedding. Now he's here. What am I going to do?" She dropped her head into her hands and massaged her temples.

"The first thing you're going to do is take a nice, long, slow breath." I modeled deep breathing for her.

Kerry sat up and inhaled through her nose.

"Where is he now?"

She looked to the fountains and off toward the entrance to Lithia Park. "I don't know. He bolted. I think he was trying to sneak around. He was probably hoping to lay low until the wedding and then—what, show up and try to walk me down the aisle?" She stuffed a loose strand of hair behind her ear.

"Okay, is there someone else you can call? Another colleague from Medford? Where was he incarcerated?"

"Pelican Bay State Prison. Not far from here in Crescent City." She motioned behind us toward the south. "How did he get out?"

Was she expecting me to answer that?

She tugged the sparkly engagement ring on her left finger. "I already called the warden. He hasn't returned my call. If I make a big deal about it and put out an all-points bulletin, there's no keeping it quiet. He's put me in the worst position, which I'm sure was his intention. I risk my job if I don't call it in, but I risk my personal happiness if I do."

That seemed like an exaggeration.

I leaned closer. "Kerry, listen. I've known Thomas and the Professor for practically my entire life. They love you. They know you. They will both do anything for you. I think we should tell them."

"Not yet. Give me some time first. Okay? Will you help me look for him?" Her voice had an unfamiliar pleading tone. "I just want to talk to him first. I need to talk to him alone. Then I'll tell them, or I'll figure something out. You have no idea how embarrassing it is."

Empathy pulsed through my body. She was right. I had been doted on by both my parents. Even though my dad had died when I was young and I had struggled with that grief ever since, I had known without a doubt that he loved me. He was a respected member of the community and beloved by everyone he met. For career day he used to bring boxes of Torte pastries to my classroom. One year he made sugar cookie cutouts of Briscoe Elementary School and brought piping bags filled with colored frosting for each of my classmates to decorate their own cookie. Another year he made ice cream cone cupcakes and shared fancy sprinkles and cake toppers with the class. Mom volunteered at school carnivals and events and was my Camp Fire Girls troop leader. Neither of them missed a performance or cross-country race. I couldn't imagine the struggles Kerry must have gone through. It gave me new appreciation for her resilience and strength.

"Of course I'll help. Where should we start, and what do you want me to say?"

She dragged her teeth along her bottom lip. "I can't believe I'm going to say this, but if we find him, do you think you can talk to Lance?"

"Lance?" I'm sure my jaw must have dropped.

"Yeah, I know. Don't look at me like that. I'm serious."

"No, no. It's not that. Lance will be here in a heartbeat if you need him. It's just that he's not always the model of discretion."

Kerry's face cracked a hint of a smile. "I know. Trust me, I know. But the thing I've learned about him is that despite his tendency to play to an audience, he can play it pretty close to the chest when he wants to, and he's so connected around here that he might be able to put my dad up somewhere out of sight until I can figure out what to do."

That was true. Much of Lance's outward persona was just that. I knew my friend had a tender heart and would do anything for Kerry or any of his friends, myself included.

"You're right; no one is more connected than Lance, and he'll definitely want to help if we need him." I glanced around the plaza, which was just starting to show the first signs of life. Shop lights had come on across the street. At a Rose by Any Other Name, Janet was placing large galvanized tins of flowers in front of the window boxes.

Two runners had finished their loop through the park and were waiting in front of Torte. Park maintenance workers rumbled past us in a converted golf cart.

"Give me a minute to go check in with my team and let them know I'm going to be gone for a little while. We can search the park together. If we find your dad, I'll get in touch with Lance, okay?"

Kerry ran her fingers through her long red curls. Her ponytail had come completely free. "Yeah, I guess that's good. I have to be back in the office for our daily update meeting in an hour. Are you sure you have time to do this? I know you're probably in the middle of getting ready to open the bakeshop."

"No, it's fine. Let me just tell Andy that I'm going to take off for a little while. Everything's ready for the day. My team is so efficient they won't even know I'm gone. In fact, sometimes I wonder if they even need me."

Kerry tried to smile. I hurried across the street to give Andy a heads-up, letting the runners in behind me. I waited for them to head to the end of the pastry counter to place their order with Rosa, our floater who managed the dining room in the mornings.

"I need to run an errand," I said to Sequoia, who worked the espresso bar with Andy. "Do you need anything?"

"We have Andy's new roast," she replied, holding up a diner-style coffee mug. "What else do we need?"

"I can't wait to try it when I get back."

"There might not be any left for you, boss. This stuff is liquid gold." Andy waved his fingers over the grinder like he was doing a magic trick. "But since you're so good to us, I'll set enough aside for you. That's a one-time deal, though. I have to keep my coffee people caffeinated."

I grinned. "Thanks. I'll be back shortly."

Kerry was pacing in front of A Rose by Any Other

Name, where tins of purple and white lilacs gave out a sweet, heady fragrance. "I can't even imagine having to face Janet if she hears about my dad." Her eyes misted.

"Janet won't care," I tried to assure her, peering into the flower shop's windows. Janet must have gone to the back. There was no sign of her near the cement workstation, which was overflowing with garlands I assumed were for the wedding.

She brushed a tear from her cheek. "It's just so embarrassing. It's mortifying. Why would he do this? Why would he want to ruin my day?"

"Do you want to talk about it?" I asked as we moved toward Lithia Park. "Maybe it would help to get some of it off your chest."

She nodded but didn't say more until we had crossed into the entrance flanked by blooming magnolias, cherry trees, manzanitas, and sturdy evergreens. "I mean, I don't know what else there is to say. Both of my parents were basically absent from my childhood. Like I said, I bounced around. I made my own way. It's one of the main reasons I was drawn to law enforcement, especially the community piece. There were a lot of people who influenced my path and steered me in the right direction. I wouldn't be here if it weren't for them. I shouldn't have told Dad about the wedding. I guess there's part of me that will always want more from him, but I should have known that it would turn into a disaster."

We passed the lower duck pond, with its peek-a-boo view of the backside of the Elizabethan theater. Light trickled from the canopy of trees, dancing on the still waters like fairies sprinkling pixie dust. "Maybe there's another explanation. Is there any chance that he's here legitimately?"

"What do you mean?"

"You said he's served eight years, right? Maybe they let him out early on good behavior? Or does that only happen in the movies?" We continued on the paved sidewalk past an open grassy field where early risers were gathering for an outdoor yoga class.

"No, it happens. But even if that's the case, I can't have him here. I can't have a former criminal as the only person who shows up for my side of the wedding. Thomas and his family are small-town perfect. Everyone here loves him. Everyone loves Janet. This is, like, the most idyllic place on the planet, and I've done everything in my power to fit in and leave my past far behind me. I can't believe he would do this to me."

"I think you should give everyone more credit. No one is going to care about your past or who your family is. That doesn't matter. We all love you for who *you* are. Thomas, Janet, everyone."

Listening to Kerry talk about her history gave me even more understanding of why she had crafted such a strong boundary around herself. I wished there was some way I could convince her that she didn't have to worry about anyone judging her.

We followed the path past the children's play area and on toward the vast network of Alice in Wonderland trails that stretched for miles in every direction. If someone wanted to hide, this was the place to do it. I made sure to scan the forested hillsides for any signs of wildlife. Spring had brought black bears down from their winter dens. It wasn't unusual to spot a bear lumbering through the park. They tended to be afraid of people. The only danger was if we happened upon a mom and her cubs.

Something flashed in the corner of my eye. I froze.

"What?" Kerry's hand immediately went to her waist. She was dressed in a pair of slacks with a form-fitting matching jacket, but I knew that she carried a gun underneath her professional outfit.

"Did you see that?" I squinted, wondering if it was just a deer.

Before I could say more, a figure bolted across the bark chip path about twenty feet in front of us. It reminded me of footage from Sasquatch sightings. The person was tall and bulky. They disappeared into the trees almost immediately.

"Jamie Crosby!" Kerry yelled, racing after the figure. "Freeze!"

Jamie? Was Jamie her dad?

I sprinted to keep up with her as she deftly straddled a fallen log and hurried down the forested hillside toward Ashland Creek. The sound of water rushing over ancient volcanic rocks echoed as the pathway narrowed. I let out a shiver. The temperature dropped near the flowing water.

When we reached the bottom, the man had stopped. He stood next to the fast-moving water holding his hands up in surrender.

Kerry had reached for her Taser and positioned it in her left hand as if ready to use it. "Freeze right there, Jamie, or I will tase you."

Chapter Three

For a minute I thought Kerry was actually going to tase him. I held my breath as she took deliberate steps toward him, with her Taser pointed straight at his chest.

"Do not move," Kerry cautioned.

Jamie kept his hands in the air. "Honey girl, I'm not moving. Put the Taser down."

"Do not call me that." Kerry moved closer. "What are you doing here?"

"I'm here for the wedding. It's not every day your baby girl gets married. I thought you'd be happy." Jamie kept his eyes glued to Kerry as he spoke. I could see a resemblance between them. Jamie had Kerry's copper hair color, but his was cut short like it had been hacked off by a dull pair of kitchen scissors. He was tall and bulky with a sleeve of tattoos running up both arms. Two large, creepy pirate tattoos, one on either side of his neck, made me cringe. How painful was it to have your neck inked with needles?

"You're supposed to be behind bars," Kerry retorted.

"No. No. I'm a free man." He dropped his hands.

"Arms up."

He followed her directions. "You didn't get my emails, did you?"

"What emails?" Kerry had stopped about two feet away from him but hadn't loosened her grip on the Taser.

"My appeal. It was approved. I'm out. My sentence is done." His weathered face was pocked with scars.

"What do you mean, you're out?" Kerry's body reminded me of the herons that sometimes landed in the Lithia Ponds. Not a muscle twitched. She held her ground with rigid posture, like she was tethered to the earth.

"I'm here for the wedding. For you, honey girl."

Her body flinched. "I told you not to call me that."

"Sorry." He started to move his arms, but stopped himself. "I emailed you about it. I told you I was coming. When I didn't hear, I decided to surprise you."

"You succeeded." Kerry lowered her Taser. "The appeal went through?"

He nodded, letting his arms falls to his sides. "Yeah, I'm a free man, and I get to be here to walk my honey girl down the aisle."

"Why did you run, then?"

"Huh? Oh, I don't know. I guess habit. I've spent my whole life running from cops. Still can't believe my kid is one."

Kerry shook her head. "It's pretty weird that you show up in town. I see you, and you bolt. It's hard to believe, Jamie."

"Check your email." Jamie took a step closer. "Call the warden. I'm telling the truth."

"I am going to vet your story, Jamie."

"Why can't you call me Dad?" He kicked a pine cone with his foot.

"Because you've never been a dad to me." Her voice was colder than the mountain runoff water gushing through the creek.

I wanted to disappear. I felt like I was intruding on a deeply personal conversation.

"Give me a chance. I'm a changed man. I've done my time, and now I'm here. I'm ready to do whatever you need. I'm ready to make it up to you. I know I did you wrong when you were a kid, but doesn't showing up count for something? I'm here. For you, honey girl. For your wedding. I did everything I could to get released in time to make it here to walk my baby down the aisle."

"I'm a thirty-three-year-old woman. I'm not a baby."

His shoulders heaved. "I get that, but at least give me a chance to make it right." Jamie's eyes drifted to me. "Ask your friend. See what she says. You think she should give her old man a chance, don't ya?"

I stepped back. No part of me wanted to be in the middle of this. Plus there was darkness in Jamie's eyes that made me uncomfortable. "I should probably get back to the bake-shop. Are you good?" I directed the question to Kerry.

"Yeah. I'm fine. Thanks for everything."

"No problem. We'll catch up later." I hesitated, trying to come up with a code. "You know where to find me if you need to talk to Lance about wedding entertainment."

She nodded, catching my drift. "Got it. I'll be in touch."

I took off before Jamie could try to loop me in to their disagreement. As I navigated the trail that led back to the plaza, I couldn't help but feel even more empathy for Kerry. At least she'd found her dad and made contact. Assuming he wasn't lying about being released from prison early, she wouldn't have to make the impossible decision of having to turn him in again. Although she was going to have to decide if she wanted him to be involved in the wedding and tell Thomas. I had a feeling I already knew the answer to her extending an invitation to her dad, but stranger things had happened.

As I rounded the corner of the trail that led back to the park entrance, hot pink rhododendrons spilled over the pathway. I brushed the blooms aside and bumped straight into Thomas.

"Jules! What are you doing here?" He stopped in mid-stride. As always, he was dressed in his blue uniform with navy shorts and hiking boots.

"Uh . . ." I fumbled for a moment. Kerry had been adamant that she didn't want Thomas to know about her dad. "Uh, early run before the rush of the morning crowds, you know."

"In jeans and a hoodie?" Thomas scrunched his forehead.

"Uh, yeah." I glanced at my tennis shoes. "I forgot to bring in my running clothes, and everything's so busy with the wedding preparations and gearing up for the OSF season, I decided I just needed to get a quick hit of fresh air."

Thomas scowled. "You're the worst liar, Juliet Capshaw."

I could feel my cheeks warm. I'd never had much of a poker face.

"You were with Kerry, weren't you?"

How did he know?

"With Kerry?" I repeated the question, hoping my voice sounded as innocent to him as it did in my head.

"Come on, Jules, where is she?" He craned his neck to see behind me, like I was trying to hide her.

"Kerry?" I shrugged. "I'm not sure where she is right now." That wasn't a lie. She and Jamie could be anywhere in the park by *now*.

"Look, Jules, I know. I know about her dad. I know about Jamie. I know he's here, and I know she's looking for him. It's nice of you to help, but I need to find her."

"You know? How?"

He tapped his chest where a deputy badge was pinned to his uniform pocket. "The prison called this morning to confirm that he had been released."

"Well, that's a relief." At least Jamie hadn't lied about that.

"Not really. Not to me. We're getting married in two days. Why would she feel like she couldn't come to me? I'm about to be her husband. She doesn't trust me?" His voice was thick with emotion.

"I don't think it's that." I tried to console him. "It's a terrible position for her. I think she's worried that she's going to embarrass you or your family."

Thomas's jaw clenched so tight that it made my teeth hurt. "Why would she think that? My family adores her."

"I know that, and you know that, but put yourself in Kerry's position. It must be so hard to feel torn about her dad. I mean, on the one hand, there has to be part of her that wants him here—wants anyone from her side of the family to be involved in the wedding—and then on the other hand, she's embarrassed about his past. She takes her work so seriously, so to have her dad, who's just been released from prison, show up unannounced right before your big day—I can't even imagine."

Thomas let out a long exhale. "You're right, Jules. I feel bad. I told her not to respond to him. I thought it would be better if she cut him off, because it felt like it was making things worse for her, but I guess I didn't think about what it must be like not to have any family here for the wedding."

"Exactly." I nodded and pointed to the trail. "Go find her. They were down by the last bridge that crosses the creek. She needs your support."

He firmed his posture and gave me a half salute. "I'm on the case."

I felt slightly relieved as I continued on to Torte. As long as Kerry and Thomas kept communicating, they would be fine. I knew from my own mistakes with Carlos that keeping an open line of communication was the most important part of any marriage.

My relief was cut short when a booming voice hollered at me from the front porch of the Merry Windsor Hotel. I turned to see Richard Lord waving at me with both arms as if he was trying to direct a plane to its landing strip.

"Juliet, come over here."

A familiar sickly feeling rumbled in my stomach. Since I had returned home to Ashland, Richard and I had been at odds for too many reasons to count. It had started when he attempted a backhanded deal to take over Torte, followed by a failed wooing of Mom, and a variety of blatant (albeit lame) attempts to copy everything we did at the bakeshop, from starting his own ice cream cart—Shakescream—to re-creating our menu item by item in the Merry Windsor's breakfast bar.

The Merry Windsor was the only hotel in the plaza. Its exterior gave off the impression of the space being a tasteful Tudor-style building, with its timber-framed siding and stone foundation, but upon closer inspection, the illusion was shattered. There was nothing Shakespearean about the hotel, as was evident by the satellite dishes on the roof, the broken blinds in the front windows, and the flat-screen TV that was always blaring in the lobby. The aging hotel was in dire need of an update. Richard would never fork out the cash for a major renovation. Instead he set out buckets to try and salvage the ugly green carpet when the roof leaked during the rainy season, and he spent the majority of his time meddling in everyone else's business.

There were only two people I knew who had managed to keep Richard's inflated ego in check—Lance and Carlos. They had teamed up to buy Richard out of his shares in Uva. I still hadn't figured out how they'd managed the feat, and both of them were tight-lipped about it.

"What's going on, Richard?"

He narrowed his eyes at me. He was dressed in his usual style—an outlandish golf outfit. I would have bet big money that there wasn't a single piece of clothing in his closet that didn't revolve around the sport. The irony was that I'd never heard him mention anything about actually hitting the links. He had a habit of lurking around the plaza, spying on our customers and annoying me. "What were you doing in the park?"

"How is that any of your business?"

He adjusted the belt on his black houndstooth shorts. "Does it have to do with the wedding? Because I've already told Thomas and Kerry that I don't want people traipsing around my property. I've checked the city code."

"What are you talking about?" The Merry Windsor sat adjacent to the Shakespeare stairs that led up to the OSF campus. A city-owned sidewalk ran in front of the hotel. Anyone could use the sidewalk to access the park.

"I warned them. I gave them a chance to partner with me, and they declined, so I don't have to play nice. If I see any wedding guests loitering around my property, I'm calling it in."

"Okay." I rolled my eyes. "I'm not sure why you're telling me this."

"Consider it your warning. I know you're working with them and catering the wedding. You better tell your staff not to come near here while you're carrying food back and forth. I'm going to be keeping an eye out."

"Good to know." I had about a dozen retorts in my head, but I had learned it was better to let Richard think he had the upper hand. "I need to get back to work. See you."

With that, I hurried across the street before he could say more. In typical Richard fashion, he was going to heckle wedding guests for walking on the sidewalk just because he was upset that Thomas and Kerry hadn't gone with him for catering. I knew I was biased about Torte's offerings, but any spot in Ashland would have been better than the Merry Windsor. Richard's idea of fine dining was purchasing mass-produced food at Costco and re-branding it as his own. His breakfast buffet that he liked to tout as being a traditional Elizabethan feast included pre-wrapped stale muffins and frozen hash browns.

I'd have loved to see him call the police on "trespassers." I doubted he'd have much luck rallying the troops, since everyone would be at the wedding anyway.

A line had formed in front of the bakeshop. I scooted past it and went straight to the pastry counter to help Rosa plate orders of our pesto egg biscuits and ricotta lemon bread. There was nothing like the first rush of the morning. I loved the humming energy of the busy dining room and getting to overhear customers rave about their lattes and orange cardamom crepes.

The first hour passed in a blur. When the line finally slowed, I took a spin around the space with a fresh pot of coffee. Two men and a petite woman with neon blue hair were seated at one of the booths in front of the windows. I recognized them right away as Heart Strings, a popular trio that played in every venue throughout the Rogue Valley.

"Good morning, can I refill anyone's coffee?" I asked.

"Yes, please." The woman held up her mug. "It is way too early for me. We're used to gigging at night. I don't think I've seen this hour in years."

I chuckled. "You're all Heart Strings, right?" Carlos and I had been wanting to book them for an evening of music at Uva.

The woman shot me a look of thanks for the refill before immediately taking a long sip. "Yep, I'm Dani—lead singer. This is Brett, our bassist."

Brett was three times Dani's size and had to be pushing fifty. He had long, straggly brown hair and looked equally shell-shocked to be awake. Like Jamie, he had tattoos on nearly every inch of open skin, including four dots next to his right eyelid. "Hey," he managed to mumble as he pointed to his coffee cup. "Can I get another, too?"

"Of course." I filled his cup, while Dani pointed to the guy sitting next to her.

"This is Randall, our pianist."

Randall didn't even bother to look up from his sketchbook. He was a bit younger than Dani. I guessed him to be closer to Sterling's age. His face was gaunt and pale. I wanted to feed him a sandwich, or two. "No coffee for me. I'm a tea guy."

"Do you need more hot water?"

He shook his head and plunged the tea bag into his cup. Skull rings made from silver, granite, steel, and what looked like ivory or bone were positioned on his fingers and thumbs. "I'm good." He went back to his drawing.

"What brings you all to Torte?" I asked Dani, who was

clearly not only the lead singer but the leader of the group, judging by the way she passed around schedules and was scribbling frantic notes in a black journal.

"We're meeting to go over the wedding set list. We have to get this nailed down because I have a very important Zoom this afternoon." She pounded her schedule so hard with the tip of her pencil that the lead snapped off.

"Right, of course, you're playing at Thomas and Kerry's wedding." I went on to explain how we were catering the event. "I won't keep you. When you have time, I'd love to chat with you all at some point about performing at Uva, our winery."

Dani reached into a black leather purse with rhinestone studs and handed me a business card. "Shoot me a text or call. We're booked through the next couple months, but have a few open slots this summer. Just be sure to do it fast, because I can't promise those spots will stay open for long. You know how it is in the summer season. Every winery wants music. Weddings, the Green Show."

Brett clutched his coffee cup. "Yeah, you're killing us with so many gigs, Dani."

"You want to eat, don't you?" she shot back, flicking the broken tip of the pencil at him.

"It's hard to eat when your fingers are bleeding from playing two or three gigs in one day. My digits don't move the way they used to." He set his coffee cup on the table and showed off his hands. His fingers were wrapped in Band-Aids, and two of his nails were bruised dark purple.

"You want to go there now? Here? At a coffee shop?" Dani glared at him. "I haven't had enough caffeine for this. Not again. If you don't want to play so many shows, you can leave anytime. Did you hear that, too, Randall? Are you listening or just zoning out again? I said you guys are free to leave the band anytime."

Randall stared at his teacup as if it was the most interesting thing he'd ever seen. "Uh, I guess. I'm not sure what you mean."

Brett hummed under his breath. "I'll tell you what she means, kid. She makes the decisions for the three of us. We're a trio, but if we're not careful, Heart Strings is going to turn into a solo act."

"You keep acting like this, and I will be a solo act." Her eyes were filled with rage.

I tucked her business card into my apron. "I'll let you guys keep talking. It sounds like this isn't the best time to chat about another booking."

Dani held out a hand to stop me. "No, really. Call me. Okay? Let's chat. If we've got space, I'll work you in. We could use the gig. People tip well at wineries, especially after they've had a few drinks."

I gave her a small nod and left to continue refilling coffees. I had heard only good things about Heart Strings, and in fairness to the band, they had admitted that they weren't morning people, but the last thing I wanted for a relaxing evening amongst the vines was infighting and bickering. From the way Dani was thrusting her finger in Brett's face, I suspected that there was more going on with the band than just a need to be caffeinated, and I didn't want any part of it.

Chapter Four

Thomas and Kerry showed up shortly after I had finished making my rounds through the dining room and downstairs. To my surprise, Jamie was with them. I watched as they spotted Heart Strings and squeezed into the booth with the band. Things must have gone well with Thomas if Kerry felt comfortable bringing her dad to the meeting. I took it as a good sign, especially since she hadn't called or texted to say that she needed Lance's help to house or hide her estranged father.

Of course I couldn't help but notice that Kerry had one eye on Jamie at all times. It made me glad that I'd never had to be interrogated by her. The intensity of her gaze sent a prickling sensation up my neck. I wouldn't have wanted to be in her line of fire.

Regardless of her warden-like behavior, I'm going to put good energy toward believing the wedding will go off without any more drama, I thought as I went downstairs to replenish two pastry trays and check on how lunch prep was coming. As I loaded the shiny silver trays with buttery chocolate-filled croissants, rhubarb custard cakes, and goat cheese and honey hand pies, Mom came in through the basement entrance.

She radiated joy. Her shoulder-length brown hair brought out the touch of sun on her skin that I knew was from her morning walks around Emigrant Lake. She and the Professor had bought a house on the banks of the lake and they made a point to start every morning with a leisurely stroll, watching birds take flight and kayakers cut through the still waters. I was so happy that she was finally taking more time for herself after a lifetime spent kneading bread dough and going out of her way to make sure that everyone in town felt cared for and comforted. Mom had a way of listening, really listening, that tended to make anyone in her presence bare their soul. It was a gift, but I knew it also took a toll on her to hold space for our collective grief and joy.

She greeted me with a kiss on the cheek, standing on her tiptoes to reach me. Mom was petite, with walnut eyes that were filled with a zest and curiosity for life. I had inherited my height and fair skin, with its tendency to burn at the slightest amount of sun, from Dad's side. "Sorry I'm late this morning, honey. Doug and I had a meeting with Judge Mimi Barbarelli—you know her, right? She's a regular after her morning Pilates class. She's officiating the wedding. You should have seen Doug's face. He's so excited to get to walk Kerry down the aisle."

"Were Thomas and Kerry there?"

"No, why?" Mom was astute at reading people. She studied me with concern as she went to the sink to wash up and get an apron.

"Have you talked to either of them this morning?"

She shook her head, lathering her hands with lemon rosemary soap. "No. We met Mimi at the park. She's going to swing by here in a few because I believe Kerry and Thomas are meeting with the band. Is something wrong? You look serious, honey."

I motioned to the seating area. "Let's go chat." I left the trays for a moment. My team was focused on lunch preparations, and since Jamie was upstairs, I figured it probably wasn't a secret anymore, but I still didn't want to betray Kerry's trust by announcing her family drama in front of the everyone.

Mom dried her hands, tied on an apron, and came out to sit on the couch by the fireplace. I took the chair next to her and leaned in. "Kerry's dad showed up."

"What?" Mom sounded as shocked as I felt. "Her dad? I didn't even know they were in contact. She never mentioned anything when she asked Doug to walk her down the aisle."

"I know. It's complicated." I paused for a minute. Mom was the soul of discretion. I knew I could trust her. "He's just been released from prison," I whispered.

"Oh, I see." She drew in a breath.

"Kerry had no idea he was going to show up." I filled her in on the morning's strange turn of events.

When I finished, she placed her hand on the Torte logo on the chest of her apron. "My heart is with Kerry. That's a lot of emotional turmoil in the midst of preparing for her wedding. I'm glad she opened up to you, honey."

"Me, too. I just wish there was more I could do."

Mom nodded in agreement. "I'll talk to Doug— discreetly of course. We can offer her a buffer. Why don't we make a pact to keep Jamie occupied? I'm sure we can put him to work, assuming Kerry decides she wants him to stay. We'd be happy to have him out at our place, and I'm sure Doug will bow out of his duties if Kerry wants her dad to walk her down the aisle."

"I like the idea of putting him to work. We can always use an extra set of hands and muscles to cart supplies between here and the park. I'm happy to include Jamie in that."

With that decided, I went to retrieve the pastry trays. I was practically mobbed while positioning them in the case.

"Is that a crinkle chocolate cookie I spy?" a woman at the front of the line asked.

I looked up to see Judge Mimi Barbarelli eyeing the fresh tray of sweets. "It is, and I believe this one has your name on it." I picked up a cookie and set it on a plate. "Would you like it warmed up, Judge?"

"Oh, Juliet, how many times do I have to ask? Please call me Mimi. I only answer to Judge when I'm sitting on the bench, and I'll take it just as it is. These cookies are my personal weakness." Her pale blue eyes twinkled. Mimi was in her early eighties with thick silver hair and a polished style. She was my personal mentor when it came to aging. Her philosophy was that you're only as old as you let yourself believe. If I had to guess, I'd have figured she believed she was still in her thirties. She did Pilates three times a week, held court twice a week, and was the most popular wedding officiant in the valley.

"One chocolate crinkle, for you," I said, handing her the cookie.

"Don't tell my personal trainer, but I might come back for seconds." She winked.

"I've been wondering if these should go in the wedding picnic boxes, and you're making my decision easy."

"Promise you won't let me see them until after they've exchanged their vows; otherwise, I might get on a sugar high and forget how to officiate." She took the cookie off her plate and pretended to hide it in her oversized purple polka-dot purse, which coordinated with her outfit.

"How are the plans coming?" I snuck a glance at the booth where the band and Thomas and Kerry, along with Jamie, were still chatting.

"Smooth as butter," Mimi replied, following my gaze. Her smile evaporated when she locked eyes with Brett. His face turned whiter than the meringues in the pastry case. Mimi gave her body a visible shake before refocusing her attention on me. "Thomas and Kerry aren't considering having Heart Strings perform at the wedding, are they?"

"Yeah, I think it's a done deal. They're going over set lists this morning. Why?"

Mimi's body shifted. "On second thought, I believe I'll take my cookie to go if it isn't too much trouble."

"Sure." I packaged the soft chocolate cookie in a bag and added in a bonus one for her.

"Do me a favor, would you?" She pressed a ten-dollar bill into my hand. "Tell Thomas and Kerry to call me when they're done. I need to have a serious talk with them."

I handed her the change, and she left without saying more. Did she know something about Heart Strings? As a judge, she must have been privy to details about people that the general public wouldn't know. Or had I read the situation wrong? Was it Jamie who had made Mimi make a quick escape?

I didn't have time to dwell on it, as the lunch rush was already starting to pick up. Thomas, Kerry, Jamie, and the band slipped out while I was taking orders and running up and down the stairs to deliver grilled BLTs and spicy Southwest chicken chowder. After we had fed Ashland's hungry noon crowd, I returned to the kitchen.

Sterling and Marty were washing dishes. Bethany and

Steph were collaborating on custom cookies in the shape of spring flowers to match our window display. They were decorating the almond shortbread cookies with our signature Torte technique. First they dipped the cooled cookies into a thin base of royal icing, coating the entire surface with frosting. Then they used toothpicks to drag pastel royal icing along the top of each cookie in straight lines. From there, they took another color of the royal icing and dragged the toothpick in the opposite direction to create gorgeous tie-dye patterns. We used the technique for holiday cookies, our Torte red and teal cookies, and for special orders. It was simple, yet elegant, our philosophy for food and life.

"Those are looking great," I noted.

Bethany beamed, her curls bouncing as she tilted her head from side to side to get a better view of the psychedelic cookies. "I'm obsessed, and I know social media is going to blow up when I post pics of these." She was wearing a classic gray scoop-neck T-shirt with the silhouette of a cupcake that read YOU BAKE ME PROUD.

"Does everyone have time to do a check-in about the wedding boxes?" I asked.

Marty dried his hands on a dish towel. "I'm a yes, and I happened to make extra paninis if anyone needs a bite to eat. There's also plenty of extra donuts if you have a hankering for something sweet. I've been experimenting with fillings for the wedding, so don't hold back."

My stomach grumbled. I realized I hadn't eaten anything since I'd had a bite of the cinnamon chips and fruit salsa. When Kerry had shown up and asked for my help, I'd completely forgotten to eat. "Yes, please."

Everyone gathered round the large island in the center of the kitchen. Marty offered us chicken Parm paninis; BLTs; and a platter of raspberry, mango, Bavarian cream, and chocolate-hazelnut filled donuts. We were surprising Thomas and Kerry with stacks of filled donuts for the reception.

Sterling had set aside enough soup for everyone to have a cup.

I munched on a sandwich and reviewed the timeline for Saturday's event. "Where are we with the wedding cake?" I asked Steph.

She continued to swirl filigree patterns on cookies from her decorating station. "We have the last layer to bake this afternoon. We can start painting tomorrow."

"And the chocolate layers are done for the groom's cake," Bethany added, snapping a candid pic of Steph with a purple-tipped toothpick in hand. Thomas had asked for a donut-themed groom's cake. It was a bit of an inside joke between them. He and Kerry shared a passion for Torte's jelly-filled donuts.

The main wedding cake would have five tiers. They had opted for spring flavors—vanilla, lemon, strawberry, coconut, and pineapple carrot. We would frost each layer in French buttercream and then drape the entire cake in off-white fondant. Then we planned to use edible paint to craft watercolor designs of Lithia Park on the fondant. Each tier would feature a different vignette from the park. Steph's initial sketches had taken my breath away. I was excited to see it come together. This wasn't simply going to be a wedding cake; it was going to be a work of art.

Torte's custom cakes were a labor of love. There were many steps involved in creating something entirely unique or an extravagant tiered showpiece. It was a process that I enjoyed, because it never failed to stretch my creative muscles. The only challenge with our custom cakes was that we had to be very detailed and organized when it came to delivery deadlines for this labor-intensive work. Custom cakes typically required carving and structural support with food dowels. Unlike our everyday cakes, the eight- and twelve-inch rounds that we served by the slice upstairs, our specialty cakes took hours, if not days, to complete.

"So it sounds like we need to finalize the picnic box items, and then we should be ready for a mad dash to the finish over the next couple days."

Sterling and Marty offered their opinions on sandwich and salad choices.

"Those clubs were out of this world, Juliet," Marty said, rubbing his stomach. Marty had retired as a baker in San Francisco, but when his wife died and he moved to Ashland, he came out of retirement to work for us. I was thrilled to have him on the team, not only for his incredible bread baking skills but also for his age and wisdom. "My stomach is begging me for a second."

"I second that," Sterling said, laughing at himself. "We're all in agreement that the clubs with potato salad and sweet chips and salsa work really well together. I'm finishing a green salad and pasta salad, so the only thing left is landing on options for anyone with special dietary requirements."

We intended to have vegetarian and gluten-free boxes to accommodate special dietary needs. Once we had finalized our menu and divided tasks, I got to work on the groom's cake.

I slathered chocolate buttercream and raspberry jam like sweet concrete between the layers and then used a long serrated knife to cut the cake into the shape of a giant donut. Once I had a round dome, I crumb-coated the outside of the cake in more buttercream and set it in the walk-in to cool.

Before I knew it, the afternoon had vanished. My team trickled out one by one, and I was back to an empty kitchen.

What a surreal day. It had started in a blur, but ended in calm. I hoped that things would remain steady for the next couple days, especially for Kerry and Thomas. I wanted their wedding to be a jubilant celebration and an opportunity for those of us who loved them to send them off into this new phase of their relationship with delectable food, gorgeous sweets, and a day of merriment. Little did I know that things were about to take a much more sinister turn.

Chapter Five

Saturday morning dawned bright. Sun streamed in through the bedroom windows. Birdsong and the fragrance of blooming dogwoods filled the air.

Carlos rolled over in the bed and rubbed his eyes. "Did you sleep in, Julieta?"

"No, but I do need to get moving." I was already halfway out of the covers.

He leaned closer and wrapped me in his arms. "Stay for a minute, mi querida."

It was tempting. I drank in the scent of his aftershave and the firmness of his gentle touch. "I wish I could." I kissed him and scooted out of bed. "There's so much to do today. We have a wedding to cater. Thomas and Kerry are getting married, can you believe it?"

"Si. Si." He sat up and ran his hands through his dark hair. "I will go to Uva and bring over the wine. Is there anything else you need?"

"No. If you take care of the wine, that's perfect. I scheduled the Scoops crew to come help."

"Excellent. I will see you at the park later, yes?"

"Yep." I tugged on a pair of shorts, a hoodie, and tennis shoes. "Can you bring my dress, shoes, and bag?" I pointed to the bathroom where I had hung the dress I was going to wear. Since the wedding was at the park, I had picked a maxi sundress with a spring poppy design in coral, aqua, and tangerine. The bold hues and romantic cut should be perfect for dancing at the reception. I would change at Torte later. There was no way I could bake in a cocktail dress and heeled sandals.

"Si. I will take care of everything."

That was for sure. I hadn't realized until recently how much I appreciated having a partner in crime when it came to running our ever-growing family businesses. Carlos and I had found a smooth working relationship. We had managed to balance our respective duties and give each other space. His primary focus was Uva, while mine was Torte and Scoops, but there were plenty of opportunities for collaborating, like our Sunday Suppers, dinner in the vines, and mentoring our young staff. Knowing that he was my equal partner had relieved a burden that I hadn't even realized I was carrying.

My step had a spring in it as I headed down Mountain Avenue and turned onto Siskiyou Boulevard. Pink and white cherry trees bloomed in tidy rows along the street. Flocks of wild turkeys scattered on grassy lawns, searching for their morning grub. Tulips and daffodils bloomed along the median that cut through the center of the street.

What a perfect day for a wedding. The morning air was cool and crisp, but by the time the festivities kicked off later in the afternoon, it was supposed to be close to eighty, with light clouds, a subtle breeze, and plenty of sun.

I didn't linger on my walk. What I had said to Carlos was true. We had the bulk of the prep work finished, but there were dozens of last-minute details to get through before we needed to be at the park to begin setup at noon.

Antique street lamps, still aglow, greeted me as I arrived at the plaza. Shakespearean banners in maroon and gold flapped in the slight breeze. Bistro tables and bright patio umbrellas lined the sidewalk in front of the pizzeria. Window boxes with cascading greenery and bunches of aromatic lavender at the apothecary made me stop and take a quick peek at their upcoming class schedule. Mom and I had been talking about trying one of their sound bath meditations.

I took note of the next one and made a beeline for Torte.

Once I'd gone through the opening routine, I went straight to work on the groom's cake. The last layer of chocolate buttercream had set, so I just needed to embellish it with miniature donut macarons. I had made a similar creation for their engagement cake. I filled a piping bag with more chocolate buttercream and began the painstaking task of adorning the colorful donut-shaped macarons all over the cake. I couldn't resist popping a couple of the bite-size sweets into my mouth as I worked. The macarons looked adorable and tasted even better. We'd done bright spring flavors—orange, lemon, raspberry, lime, cherry, banana toffee, and my favorite: Fruity Pebbles, made with the actual cereal—each sandwiched together with fresh jams and buttercream. After making them for the groom's cake, we had unanimously decided that every picnic box needed a trio of the tiny delicacies included, along with chocolate crinkle cookies and mini tartlets.

No one could accuse us of not having a plethora of dessert options.

By the time the team arrived, I had finished the groom's

cake and had started organizing the wicker picnic boxes. The boxes were lined with blue-and-white-striped gingham and included a four-piece set of dishes, silverware, and wineglasses. They were going to serve two purposes—at the actual picnic feast, and as take-home gifts for each of the guests from Thomas and Kerry.

"Did you get here at two a.m.?" Sterling asked as he came in, tugging off the hood on his gray hoodie and motioning to the rows of picnic boxes.

"Someone's excited about a wedding," Andy teased. He had followed Sterling in. When he stopped to swipe a raspberry macaron, he froze and used both hands to waft air beneath his nose. "What is going on in here? I don't smell anything. Not even coffee. You haven't had java yet, have you, boss? That's a tragedy. A real tragedy."

"It's true." I grinned. "I waited for you. I heard a rumor that you might have a wedding day special in mind."

"You know it." He gave me a two-fingered salute. "Be right back."

"What's the game plan for the day?" Sterling asked.

We talked through details and then went our separate ways to get production started on the picnic boxes. The morning flew by in a blur of packing potato salad into cute to-go tubs, storing them in the walk-in with the other perishable food, and adding the desserts to each of the boxes.

When I glanced at the clock above the sink, I expected that only an hour or two had gone by, but instead it was close to eleven.

"Where has the morning gone? I need to run over to the park and go through the site setup with Nat Bennett," I said to Sterling. "He's the head of maintenance and is our point person today. Some of it is going to depend on weather. We don't want the cakes sweating in the sun, but any pre-prep we can do will help. Nat's going to help me assess where best to store everything and where the food tables are going to be set up."

"Got it." Sterling leafed through his task list. Rows and rows of our wedding club sandwiches were stacked on the island. "We'll go ahead and get these in the walk-in and bust out the last of the to-do list. The plan is still to close at noon, right?"

"Yep." I could have scheduled additional staff to keep Torte open for the afternoon, but everyone on the team had been invited to the wedding, and aside from tourists, *everyone* in town was going to be at Lithia Park to celebrate Thomas and Kerry's nuptials.

I glanced at my watch. "Okay, since you have things rolling, I'm going to head over to the park for a few. Be back shortly."

Andy was waiting with a latte in hand when I came upstairs. "You weren't trying to sneak out on me without tasting the wedding day special, were you, boss? We got slammed up here; otherwise, I was going to bring you one. Sorry about that."

"Don't sweat it. I haven't even needed caffeine this morning. If you can believe it, the wedding-day adrenaline has kicked in." I attempted a wink, which I'm sure resulted in contorting my face into a goofy grin. I'd never been able to wink without scrunching half of my face. My team teased me mercilessly about it, which only motivated me to do it more.

"You could always use caffeine, though." Andy handed me a latte in a to-go cup. "Give this beauty a taste."

I did as instructed. The latte was strong on the coffee flavor with touches of semisweet cocoa powder and dark chocolate curls, but there was something underneath the traditional flavor I couldn't quite pinpoint. "Is this almost bubbly? I'm getting a hint of effervescence."

"Well done." Andy clapped twice. Then he reached beneath the espresso counter and pulled out a fluted champagne glass. "It's a champagne latte. We've been serving them in these glasses with foam hearts."

"There's champagne in this?" I took another sip.

"Just enough to make it feel like a celebration in a glass, but not enough to give you a buzz." He pointed to a collection of bottles at the end of the counter. "Not to worry, I have sparkling cherry cider for a nonalcoholic version, too."

"This is so fun, and so original."

Andy's cheeks spotted with pink. "Thanks, boss. Have to keep it real, you know."

"For sure." I grabbed a lid for my cup. "I'm off to finalize details with the park maintenance director, but I have a feeling you might finish off all those bottles by the time I'm back if the size of the line is any indication." I nodded to the queue waiting to put in their orders and held up my coffee in a toast. "Cheers."

I took another drink as I crossed past the Lithia bubblers. Andy's champagne latte was a perfect example of how fortunate we were to have such highly skilled and creative staff. I never would have thought to spike my morning coffee with a little hit of bubbly, but it worked beautifully. And I wasn't kidding about selling out. Andy's ode-to-love creation was original and delicious.

The park was alive with spring colors as I took the short pathway through the canopy of greenery toward the band shell. Dozens of workers were setting up for the wedding. Squares for the blankets had been roped off in four-by-four-foot sections throughout the sprawling lawn. A temporary dance floor was being erected in front of the stage. Long folding tables were being carted from the underground storage space attached to the band shell.

Janet and her floral team were hanging garlands of fragrant stargazer lilies and blushing pink roses from the eaves. Judge Mimi was chatting with Dani and Randall from Heart Strings on the stage where more park workers were setting up microphone stands and running sound checks.

I wondered where Brett, their third member, was as I scanned the blur of activity for any sign of Nat. He didn't appear to be anywhere, so I headed for the band shell to ask if anyone had seen him recently.

As I approached the side of the band shell, a commotion broke out. Nat, the park maintenance director in a khaki uniform, was nose to nose with Brett, who used his large bass instrument as a barricade between them.

"I told you to chill out. I will get to you when I have a minute." Nat thrust a finger in Brett's face. "There is a checklist a mile long that I need to get to. Stop acting like a toddler and wait your turn." Nat bent over and picked something up from the grass. He proceeded to stuff it in his pocket.

I couldn't see the object. Nat kept one hand in his pocket as he faced Brett again. "Get out of here and go sober up."

Brett swayed slightly as he spoke. "Listen, old man, you need to shut it. If you're not careful, you know what I'll do." He paused and rocked to the left as he tried to steady his arm to stare at his watch. His bass almost toppled over. Had he stopped by Torte and imbibed one too many champagne lattes?

That wouldn't be good for Thomas and Kerry. Heart Strings might have to quickly become a duo if the lead bassist was drunk at noon.

Nat lunged at Brett. "Get off my stage. Get out of my sight, or you're going to regret it."

"Whatever. It's your funeral, old man." Brett yanked his instrument with one arm and dragged it off the stage toward the storage area.

Nat let out an audible sigh, shaking his head in disgust as he watched Brett disappear.

"Hey, Nat." I stepped closer to the stage. "Sorry to bug you. This might not be a good time to chat about food setup."

Nat tried to regain his composure. He sucked in a breath through his nostrils and rounded his shoulders. Then he flipped through notes on a clipboard, crossing something off with a red ballpoint pen. "Juliet, no, not at all. *You*, unlike other people—" He paused and shot one last glance in Brett's direction, as if to make sure he really had taken off. "Are on my schedule." He removed a spiral notebook from his shorts pocket. "Let's see, we want to look at the angle of the sun to make sure the food tables are in the shade come four o'clock, correct?"

"That's right."

He hopped down from the stage in a deft move for someone his age—I guessed Nat to be in his late sixties. He had long gray hair that he wore in a ponytail and tanned skin that had definitely seen its fair share of the sun in his years of managing the park. "Come this way." He walked with a purpose to the far side of the lawn. "The sun's going to set over here." He used his finger to trace the sun's angle in the sky. "The problem is that four o'clock is peak heat of the day, and this grassy area is designed to be in full sun, hence the surrounding trees. I don't think there's any way to completely avoid some sun, but you had mentioned wanting to bring over nonperishable items soon, correct?"

"If it's possible, but if not, it's okay. We can do a mad dash at the last minute. Most things are going to be in the boxes anyway. I was thinking if we could set up the drink stations, that would help."

"Not a problem." Nat got a call on his walkie-talkie. "Be there in five," he said through the static. "Come this way," he said to me.

I followed after him to the opposite side of the band shell.

"You can stage the tables here," he suggested. "This area is permanently shaded by the band shell. Then I can get some of my guys to help you move the tables out right before the guests arrive."

"Oh, yeah, that's a great idea." The section was completely shaded and a few degrees cooler. "Where will the drink tables go?"

Nat pointed to where we had just been standing. "Right there. In fact, they should be set up in the next few minutes, so feel free to start getting your stuff together whenever you're ready."

"Great. Thanks so much."

He started to move on to check in with one of his team members flagging him down for help with lighting. "If you need extra tables or chairs, feel free to let me know, and if you can't find me, you can help yourself to any of the tables in the storage area beneath the shell, okay? I left it unlocked for the time being."

"Perfect." I could tell that he was anxious to continue with his tasks, so I left him to his work.

As promised, the tables for our drink buffet went up in minutes. That meant that we could start prepping them with our linens, silverware, and glasses, and begin bringing over large tubs of cookies, house-made chips, and anything else that didn't require refrigeration. The wedding cakes would be the last thing we moved, but we could set up the cake table in the meantime.

I hurried back to the bakeshop to gather the first load

and recruit some staff to help me. Marty and Bethany were both free, so we stacked boxes of supplies on a dolly and wheeled it to the park.

The excitement was almost palpable. Happy energy hung in the air.

"This is quite the production," Marty noted, taking in the whirlwind of activity around us when we arrived at the band shell. "And I thought Kerry had said she wanted a simple park wedding."

"But it's so romantic." Bethany placed her hand on her heart and batted her lashes. "It's like something straight out of Shakespeare."

"Maybe that's the actors in tights you're thinking about," Marty teased, pointing to the stage.

In the short time I'd been away, Lance and his acting troupe had arrived and were marking out their spots on the band shell's stage. Mimi, Dani, and Randall had moved offstage.

"Drink table first?" Marty asked.

"Yeah. Let's get that set up. Carlos is bringing cases of wine soon. Then we can move on to the food tables."

Marty unloaded the first box while Bethany and I stretched light and airy sheer tablecloths in spring pastels. One table would be reserved for our Uva wines. The other would have pineapple-shaped glass drink dispensers filled with strawberry guava lemonade, virgin piña coladas, and summer berry punch, along with citrus-infused water and champagne and sparkling ciders for the official toast.

Once we set out the linens, we stood back to survey the tables. "What do you think?" I asked.

Bethany frowned. "I don't know. It feels pretty tight, doesn't it? I'm trying to imagine glasses and guests crowding in to get their drinks. I feel like we might need one more table."

"I agree," Marty said.

"Me three." I chuckled. "Flow is everything when it comes to events. We don't want guests to have to feel scrunched together while they're waiting to get a drink." I glanced around to see if Nat was nearby. I didn't see him. "I'll go get another table. Why don't you start setting out the drink dispensers?"

"Do you need a hand?" Marty asked.

"I'm not even sure if there are any extras. I'll go check and let you know." I headed through the dewy grass around to the back of the band shell. Ashland Creek gushed to my right. This side of the park was cooler, shaded by the rounded dome of the band shell and the towering redwood trees.

The storage area door was to the left of the stage. No one was around, but the door was propped open. Nat had said we could help ourselves to anything, so I figured it was okay for me to grab a table.

A short set of cement stairs led into the underground storage area. The temperature dropped as I descended into the dark unfinished basement. A strange chill ran down my spine. My arms broke out in goose bumps. Something felt off.

What's wrong with you, Jules? I asked myself as my eyes tried to adjust to the darkness.

I wasn't typically prone to freaking out over nothing, but I couldn't shake the uncomfortable feeling assaulting my body.

Maybe it was the musty smell or the fact that all of the chatter and noise of setup on the other side of the park became muffled as I ventured farther beneath the ground.

My feet tripped on something on the floor. I caught myself on the wall, blinking hard to see in the dimness.

Suddenly I realized why I was feeling so off.

Brett's bass had been smashed. Large pieces of the expensive instrument were scattered on the ground.

"Oh no," I gasped.

Shards of mahogany and strings littered the dirt floor.

Had Brett fallen down the stairs and shattered his bass in the process? His balance had been off on the stage. Maybe he really had imbibed too much already and taken a tumble down the stairs.

I tried to make sense of what I was seeing as my eyes drifted farther into the cave-like room.

Along the far wall were carts holding metal folding chairs the city used for concerts in the park. There were a few folding tables next to the chairs, along with extension cords, a box of flashlights, and a tub with rope, duct tape, and caution tape.

I was about to lift one of the smaller folding tables when my eyes landed on the back corner of the storage area.

I blinked again, hoping I might wake myself from this nightmare.

Then I let out a scream.

Brett's body was sprawled out on the dirt floor with the spike from his bass piercing his chest.

Chapter Six

My knees went weak. I thought I might collapse.

Breathe, Jules.

Breathe.

A coldness spread from the top of my head all the way down to the tips of my toes. I squeezed my fists as I took a timid step closer.

Maybe I was wrong. Maybe he wasn't dead.

My chest tightened as I bent down to his body. Blood fanned out in a large circle on his chest. I checked for a pulse or a sign that his heart was still beating. There was nothing.

I stumbled to my feet, swaying as the ceiling began to close in on me.

You have to get out of here, Jules.

I forced air through my lungs and ran up the stairs for help. Sunlight flooded my face, making me squint. Bright spots filled my sight line. It wasn't just the blinding light of the sun; it was Brett's lifeless body. This couldn't be happening. He couldn't be dead.

I took a second to steady myself against the door frame. *Keep breathing, Jules. You've got to get help.*

I pushed myself forward and ran straight into Jamie, Kerry's dad. He was holding a broken section of bass strings.

"What is that?" I asked without thinking.

His dark eyes darted from the mangled mess of strings he was holding to the storage area behind me. "I don't know. I found them on the grass."

Instinct kicked in. "Don't move," I said, holding up a finger. "I need to call for help."

Jamie shrugged.

There was something about the way he kept looking down into the dark basement area that made the tiny hairs on my arms stand at attention.

I reached into my jeans for my phone. My hands quaked as I punched in 911 and waited for an operator to answer.

This couldn't be happening on Thomas and Kerry's wedding day. How were we going to keep a murder from them?

The operator explained that an ambulance and squad car were on their way.

"Somebody died?" Jamie asked when I hung up.

"Yes." I pointed to the storage area with a quivering finger. "Brett, the bass player. He's on the floor down there with his bass in pieces." My eyes drifted to Jamie. Where was everyone? All of the activity was taking place on the other side of the band shell. It felt like we were in some other dimension, like this wasn't reality.

He dropped the strings on the ground like they had suddenly zapped him with electricity. "He's dead? The dude is dead?"

I squeezed my eyes shut, trying to force the image of his bloody chest away. "It looked like someone stabbed him."

"No. That can't be. I just saw him. We were talking, like, a minute ago. He was good. He was pretty drunk, but good."

My stomach dropped. This wasn't good for Jamie. He was on the scene of the crime, he was holding pieces of Brett's bass, and he was admitting that he was likely the last person to have seen the musician alive.

What should I do? The operator had told me not to move until the police and paramedics arrived, but I wanted to scream for help. There were dozens of people just a few hundred feet away from me, but none of them had any idea that a murder had just occurred. It was as if I was living with my feet in two different worlds. There was the carefree world of wedding setup, and the nightmare of a man being brutally murdered.

Not only was I worried about being face-to-face with a potential killer, but this was the worst possible outcome for Kerry. A man had been killed on her wedding day at her wedding venue, and now it was looking like her estranged father was the most likely suspect.

"Where did you see him?" I asked, placing my hand over my stomach to try and steady myself.

"Right out here. He needed a hand with his bass. I helped him carry it downstairs. He said he needed to store it for a few while he took care of something before the wedding."

"When was this?" I wanted to keep Jamie talking until the police arrived.

Please hurry. I said a silent prayer to the universe and kept my eyes locked on Jamie. I didn't want him make a run for it. Come to think of it, it was odd that Kerry had let him out of her sight, given the tight leash she'd had on him at the bakeshop.

He shrugged. "I don't know. Like I said, a couple minutes. I helped him and then I went to see if I could find a drink. I thought maybe the bar would be pouring by now, but no luck."

"Did Brett say anything?"

"Not really. He seemed pretty wrecked, though."

"Wrecked?"

"You know, drunk. I asked him where he scored, but he said he hadn't been drinking. Yeah, right. The dude was wrecked."

Sirens wailed nearby.

Thank goodness.

The Professor and an EMS crew arrived a few minutes later. Their flashing red and blue lights and police sirens had brought the crowd of workers behind them, and suddenly my nightmare and dream worlds collided. I felt like I was in the middle of a circus performance as two officers worked to keep everyone back while the rest of the team raced toward us.

I directed them to the body and waited for further instructions.

Jamie twitched and kept cracking his knuckles. "Man, this isn't good. This isn't good for Kerry. She's gonna be pissed."

I wondered if he meant at him or the situation. I wanted to keep an open mind. It wasn't fair to assume that he was a killer just because he'd recently been released from prison, but given the circumstances, I had a feeling the Professor was going to want to talk to Jamie first.

Time slowed to a thick sludge, like the dredges of a coffeepot left sitting for too long.

I tried not to look as the EMS workers carted Brett's

body away. The Professor approached us. He was dressed in a pair of casual slacks and a short-sleeved button-down shirt with a lightweight blazer. After removing a Moleskine journal from his front pocket, he gave me a pained smile.

"Juliet, alas, this is not the outcome I was hoping for today. Could you please fill me in on everything that has transpired?"

"Of course." I explained how I'd come to see about another table and had discovered Brett's body. Everything poured out in a jumbled mess. I concentrated on remembering every detail that I could while it was still fresh in my mind.

The Professor took copious notes. Jamie rocked on his feet while I relayed what I'd witnessed. When I finished, the Professor turned his attention to Jamie. I watched as his eyes took a brief survey of the space around us, noting the wadded-up bass strings on the ground near Jamie's feet.

"Can you tell what happened from your perspective?"

Jamie repeated what he'd said to me, leaving out the part about finding the strings. The Professor made more notes. Then he motioned for one of his officers to come over. "Can you bag this?" He pointed to the broken strings.

The police officer used a gloved hand to pick up the bass strings and place them in a large evidence bag.

"What about the wedding?" Jamie asked. "This is going to ruin my honey girl's day."

A frown tugged on the Professor's cheeks. "We'll work to do what we can to ensure the wedding can go on as planned, but I will need your assistance. I'd like you to come take a walk to the station with me, so I can get a formal statement."

Jamie flinched. "You gonna arrest me? Because I'm a felon, you think I'm a killer? That's the deal? That's how we're going to play this? Why would I kill someone I don't even know—on my girl's wedding day?"

"I assure you that I didn't say that. I simply need to take a formal statement." The Professor's tone was firm.

"You don't need to take her statement, and she found the body." Jamie glared at me.

"I believe that we share a common wish for Kerry and Thomas to be able to revel in their day, and I ask that you join me in cooperating so that we may ensure that the wedding can go on as intended."

That shut Jamie up. "Fine. Let's do this. I've got nothing to hide."

The Professor gave me a short nod. "Juliet, I'll be in touch shortly." He directed his team and then escorted Jamie away.

I wasn't sure what to think about Jamie, but the one thing that was evident was that he cared about Kerry. His aggressive attitude had vanished the minute the Professor had mentioned his daughter's name. I wanted to believe that he wasn't a killer. He raised a valid point. Why would he kill a stranger? If he had really done everything he could to make sure he was released from jail in time to attend the wedding, why would he jeopardize that? Unless he was a more serious criminal than I realized. Kerry had been distraught about his arrival. Maybe I had mistaken her reaction. I had thought that she was torn—that part of her was excited to have her dad at the wedding. But what if she was actually scared? Maybe she knew that he was dangerous.

I sighed and started to walk around to the front of the bandstand. Word had obviously already spread. A large crowd of workers had gathered in front of the stage. People were trying to get a glimpse of the police activity. They whispered in hushed tones.

"Is it true, Jules? Someone's dead?" Bethany asked. She and Marty were still unpacking our supplies, but both of them were keeping an eye on the commotion.

"Yes." My body shuddered at the memory of seeing the blunt point of an instrument jabbed into Brett's chest.

Marty reached out to steady me. "Do you need anything? Bethany, can you grab her a water?"

Bethany was already pouring me a glass of our lemon-infused water. She handed it to me. "Jules, I'm so sorry. That's terrible."

I took a sip. It glided down my throat, spreading a much-needed coolness throughout my body. A heavy weight sank like a rock in my stomach.

"Would it help to talk about it?" Marty asked.

I gulped another sip. "I think I'm in shock."

"I'm sure you are," he agreed. "Rumors are swirling that it was one of the band members who was killed."

"Yeah, I recognized him right away. It was Brett, the bassist. I found him in the storage area. Someone smashed his instrument and stabbed him with the spike."

"Yikes." Bethany grimaced. "That's dark."

The twirling feeling in my stomach returned. "It was pretty gruesome." I tried to blink away the image of the pool of blood on his chest and the way his mouth hung open. "I don't understand why anyone would kill him, and here—at a wedding. Why?"

"There's no explanation when it comes to murder," Marty wisely offered.

"It's so true. Why did he need to die? And poor Thomas and Kerry. Can you imagine showing up to your wedding and learning that one of the band members you hired was brutally murdered?" I picked up a wineglass and set it back down again. My mouth felt like I had swallowed sand. My hands were clammy and damp. "I don't know what to do next. Do we keep setting up and pretend like the show must go on, as Lance would say, or are they going to postpone the wedding?"

"All good questions," Marty agreed.

"I don't envy being in the Professor's position. Does he tell them? Talk about a dark cloud over your special day. But then if he doesn't tell them, how are they going to feel when they eventually find out? Because this is Ashland, and they *will* find out."

Bethany refilled my water glass. "Totally. There's no way to keep a secret around here. In fact, odds are probably pretty good that they've already heard."

She had a point.

"I wouldn't tell them, though. What good does that serve?" She handed me the water, placing a lemon slice on the side of the glass. "It's their wedding day. They can just show up in a happy blissful state. I mean, you're right, they'll hear it about it later, but aren't they taking off for their honeymoon tonight anyway?"

I nodded.

"See, so why can't the wedding go on as planned? When they get back, they'll hear about it, but it shouldn't have to ruin their big day."

I tended to agree with her, but I wondered what the odds were of getting through the ceremony and reception without anyone mentioning the murder.

As if reading my mind, Marty chimed in. "We'd have to make a pact amongst the guests that mum's the word about the murder, though."

"Right." I plunged the lemon slice into the water. "I was thinking the same thing. Is it even possible?"

He threw his hand out toward the park, which had been completely transformed. It looked like a scene from one of Lance's most extravagantly romantic productions at OSF. "This is Ashland, magical Ashland. Anything is possible."

I hesitated. "Do you think they'd be mad, though?"

Bethany answered first. She had finished lining up the first crate of wineglasses in symmetrical rows. "Maybe, but after the fact, who cares, right? If we all rally around them to protect their day, isn't that sweet? Isn't that what they do for us as a community? They made an oath to serve and protect. We're reciprocating that. I think it's a gesture of kindness. Give them their day. Let them take off on a honeymoon. Work will be waiting for them when they return. They already have to deal with such heavy stuff every day, I vote let the wedding go on."

Janet had come up behind us. "I second that. Thomas and Kerry have been looking forward to this day for months. I would hate to crush their dreams, or have them feel like the marriage is tainted before it even starts." She held a pair of gardening shears in one hand. "We can't let these beautiful flowers go to waste. And, I know that if we ask, this community will hold them in their hearts, while also honoring this terrible loss."

"What do you think the Professor will say?"

"I think he'll agree. He had intended to walk Kerry down the aisle. I don't know if that's changed now that her dad is here, but he knows how tremendously hard they've worked these last few months. They deserve all the happiness today."

I didn't mention that the Professor had taken Jamie in for further questioning. If he ended up arresting Kerry's dad, he was going to have to come up with an excuse as to why Jamie wasn't going to walk her down the aisle.

Janet's phone rang. "This is Doug now." She answered

the call. Their conversation was brief. When she hung up, her eyes brimmed with tears. "Well, that settles it. Doug said the wedding can and should go on as intended. He's not going to say anything to Thomas or Kerry, but he wanted me to know that Jamie has been arrested for Brett's murder."

Chapter Seven

That was terrible news. It didn't make sense that Jamie did everything in his power to make parole in order to attend his daughter's wedding, only to kill someone and land himself back in jail. He might have been a criminal, but I had seen the way he had looked at Kerry the other day with such pride and affection. Why would he jeopardize the relationship he was building with his daughter and risk missing out on arguably one of the most important days of her life?

Janet sprang into action. She held her gardening shears in one hand and pulled a pencil from her apron pocket. "Okay, I'm going to start spreading the word to vendors about keeping quiet on what's happened. Juliet, can you talk to your mom? There's no one better than Helen to tackle getting the word out to the community."

"I'm on it." I needed to get the next load from Torte anyway, and maybe getting away from the scene of the crime for a few minutes would help settle my nerves. After making sure that Bethany and Marty were okay, I headed for the bakeshop. On my way I bumped into Lance, who had completed his dress rehearsal.

"Darling, how are you? I heard that you found the body. Shocking. Absolutely shocking." His words were in his normal tone, but his jaw was firm and his eyes serious. He pulled me into a long hug.

I almost broke down, but somehow I managed to inhale through my nose and exhale through my mouth in a rhythmic pattern.

"Was it awful?" He pulled away and studied my face. "I've been looking everywhere for you, but the park is a mob scene."

I gulped. "It was pretty bad."

"Juliet Capshaw, you are built of strong stuff." Lance tried to give me a pep talk. "Don't let this take you down."

I bobbed my head in agreement. "I know. I just keep replaying it. I can't stop seeing his body and the blood . . ." I trailed off.

Lance reached for my hand and squeezed it tight. "Stiff upper lip, darling. We'll get through this together, and you know the best way forward is to face this head-on. We must solve this case ourselves. It's the only way you'll recover."

I wasn't sure about that, but he did have a point about facing my fear.

He straightened his skinny tie. "I can't linger. I just had to come check in with you, but I promised Dani and Randall that I would reach out to our company bassist to see if he can fill in tonight. As soon as I remedy this music crisis, we need to put our heads together about the real tragedy." He nodded to the side where the police had roped off the area behind the stage.

"I feel so terrible for Kerry."

He twisted his wrist. "She'll never know. Haven't you

heard? We are already implementing Operation Donut Break Her Heart."

"Wait, what?"

"It's a pun. Donut Break Her Heart. Donut Ruin Her Wedding Day. I could go on and on. Get it? Kerry loves donuts, and we will not allow this dastardly deed to ruin her day."

"I get it, Lance, but what does it mean?"

"It means that you, me, and everyone—everyone—in town are going to zip our lips and pretend that setup this afternoon has been nothing short of a dream." He made a zipping motion across his lips.

"I'm with you on that. We were just chatting with Janet, but I hadn't heard that there was an official name in place. In fact, I'm heading to Torte to recruit Mom to take the lead, but I meant that I'm more heartbroken for Kerry about her dad."

Lance snapped his head. "Her dad? Do tell."

Of course he hadn't heard yet. "Jamie's been arrested for the murder."

"What?" Lance gasped. "Now we're entering Shakespearean territory. The father of the bride arrested for *murder* on his daughter's wedding day? If that doesn't have the makings of a classic tragedy, I don't know what does. But why?"

"That's my question. I don't get it. I know he was just released from prison, but if anything, that makes him the least likely suspect in my book."

"Could it be a buried secret from their family's past? What if Brett and Kerry had a fling? Perhaps they're old lovers and Jamie showed up to exact his revenge."

"I don't think so. That's a stretch. Brett doesn't seem like Kerry's type. All those tattoos. The late nights gigging. He's the opposite of Thomas, and substantially older, too."

Lance held up his index finger and cut me off. "No, wait, I've got it. Maybe it was unrequited love. Brett intended to declare his undying love for Kerry. When Judge Barbarelli asked whether there was anyone in the audience who had a reason that Kerry and Thomas shouldn't be wed, Brett was planning to jump to his feet, declare his love, and hence destroy Kerry's only chance at happiness."

"That sounds like a great piece for the stage, but I don't think so. Kerry hired Heart Strings and I saw them interacting. She didn't show any signs of harboring old tension. You know as well as I do that Kerry is one tough cookie. She doesn't need her estranged father to sweep in and save her. She's a strong, capable woman. I hardly see her as a damsel in distress."

Lance blew out a breath and shook his head. "You're absolutely no fun, darling. No fun. Where's your sense of theatrics?"

I pointed to the crime scene. "We have real theatrics, we don't need imaginary ones."

"Touché." He gave me a half bow. "On that note, let's begin the implementation of Donut Break Her Heart and reconvene here shortly. Remember, chin up, stiff upper lip. You've got this." He patted my jaw in a show of support before taking off in the opposite direction toward the Shakespeare stairs.

I crossed into the plaza. As much as Lance liked to play up the dramatics, I knew that he would do anything for Kerry. No one was a more loyal friend than Lance. He was who I wanted by my side in good times and bad. I was so grateful for our friendship and how it had developed since I'd been home.

Carlos adored Lance as much as I did, and he and Lance's current love, Arlo, had become fast friends. I felt so lucky to have such an amazing community around me, and I, too, would do anything in my power to make sure that Thomas and Kerry received that same support today.

With that in mind, I headed into Torte. Andy had a dozen champagne glasses lined up on the espresso bar and was pouring pink sparkling bubbles into each of them. "Whoa, I take it the champagne lattes are a hit?"

Sequoia dabbed a spill with a dish towel. "You wouldn't believe how many we've sold. People love the idea of something sparkling in their coffee. It's given us an idea to play around with some infused sparkling waters next week, but this order is for a large party that's taking over two tables on the Calle. They're not even connected to the wedding, but in their words, not mine, these drinks are 'brunch goals.'"

I tried to laugh, but it fell flat. "Yeah, that doesn't sound like your vibe."

"Hey, speaking of vibes," Andy interjected. "What happened at the park? Everyone coming in is saying there's a ton of police activity, and we're hearing rumors that someone was killed. That can't be true, can it?"

Another wave of sadness washed over me. I still couldn't believe it was true. I wanted to pinch myself. Brett was dead. He was really dead. "Unfortunately, it is." I gave them a brief recap of what had happened.

"That's terrible." Andy finished filling the glasses with champagne. "I just served Brett and Heart Strings the other day. How can he be dead? It doesn't seem possible."

"I know." My hand instinctively went to my stomach. "It's awful, but the consensus is that the wedding should go on. I'm actually looking for Mom. Is she around?"

"She was downstairs a minute ago," Sequoia said. "Is there anything we can do?"

"The goal is to try and preserve the day for Thomas and Kerry, so if either of them happen to come in, which

I can't imagine they will, just try not to bring up the murder."

"No problem, boss." Andy began adding shots of espresso to the champagne glasses. "We're going to close any minute now. We were going to a while ago, but the news of the murder brought more and more people in."

"I say flip the sign as soon as you can." I left the espresso bar in their capable hands and went to find Mom. She was helping Steph put the finishing touches on the wedding cake.

"Wow, that is incredible. It's like a work of art." I stopped to admire the watercolored tiers with sweet vignettes from around Lithia Park. The bottom tier captured the flush of spring colors and the view of the Elizabethan theater from the duck pond. The second tier depicted a family of black-tail deer nibbling on the grass. The third tier traced Ashland Creek as it wound through the forested trails. Next came the elegant Lithia fountain, which resembled Grecian architecture. And finally the top tier showcased a bride and groom, who bore a striking resemblance to Thomas and Kerry exchanging vows at the band shell.

"This might be my favorite cake of all time," I said.

Steph cracked a grin. "It's pretty sick."

Mom placed her arm around our young designer. "'Pretty sick' doesn't even begin to capture your talent, my dear." She turned to me. "I don't know how we're going to convince her to stay here once she graduates. Every cakery and pastry shop in the world is going to want her. We're going to have to take out a second mortgage to keep her."

"It's true."

Steph shrugged. "We'll see."

She had been noncommittal about what was next for her. I knew that she and Sterling were getting even more serious since moving in together. Like Mom, I'd been wondering if they were thinking of leaving Ashland once Steph was finished with school. I wouldn't blame them. In fact, as much as I would hate to lose them, part of my role as their boss and mentor was to push them to new challenges. I would cry for sure, but I would also send them on to their next adventure with glowing recommendations.

Don't think about that now, I told myself.

"Listen, have you heard the news?" I asked them.

Mom's face turned solemn. "Doug texted. We've been worried about you. How are you?"

If anyone could bring the tears I had been trying to hold back from the surface, it was Mom. "I'm okay," I lied.

She frowned. "I've been trying to keep busy while waiting to hear more. I can't imagine how you must be feeling, honey."

"I'm trying not to think about it."

"Okay." She gave my hand a light squeeze.

"Janet told me that they arrested Jamie."

"Oh dear." Mom placed a paintbrush into a cup of water. "I was worried that might happen. When Doug texted me, he mentioned that they found some incriminating evidence on Jamie."

My mind went to the bundle of bass strings. "Really? Did he say what?"

Mom shook her head. "No. It was a short text. I'm sure he's feeling terrible for arresting Kerry's father, and on her wedding day, no less."

"I know." I paused. "Anyway, Janet said that everyone is in agreement that the wedding can and should go on, and she wondered if you could take the lead on spreading the word. She's going to talk to the vendors and everyone who's at the park now. I don't know, do you think Kerry and Thomas will be angry if we don't tell them? But on the other hand, I can't imagine that they would want to go through with the wedding if they hear what happened."

She was thoughtful for a minute. "I suspect they already know."

"You do?"

"If they're anything like Doug, and I think they are, because he's trained them, detective work is who they are. I can't imagine that either of them has completely cut themselves off from work updates today. I could be wrong, but I doubt it."

I hadn't thought of that possibility. "That's a really good point."

"Kerry is getting ready at Lithia Springs. I will start making some calls to let everyone know the wedding is a go, but maybe you should pop in and check on her. I think she would appreciate a friendly face right about now, and it might help get you out of your own head."

"Yeah, okay, I'll do that, and then as soon as I get back, we can start bringing everything to the park."

Mom gave me a tight hug. "Keep breathing, honey. You're going to be fine, and Kerry needs a girlfriend today."

The thought made me tear up. I left for the hotel with a new mission—to be there for Kerry in whatever way she needed me. Instead of trying to direct her day, I just needed to be a friend, whether she wanted a shoulder to cry on, someone to vent to, or just company while she transformed herself into a bride.

I walked with purpose up Main Street, wondering whether she already knew that her father was behind bars again. Either way, we could face it together. Every woman needed a friend by her side on her wedding day, and Kerry was no exception.

Chapter Eight

Ashland Springs was the only "high-rise" in town. The landmark Art Deco hotel, built in 1925, was designed in European style with a pale buttercream exterior and white-trimmed windows. Tourists often stopped to snap selfies in front of the hotel's extravagant entrance and historic lobby. Ashland Springs' exterior was a photo-worthy architectural gem, and its interior was equally impressive. Stepping into the lobby always made me feel like I was on the set of Agatha Christie's *Death on the Nile*. Leafy potted palms, soft yellow walls, whirling ceiling fans, and an iron veranda greeted me.

I stopped at the front desk to confirm that Kerry was getting ready in the wedding suite, and then took the elevator to the top floor.

Kerry answered the door wearing a silky robe. Her hair had been curled in loose waves, and her subtle makeup accentuated her gorgeous cheekbones and bright green eyes, while still allowing her to look natural.

"You look amazing." I greeted her with a hug.

"Thanks." She gave me a hard stare. "I know, Jules. You don't have to hide it from me. I heard everything."

"I kind of figured. We were going to try to keep it from you and Thomas—let you have today. I'm so sorry."

"It doesn't really change anything for me. It's not going to stop me from marrying Thomas. I knew I couldn't count on Jamie." She walked over to the bathroom door where her wedding gown hung, pressed and ready for its big appearance. For a minute I thought she was going to cry, but instead she pursed her lips tight and turned around to face me. "Can you do me a favor?"

"Of course. Anything."

"I want you to help Doug with the case." She fluffed the hem of the empire-cut dress. The style suited her. A band of delicate organza flower embellishments lined the waist, bodice, and hemline. The chiffon fabric gave the dress an airy feel. She was going to look amazing in it.

She wanted my help? I cleared my throat and tried not to choke.

"You and Lance are always snooping around. This time I give you my blessing. Jamie has spent a lifetime disappointing me, but he's not a killer. I know that much for sure. I want to go on our honeymoon tonight and sip margaritas on the ship for a week and not worry about anything. I know that Doug is going to do everything he can, but I would feel better if you helped, too."

"Consider it done." I couldn't believe that this was happening. Out of everyone, Kerry had been the least receptive to any input Lance and I had offered. Not that I blamed her. She took her job seriously, and hadn't approved of our meddling.

"He's not a killer," she repeated. I got the sense she was saying it as much for herself as for me. "He's not."

"I agree. It doesn't make sense. He obviously wanted to be here for you. Why would he ruin that?"

She moved to the window. "I don't know. I'm not sure that he didn't have an ulterior motive for showing up, but he can't be a killer."

The wedding suite offered panoramic views of all of downtown and the rolling hills to the east, where vibrant patches of yellow and purple vetch bloomed in colorful swaths.

"Can I ask what he was in jail for? You don't have to tell me if you're not comfortable."

"No, it's fine." She kept her gaze focused out the window. "Like I said before, he was in and out of prison my entire childhood. Petty theft, that sort of thing, but things took a turn about ten years ago when he was arrested for armed robbery. He and some of his buddies decided to set their sights higher—on a bank. He was driving the get-away van. I don't think he would have ever hurt anyone, but he got caught with weapons in the back. His friends left. He shouldered the blame for the entire thing."

"That's terrible."

She held her chin high as she flexed her fingers, letting the light from the window reflect off her engagement ring. "He never should have been involved to begin with. He made that choice."

I couldn't argue with her on that.

"Kerry, I promise that I'll do anything and everything I can to help the Professor and clear your dad's name. Lance will, too. You and Thomas deserve to get away and not worry about any of this, okay?"

She nodded.

"So, with that in mind, what can I do to help get you in the wedding spirit?" I glanced around the wedding suite. Kerry's luggage was packed and waiting by the door. Her makeup and hair were done, and her rustic bouquet filled with roses, ranunculus, hellebores, crabapple, and cherry blossoms rested in a box on the bed.

"Nothing. I'm going to get in my dress soon, and then we're supposed to meet at the park early for photos. It's weird that they take photos before the ceremony, but the photographer says that's the way it's done now."

"Actually, I think it's good. You and Thomas can have a moment together just the two of you before everything gets crazy."

"Yeah." She sounded wistful.

"Are you sure there's nothing else you need?"

"Nope. Janet is going to come by and take me to the park. That will be nice."

I was glad that she wasn't going to be alone. "I can stay if you want company."

"No, I'm fine, and I know you must have tons of setup to do. I really appreciate you stopping by, and it is a relief to know that you and Lance and Doug have my back while we're gone."

"We always have your back, Kerry."

She blinked away tears. "Thanks, that means a lot."

I hugged her again. I knew that physical displays of affection weren't really her thing, but I couldn't not hug her. Even with Kerry's strength and resilience, she had to be feeling a weight of emotions.

To my surprise, she hugged me back. "Thanks, Jules," she said when she pulled away. "You're a good friend."

"You are, too. I can't wait to watch you marry one of my oldest friends today. It's going to be beautiful, okay?" The sting of happy tears hit my eyes. I blinked them back.

She bobbed her head in agreement as her eyes misted, too. "I hope so."

"I know so. See you at the park soon." I blew her a kiss and took off.

Mom's advice had been right. I felt better after our talk. Even though it was terrible that Brett's murder and Jamie's arrest had happened on Kerry's wedding day, I felt relieved that she knew and that we didn't have to try and dance around the subject. Hopefully she could enjoy the wedding and their honeymoon.

That's your new mission, Jules, I told myself as I walked down Main Street. Make today the most magical experience for both of them. I could focus all of my nervous energy on that.

At Torte it was all hands on deck. The bakeshop was closed for walk-in customers and everyone was pitching in. Andy and Sterling were in charge of transporting the wedding and groom's cake. Mom, Steph, Rosa, and Sequoia had created an assembly line to pack the picnic boxes.

"Where do you want me to jump in?" I asked.

Mom pointed to the back door where Andy and Sterling stood, balancing the groom's cake. "Can you help them?"

"You bet." I propped the door for them and tried to remember to breathe as they carried the heavy donut-shaped cake up the stairs. "What can I do?" I asked once they made it safely to the top.

"Just clear a path, boss." Andy kept his arms firmly gripped on the cake box.

Transporting custom cakes was perhaps the most agonizing part of being a professional baker. So many things could go wrong. From tripping over the sidewalk to having to pump the brakes when delivering a cake in our van. Over the years I had learned some invaluable lessons in wedding cake deliveries that I imparted to my team.

First was making sure that all of the decorating was finished before stacking the tiers. There was nothing worse than trying to do touch-up on the top tier once a cake was stacked. My second piece of advice was to stack the tiers at the bakeshop whenever possible. Trying to stack a cake on site came with inherent issues like time. Often venues scheduled back-to-back receptions during the height of wedding season. I had been burned on more than one occasion, trying to get into ballrooms to stack tiers as the bride and groom were about to make their big entrance. Plus having event staff milling around and watching you attempt to level a cake was nerve racking, to say the least. It was like putting yourself on full display.

Making sure each layer was properly doweled was another important element. Dowels offered structural support so that the tiers didn't slide during the delivery process. And finally, my last requirement was chilling cakes for at least twenty-four hours before moving them. Cold buttercream was like armor, and both the wedding cake and groom's cake were fully armored after a long night's rest in our walk-in.

I made sure to give Andy and Sterling a wide berth as we crossed into the park. The police were still surveying the crime scene, but they had removed the yellow tape. That was a step in the right direction.

The transformation of the band shell took my breath away. Hand-sewn quilts created a patchwork pattern on the grassy slope. Flower garlands and paper lanterns blended in with the park's natural greenery. Fairy lights and topiaries enclosed the wooden dance floor. Our food and drink tables had been accented with vases of pale purple lilacs, willow branches, spray roses, and berries.

"This looks like a set from OSF." Andy sounded impressed.

"It's amazing," I agreed. "Let's just say it didn't look like that a few hours ago."

I showed them where to put the cake and then went to check on Bethany and Marty's progress. In the time I had been gone, they had managed to set up the drink station, and Carlos had finished the wine table. Dozens of our wine bottles shimmered beneath the afternoon sun. Stemmed glasses in neat rows awaited guests. Steph had created signage for the tables in calligraphy. Cream note cards highlighted the different flavor profiles in each wine we were serving, as well as descriptions of the nonalcoholic beverage options.

"This is looking so great," I said.

"I can't wait until the cakes and picnic boxes are all set up, too," Bethany said. "I'm dying to take photos of everything." She cringed. "Sorry, that's totally the wrong choice of words today."

"Don't worry about it." I told everyone about my conversation with Kerry. "Of course, she's devastated about Brett's murder, but like Lance says, the show must go on, so I think the best thing we can do is try and make this a memorable night for both of them."

"I'm glad we don't have to tiptoe around the murder." Marty placed folded cocktail napkins at the far end of the drink table.

"Me, too. It's better this way."

"She is in good spirits?" Carlos asked.

"Yeah, I think so. I mean, obviously having a murder occur on your wedding day puts a cloud over everything, but considering that, she seemed good, and she definitely wants to go forward."

"Si. I think this is good, too," Carlos agreed. "We must focus on the love."

Our eyes met across the table. I wanted to fall into the

comfort of his arms, but instead I swallowed and concentrated on the task in front of me.

For the next hour we took at least a dozen trips between the park and Torte. By the time we finished setting out our romantic boxes and putting the finishing touches on the wedding cake, it was time to get ready.

"Great work, everyone. Go change, and we'll see you back here soon," I said to the team.

Carlos and I walked to Torte together. "Julieta, how are you holding up?" He secured his arm around me. I drank in the scent of his woodsy aftershave.

"I'm okay. I'm trying to concentrate on the wedding. I can fall apart later, and there's going to be stuff for us to do starting tomorrow, but for the moment, I'm trying to forget about that."

"I understand, mi querida." He squeezed my shoulder. "I will be by your side every step of the way."

I knew that. I felt an immense sense of relief knowing that I had a partner in Carlos. We could get through anything together. Thomas and Kerry were about to embark on the same adventure, and I wanted to do everything I could to make sure we sent them off surrounded by love.

Chapter Nine

The wedding was nothing short of enchanting. I almost forgot about Brett's murder as I watched my friends exchange vows and seal their marriage with a tender kiss. Thomas looked handsome in his tux, and Kerry was a vision in her ethereal dress. The layers of chiffon fabric reminded me of a traditional wedding cake. Her hair caught the late afternoon breeze a couple of times, flowing out behind her like the scene was being staged by a professional photographer.

The Professor played the part of proud father as if the role had been scripted for him. I knew he wasn't acting when he teared up giving Kerry away and hugging Thomas tight.

Fortunately the police had managed to clear away any evidence of the crime scene, allowing everyone to bask in the fragrant aroma of the wedding arrangements and the feeling of love.

After the newlyweds had exchanged rings and shared their vows, Heart Strings took the stage for their first set and the wine began to flow. I found it odd that the band was continuing on after the news of Brett's death. They were either callous or the upmost professionals who could compartmentalize in a way that I couldn't understand. Seeing them perform gave new meaning to "the show must go on."

There was a jovial atmosphere as people swayed to the music and toasted to the happy couple, oblivious about what had transpired before their arrival. It was hard to believe a man had been murdered only a few hours ago.

Lance and Arlo were seated next to us. "This is absolutely wonderful," Lance gushed, raising his glass of blushing pink rosé. "Talk about divine. I say here's to Thomas and Kerry, but also here's to us, Juliet. This is a vision. And to think Kerry wanted to sneak off to the courthouse." He threw his hand to his forehead.

"I don't know. I think a courthouse wedding has a nice ring to it." Arlo caught my eye and winked.

Lance punched him in the shoulder. "Don't you dare. Don't even think of it. You'll have to find some other charming, witty, and ravishingly handsome man."

They looked like they could be the ones tying the knot in their matching black tailored suits. Lance had accented his with a freesia floral navy tie and pocket square. Arlo's tie was the mirror opposite. I was pretty confident that they had planned the look.

"Are you two thinking of marriage?" Carlos asked with a wide smile.

"Us? No, no. We're having fun, aren't we, Arlo?" Lance tried to play it off, but I could tell by the longing behind his eyes that he had probably given more than a passing thought to the idea.

"Speak for yourself, Rousseau." Arlo leaned against the

edge of the quilt with one hand anchored to his hip. He shot me a confident smile.

Lance's eyes widened. His mouth fell open. He clutched his wineglass in one hand and swatted at Arlo. "Don't tease."

Arlo tilted his head to the side. "Who said I was teasing?"

Carlos squeezed my knee.

Lance was about to say more when Mom and the Professor strolled toward us.

"May we join you?" The Professor pointed to the edge of the quilt. They looked equally regal. Mom's Aegean blue A-line dress with fluttering sleeves and accompanying shawl made her look like the mother of the bride. The same was true for the Professor in his stone gray suit with his orange sherbet and navy paisley tie.

"Absolutely." I scooted closer to Carlos to make room.

Mom sat next to me. "I don't know about you all, but my eyes are completely dry." She dabbed the side of her eyes with the Professor's monogrammed handkerchief.

"Who's crying?" Lance fanned his face. "I'm not crying. You're crying."

We all laughed.

Carlos stood. "Is everyone ready for food?"

"I thought you'd never ask. This emotional roller coaster has me famished." Lance placed a hand on his taut stomach.

"Appetite, an universal wolf," the Professor quoted Shakespeare to Lance, then turned to Carlos. "Shall I help you?"

"No, no. It is no problem." Carlos waved him off. "I'll be back shortly." He left for picnic provisions.

"That truly was a touching ceremony. I, too, may have

shed a tear." The Professor removed his jacket and rested it on the quilt. He unbuttoned his shirt and rolled up the sleeves an inch.

In my lightweight summer dress, it was the perfect temp, but I could imagine that standing under the heat of the sun on the stage in a jacket must have made him hot. A slight breeze rustled the leaves on the white birch and leafy oak trees, sending the paper lanterns swinging.

"Weddings always make me sob like a baby," Arlo added. "I don't even know Kerry or Thomas that well yet, and I'm a blubbering mess."

"It seemed especially poignant after this morning." Mom voiced what I was sure everyone was thinking. "I didn't realize how much I needed a little hit of happiness. I just hope that Thomas and Kerry feel that way, too."

I glanced around the park. The mood had lifted. Guests swayed to the music and nibbled on our sweet chips and fruit salsa and raspberry-filled donuts. Kerry and Thomas circulated through the crowd, their hands entwined, greeting guests and stopping for impromptu photos. Their eyes were bright, and their smiles lit up the already airy park. I doubted that they had forgotten about the horrific turn of events earlier, but it was obvious that they had found a way to put Brett's murder in the back of their minds and soak up the reception.

Carlos returned with a stack of picnic boxes and two bottles of wine tucked under one arm. "Who's ready to eat?"

"I am absolutely famished. Love will do that to you, won't it?" Lance shot a steamy look at Arlo before getting up to help him distribute the boxes.

Arlo opened his box. "These are too beautiful to eat. I don't even know where to start."

"Everything is made to be enjoyed together," Mom replied. "Like with a regular picnic, you can have tastes of everything."

"Be sure to try her potato salad." I held up the container of creamy potato salad loaded with pickles, hard-boiled eggs, and Mom's special secret ingredient. "It's legendary."

"This sandwich looks amazing, too." Lance took a bite of the club.

"Do you know what club sandwich stands for?" I asked.

Everyone shook their heads.

"Chicken and lettuce under bacon." I grinned. "Well, at least that's the food lore passed on from my culinary school instructor."

"What?" Lance put his sandwich down momentarily so he could mime having his head explode. "Now I'm never going to look at a club sandwich the same way again."

"It blew my mind, too."

"Anything under bacon is good in my book," Arlo teased.

"I will drink to that." Carlos opened a bottle of our pinot noir. "Can I top anyone off?"

The Professor held up his glass. "I don't mind if I do this evening. My colleagues in Medford are taking calls tonight, which means I'm off duty and going to imbibe for once."

Mom rested her hand on his knee. "And don't forget dancing."

"Ah yes, I did promise my lovely bride a turn around the dance floor." His eyes shone, becoming almost glossy as he offered her his hand.

"Oh, we're all going to cut loose later." Lance shot a

glance to me. "I expect our squad to set an example for everyone else. After the performance, I'm dragging each of you onto the dance floor."

Carlos caught my eye and smiled. "Si, count us in. It has been a long time since Julieta and I have shared a dance."

My heart fluttered as he held my gaze. Maybe it was the wedding, the dazzling light filtering through the trees, the romantic music, or the wine, but there was nothing I wanted more at the moment than to be swept up in his arms.

I unpacked my picnic box instead.

The conversation turned to lighter subjects as we ate and drank more wine and enjoyed the open air and being together.

Lance excused himself to go check in with his actors. Thomas and Kerry made their way over. We all greeted them with hugs.

"It was such a gorgeous ceremony." Mom beamed.

"Thanks," Kerry returned her smile. "It turned out better than expected." She and I exchanged a quick glance.

Thomas couldn't take his eyes off his new bride. "Now we're ready to cut the cake and hit the dance floor."

"I think Lance has other plans in mind." I nodded to the stage, where Lance was tapping on the mic.

"Everyone, may I have your attention, please?" He was in his element. "First, a toast to the happy couple."

I thought he was going to launch into a speech, but instead the Professor reached for another microphone that they must have stashed on our blanket. He cleared his throat and spoke directly to Thomas and Kerry, who were by his side. "This occasion has filled my heart and every heart here that had the chance to bear witness to your love. This sea of faces around you is the reflection of your love and how you show up for this community. Let us reflect that back on you tonight and every future night."

Mom reached for my hand. I leaned into her.

"My wish for you both is to release doubt. As the Bard so wisely said,

Doubt thou the stars are fire;
Doubt that the sun doth move;
Doubt truth to be a liar;
But never doubt I love.

"No one here tonight can doubt your love. Hold that in your hearts, and your future is written in the stars. To Thomas and Kerry."

"To Thomas and Kerry," we all responded, raising our glasses.

"Kiss, kiss," Lance said into the mic.

As their lips touched, applause broke out.

Lance pulled the crowd's attention back to the stage. "And without further ado, let's continue this love fest with a scene featuring Beatrice and Benedick from *Much Ado About Nothing*." He clapped and waved the actors forward.

We watched with rapt attention as the OSF duo performed arguably Shakespeare's most memorable romance. It was impossible not to get caught up in the dreamlike atmosphere as the sun began to set and twinkle lights and paper lanterns illuminated the park. Kerry and Thomas cut the wedding cake and shared their first dance.

As promised, Carlos led me to the dance floor and whispered Spanish sonnets in my ear as we held each other close and moved to the music. The party continued long after the first stars appeared in the sky. I nearly forgot about Brett's murder.

Tomorrow the investigation could continue in earnest, but for the rest of the magical evening, I let myself become enchanted under the spell that Thomas and Kerry's love had cast upon us all.

Chapter Ten

The next morning I woke up groggy. We had decided to open Torte late in order to give everyone time to recover from the wedding. Carlos had woken before me. I was shocked to roll over in bed and find him gone. But the scent of fresh-brewed coffee beckoned me from beneath the covers.

I tugged on a pair of sweats and padded downstairs.

"Good morning, mi querida." Carlos stood in front of the stove with an apron tied around his waist and a whisk in one hand. "I knew that you would never resist the smell of coffee." He poured me a mug and pointed to the island. "Sit. I am making breakfast for you."

"Mmmm, it smells delish." I cradled the coffee in my hands. "Thanks for this. That was a late night."

"Si, especially for you, my early morning baker."

"I know." I rubbed the corner of my eyes. "I'm glad I told everyone to sleep in and to leave cleanup for this morning. It was so fun to be able to enjoy the reception and dance until after midnight."

"I'm glad you allowed yourself to sleep in. You work too much, you know this." He cracked eggs into a glass bowl. "You need to take more breaks."

"You're right, but I love my work. It's hard to let go, especially when there's so much going on."

He whisked the eggs and added chopped peppers, onions, garlic, and salt and pepper. "But you and I could have more time together."

"I'd like that."

"I would, too, mi querida." His voice was thick with emotion. "I got a call from Ramiro yesterday."

"How is he?" Carlos's son was living in Spain with his mother. I knew that Carlos missed him desperately. We had talked about having Ramiro come stay with us for the summer.

"He is good. He is almost done with his schoolwork, and I have good news."

I took a long drink of coffee. "He's coming?"

"Si. He will arrive the second week in July and stay through August. His mother is happy to have him come, and he even mentioned that he might think about the possibility of doing a term of school here. He would like to improve his English and has been wanting to do a study abroad program. What do you think about that?" He sounded almost nervous.

"I would love it! That would be great. We have so much extra space here. It will be good to have a kid in the house. I mean, I know Ramiro is a teen, but still. I've been wanting to share our space."

"You have?" Carlos's eyes brightened.

"Yeah, I mean I've been thinking a lot about kids lately. I'm not getting any younger, you know?"

He dropped the whisk and came closer. "You have been thinking about babies?"

My breath felt heavy. I bit my bottom lip. "I have. What do you think?"

"Julieta, I would love to have a baby with you." He reached for my hand and caressed it with his thumb. "You have not said this to me, so I didn't know that you felt like this. We had talked it about it on the ship years ago, but the timing wasn't right then."

"It's been running through my mind since you moved in. I guess I just wanted us to have time together first, to make sure that you were really comfortable here and that this was going to work." I rubbed the back of my neck. A tingling sensation spread down my arms. We were really having this conversation. I couldn't believe it, but I knew it was time.

"And?" Carlos leaned in.

"And it seems like it is. I've never been this happy. You seem so happy, too, but I don't want to do anything to throw that off." I paused, trying to stop my knee from bouncing. "A baby is a huge commitment, and like you said, we're both working a lot, and I don't want to add stress, but at the same time I feel like I'm ready."

"I am ready!" Carlos didn't hesitate. A grin that refused to be contained spread across his face. "I have been ready for a while."

"You have?" My breath felt quick.

"Si." He cupped my face in his hands, his body becoming as still as a statue. "Yes. Yes."

I could feel heat building in my cheeks. "I guess I just thought you already have Ramiro."

"Yes, but that doesn't mean I cannot love our child, and I would like a chance to do it myself." He pulled back so he could study my face. "I missed so much with Ramiro.

It is not the same. I was gone for his childhood. But it is different now. We are here together in Ashland, and we have so much help from our friends. We can build a family here." His lips brushed across mine.

I savored the moment. Why had it taken me so long to broach the subject? I guess I hadn't realized until now how much I really did want to be a mother.

"Can you imagine how much Mom and the Professor would spoil our baby?" I said after pulling away from him. "In fact, come to think of it, you should probably warn Ramiro they're going to be over the moon that he's staying for the summer."

Carlos laughed and kissed the top of my head. "I will warn him, Julieta, but I also must tell you how happy I am that we are having this talk. I would like nothing more than to have another child with you."

My stomach flopped with excitement and nervousness. "Okay, but let's keep this between us."

"Of course." He kissed me again, this time with even more tenderness. "I will not mind the practice either."

I grinned.

He returned to the stove. "Now I must really cook for you. This frittata is going to be packed with protein."

My mind drifted to thoughts of decorating one of the bedrooms upstairs like a nursery and planning for Ramiro's arrival. I wanted him to know that he was part of our little family and make sure he had his own space. Talking to Carlos about the possibility of having children of our own took a weight off, and I was glad that we both felt the same way.

After breakfast Carlos dropped me off at the bake-shop on his way to Uva. Normally Sundays have a slower rhythm, but not today. From the minute I opened the doors, I was slammed with projects. The first and most important project was organizing. We'd left everything in a rush to set up for the wedding, and after sending Thomas and Kerry off with cheers and sparklers, we had literally tossed everything in tubs and dumped them in the kitchen to deal with today.

Marty, Rosa, and I were going to tackle the task of getting the kitchen back in shape and putting away the supplies left over from the event. Sterling, Steph, and Bethany would be responsible for stocking the pastry case and prepping breakfast specials, and Andy and Sequoia were going to be slinging strong shots of espresso and hand-crafting foamy lattes.

Since I was the first to arrive, I went through the morning checklist—firing up the ovens, proofing bread dough, and making sure our inventory was stocked and ready for a day of baking. Fortunately Sundays tended to be light on custom orders, and we didn't offer wholesale bread deliveries either, so even with a late start, we would be able to handle the coffee and brunch crowd.

I managed to make a decent dent in sorting through the stacks of dishes and supplies before Andy showed up.

"Cool wedding last night," he said, taking off his baseball hat and hooking it on the coatrack. "I'm glad you told us to come in late. I don't think I fell asleep until sometime after two."

"I know." I returned a jar of silver sprinkles to Bethany's workstation. "I can't remember the last time I was out that late. I don't think I've seen the other side of midnight in years. Baker's hours, you know."

"Don't worry. I've got you covered." He lifted a small container of beans. "I made a special highly caffeinated roast just for the occasion."

"Ohhh, I can't wait." I gave him a thumbs-up.

"I'll holler when it's ready." He left to craft his brew

while I continued washing flat spatulas and returning the extra supplies we'd brought to the reception to their spots in the kitchen.

It didn't take him long to work his coffee magic. When Sequoia and the rest of the team arrived, I went to take stock of our milk supplies upstairs and Andy had a coffee waiting for me at the bar.

"Here you go, boss." He waved his fingers over the ceramic mug. "I call it the Wedding Hangover. It's a triple-shot latte with extra foam, a touch of dark chocolate sauce, and dark chocolate shavings. Caffeine and chocolate are the cure for anything."

"Don't say that around Bethany," Sequoia teased. "She'll put it on a T-shirt."

"This sounds strong," I said to Andy, gladly accepting the drink. "But I'll take it today."

"I figured everyone might need a coffee boost today." He gave me a knowing look as the Professor's frame appeared at the front door.

"Yeah." Reality was setting in. We had sent Thomas and Kerry off with a show of sparklers and fireworks erupting over the band shell, but now that they were on their way to the Caribbean islands, the real work of solving Brett's murder had to begin.

"Morning." I opened the door and motioned the Professor inside. "Andy is pouring strong shots of espresso. Can I get you a latte? A classic cup of Joe?"

"A black coffee would be wonderful." He nodded to the window booths. "I realize it's early, but might I beg a couple moments of your time?"

"Of course." I went to pour him a cup of our house roast and join him at the table.

Instead of jumping into the murder case, his eyes were focused on the plaza where a pale pink blush from the rising sun shimmered on the fountains and the copper roof of the information kiosk. "What an enchanting evening. I don't believe your mother and I have danced like that since our wedding."

"It turned out beautifully, didn't it?" I agreed. "And Thomas and Kerry seemed so happy."

"Indeed." He tore his gaze away from the window. "They texted this morning. They're in Florida and will board the ship later this afternoon. It was so kind of Carlos to arrange the cruise for them."

"He was thrilled to be able to do it." I took a drink of Andy's wedding hangover cure. He hadn't been lying about it being strong. The latte's bitterness was balanced by his use of dark chocolate. I picked up notes of vanilla and dried cherries. My taste buds hummed with each sip. I had a feeling my body would soon follow.

"They said he arranged for the honeymoon suite, a balcony and all."

"Yeah. I hope they enjoy it. As you know, the *Amour of the Seas* is a romantic ship, and staying in the honeymoon suite is truly cruising in luxurious style." Carlos had reached out to the captain, who had become a dear friend over the years of both of us working on the ship. Having friends around the world was a perk on many levels, but in this case, it allowed us to offer Thomas and Kerry a deep, deep discount on their honeymoon. No one deserved it more than they did, and the captain eagerly agreed to host them for dinner at his table and make sure that they were treated like royalty while on board.

"Yes, in fact, I was feeling a bit wistful this morning about our time together on the ship." The Professor cradled his coffee mug in his hands and took a slow sip. "I think it might be time again soon to whisk your mother off for another getaway."

"Oooh, I love that idea. Are you thinking another cruise?"

"No, I've been toying with something more Shakespearean in nature?"

"Really, what? Like Stratford-upon-Avon?" I glanced out the window toward the Merry Windsor hotel. The final "r" in "Windsor" was hanging down from the rest of the sign. Something else I'm sure Richard would never pay to have fixed. How great would it be for Mom to have a real Elizabethan experience?

"Mmmm, good suggestion." He ran his fingers along his chin. "I've been leaning toward Verona."

"Italy!" I covered my mouth. "That would be incredible. She'll love that. Can Carlos and I tag along?"

"Certainly." He lifted his coffee mug. "Join us."

"No, I'm kidding. We wouldn't want to barge in on your romantic getaway, but Verona is so lovely. Mom will freak out."

"Agreed." He chuckled. "Let's keep it our secret, shall we?"

I nodded.

"And a family getaway would be even more delightful, so I will be sure to keep you and Carlos abreast of my plans on the chance you might be able to join us for a few days."

"Sounds great." As I thought about it, depending on the timing, Carlos and I could fly over and pick up Ramiro, and then the three of us could meet Mom and the Professor in Italy for a few days before coming home. I hadn't been to Italy for a few years, and the thought of going to one of the most picturesque countries on the planet was definitely appealing.

"Alas, I suppose we should shift our conversation to other things." The Professor sighed.

"I'm guessing you're talking about Brett's murder. Any updates?"

"Not much as of yet." He shifted in his seat and removed his Moleskine journal from his jacket. "The coroner confirmed that the stab to the chest delivered a fatal blow and has given us a window from ten thirty to eleven thirty as the most likely time of death when blow was delivered."

"That seems like a pretty tight timeline. There were so many people setting up that there had to be plenty of witnesses who saw him shortly before he was killed, right?"

"Yes." He flipped through the notebook. "My team canvassed the area and took everyone's statements. The last person to have seen Brett alive, aside from Jamie, who as you know is currently behind bars, was Judge Mimi Barbarelli."

That was a surprise. "Really?" I remembered seeing her at the band shell with Dani and Randall before I found Brett's body, but everything after that was a bit of a blur.

He glanced around us to make sure no one was paying attention. Andy and Sequoia were the only other people upstairs, and they were both focused on organizing beans and brewing extra pots of our house roasts. "I will share this with you in confidence—that information doesn't come from the judge, but rather someone who observed her and Brett involved in an altercation."

"An altercation?"

He raised one brow. "Odd, isn't it? According to the witness, Mimi threatened Brett and attempted to hit him."

"Mimi?" I couldn't believe it.

"Yes, which is why I'm here, at least in part." He motioned to his coffee. "No day can truly begin until one has had a cup or two of Torte's signature blend."

I smiled and raised my latte in a show of solidarity. "Agreed."

"In any event, I digress. There is unfortunately compelling evidence tying Jamie to the crime."

"Is it the strings?" I asked.

"Strings?" His brow crinkled in confusion.

"The bass strings. Jamie was holding them when I found Brett's body."

"Ah." He paused to take a quick note. "It's more than that. Again, I'd ask that this stay between us."

I nodded with sincerity. "Yes. Absolutely."

"We found a definitive connection between the two men."

I felt my breath catch in my chest. "What kind of connection?"

The Professor put his notebook down and removed his phone. It took him a minute to find the picture he was looking for. "Here, see the tattoo on Brett's forearm?" He held his phone so I could see.

"Yeah." I had seen the same creepy pirate tattoo before.

"Jamie has the same tattoo."

"That's right." I still wasn't making the connection.

"It's a standard inking that members of the same prison gang get to mark themselves."

"Wait, what? Are you saying that Jamie and Brett were in the same prison gang?"

The Professor's lips pressed together in a solid line. He frowned as he nodded. "That's exactly what I'm saying."

"Are prison gangs even a real thing? I've seen references to them in movies, but I guess that I just assumed they were fictional."

"They most certainly are not fictional," he replied with a shake of his head. "Unfortunately there are thousands of members of criminal organizations that originate in the penal system throughout the United States. These entities operate inside and outside of the system. Many of them are highly structured, with hierarchies and codes of conduct. They pose a real world threat to all of us in that they have an extremely organized system of transporting and distributing narcotics. Gang members have been responsible for assassinations of prosecutors and judges, and other murders in cold blood."

"I had no idea." I massaged my temple. "That can't be good for Jamie, can it?"

The Professor inhaled deeply through his nose. "No."

Chapter Eleven

I nearly spilled my latte upon hearing the Professor's revelation. This changed everything. I'd been grasping for answers about why Jamie would risk his reconciliation with Kerry, but if he and Brett had done time together and been in the same prison gang, then he had plenty of motivation to kill the bassist.

"Yes, so you see why bass strings are the least of Jamie's worries," the Professor continued. "We have been able to confirm that the two men not only served time together in the California state prison but were cellmates for two years."

"Oh no." My thoughts went to Kerry and my promise to her.

The Professor's tone mirrored my feeling of concern. "Indeed, which is why we have him in custody while we gather more information and sort through evidence. However, that is not to say that I believe Jamie is the killer."

"Kerry will be devastated if it turns out that he did it."

"Yes, which is why I'm here. I'd like to beg a favor."

"You know you never have to beg. I'll do anything to help."

He shook his head to the side. "Yes, I do know, and I hope you know how grateful I am not only to be a part of your family, but for your ongoing support of this community. Detective work can feel lonely sometimes, and there's never a day when I don't revel in the fact that we are all so fortunate to live and work in such a place."

I reached for his hand. "I agree, and I'm happy to do whatever I can to support you."

A sad smile formed on his kind face. "I must stay on topic. The reason why I dropped by was to ask if you might be willing to have a chat with Mimi. My team has already interviewed her, and I'll be following up on some additional leads, but it would be most helpful to have your insight."

"Sure. Is there anything specific you want me to ask?"

"No. In fact, the opposite. I know the trust this community has in you and your mother. I have it on good authority that Mimi tends to stop by on Sunday afternoons for a late lunch after her Pilates class. I'm hoping that you might take it upon yourself to wait on her, and perhaps strike up a conversation about the wedding and see where it leads."

"You bet. I'm on it." I didn't tell him that Kerry had already asked me to learn what I could, too. Not that he would care, but I had promised her to keep that between us.

"I greatly appreciate it, my dear." He finished his coffee and stood.

"I'll let you know what I learn," I said, picking up our empty cups.

"Most excellent." He left me with a kiss on the cheek. "And let's do put our heads together about an Italian getaway—quietly of course."

I pressed my finger to my lips. "Your secret is safe with me. I'll talk to Carlos about it." He left, and I took our dishes downstairs. It was almost time to open, and I needed to get back to work. As I sorted through containers from the picnic boxes, I couldn't stop thinking about Jamie. He and Brett had served time together. Did that mean that his reason for coming to Ashland had nothing to do with Kerry's wedding after all? Could I have gotten that completely wrong? I'd been convinced that he really cared about her, but what if I'd been mistaken? Maybe the wedding was just an excuse for him to come and exact his revenge on his old cellmate. I wanted to believe that he was well intentioned and trying to make a fresh start, but this new information threw everything into question.

The news that Mimi had tried to attack Brett was equally perplexing. Why would an eighty-year-old woman get in a physical fight with a man three decades her junior? I was glad the Professor had asked for my help, because I was quite curious to hear what the judge had to say.

For the next three hours, we cleaned, sorted, organized, and tested the strength of our industrial dishwasher with load after load of wedding place settings and cutlery. There was nothing as satisfying as a clean and organized kitchen. I had embraced the philosophy of mise en place since culinary school. The French term translated to "everything in its place." Working in a disorganized and messy kitchen impacted the food. Even with our larger operation in the basement, space was always at a premium, and knowing that everything and everyone in my kitchen had their own space brought a sense of calm to the workday.

After I tucked the last set of piping tips into their drawer, I stood back to survey the spotless space as Sterling squeezed past me with a tray of paninis headed for the pizza oven. "What yummy delight do you have there?"

I'd been so focused on re-acclimating from the wedding that I hadn't paid much attention to what the rest of my staff was doing. Yet another reminder of how lucky I was to have such a self-sufficient team.

"It's panini madness for lunch today," he said, using his free hand to point to each of the sandwiches on the tray. "We've got a Reuben with house-made Thousand Island and brined onions and sauerkraut. A turkey pesto with Havarti, red onions, fresh basil, and heirloom tomatoes, and a veggie option with eggplant Parm, mozzarella, and tomato jam."

"Can I have one of each please?"

"Save room for soup, though. I made a French spring soup with potatoes, leeks, and asparagus."

"Good thing I've worked up an appetite with all this cleaning."

Sterling tapped the edge of the tray. "I'll save you one." Each panini had already been grilled in our panini press, giving the sandwiches those classic char lines. We liked to finish them off with just a few minutes in the pizza oven to add a nice smoky aroma.

Steph was spreading vanilla buttercream on two large chocolate sheet cakes.

"Did we get a last-minute custom order?" I asked. Our sheet cakes were a popular option for office and birthday parties, since they could feed a large crowd on a reasonable budget.

She used a flat-edge spatula to even out the buttercream. "No, this was Bethany's idea. Leftover wedding cake for today's special. Although technically speaking, it's not leftover."

"That's so great."

Bethany rolled balls of snickerdoodle dough in cinnamon and sugar. "Do you love it? We were talking about how the best thing the day after a wedding or any festive occasion is leftover cake. Plus sheet cakes are super easy and quick to bake and decorate."

"It's brilliant."

I had to resist sneaking a piece for myself. The moist chocolate cake slathered with light and airy buttercream was like a siren song, calling for me to grab a fork and dive in.

Instead I figured I should probably go check in upstairs. It had been a few hours, and now that lunchtime was upon us, I wanted to stay on the lookout for Mimi. The Professor had mentioned that she was likely going to stop after her Pilates class.

I didn't have to do much looking out. As I came upstairs, I spotted the judge in line to order. After setting out a tray of oversized peanut butter chocolate chip, snickerdoodle, and lemon sugar cookies in the display case, I grabbed a carafe of coffee and circulated through the dining room. Refilling customers' drinks was a service we liked to offer when we had the chance, but secretly I was keeping an eye out to see where Mimi was going to sit. She took her coffee outside, so I followed her. Our red and teal patio umbrellas provided shade for guests, along with the miniature Japanese maple trees we had planted in large galvanized tubs to create a natural fencing for our outdoor space.

Fortunately Mimi must have been waiting for a friend to join her because she took a seat at one of the large tables and placed her yoga bag on the empty seat across from her to reserve it.

I seized the chance to get a word alone. "Hi, Mimi, can I top you off?" I asked, knowing that her coffee was still full to the brim.

"Wow, what service. I just placed my order, so thank you, but I'm fine." She tugged on her loose-fitting wrap that covered her black yoga gear.

"What a wedding last night." I jumped right in. "I'm still buzzing from it so much that I don't even need caffeine."

She smiled. "It was beautiful, and trust me, I don't say that lightly. I've seen a lot of weddings in my day, and last night stands out for sure." She pointed to the empty bench across from her. "Do you have a minute to sit?"

"Sure." I set the coffee carafe on the table and sat down. "I was so relieved. After the way things started, I was worried that the wedding might not even happen."

"I wouldn't have allowed that." She made a dismissive motion with her hand. I noticed that it was deeply bruised and slightly swollen. "I would have gotten Doug involved if it had come to that. We couldn't allow a hoodlum to cancel Thomas and Kerry's wedding."

A hoodlum. That wasn't a term often used. And also hinted that Mimi was aware of Brett's past.

"Did you know him well?" I asked.

She choked on her coffee, coughing violently before finally placing a hand on her throat.

"Do you need help?"

She shook her head. "I swallowed wrong, that's all."

I waited for her to regain control of her breath.

"Are you asking me about the victim? He's well known around the valley. Heart Strings has performed at dozens of weddings that I've officiated, so our paths have crossed." Her face shifted. I had the sense that the intense stare she was giving me was the same one she used on the bench to intimidate those on trial. "Why do you ask?"

"It's so odd that he was killed at the park, with so many people around. In the middle of the day, no less." I reached over to pick a weed from the planter box.

She twisted her yoga wrap in a tight knot around her chest. "When you're in my line of work, nothing is surprising anymore."

"Did you hear that they already made an arrest?"

"Is the sky blue?" She craned her neck toward the powder blue sky dotted with white fairy-like clouds. "Who do you think initiated the arrest?"

"You?"

"As a judge, I obviously am not involved in that aspect of the criminal justice system, but I did put a bug in Doug's ear. I happen to have some background information on the deceased."

I decided there was no point in trying to play it cool. "You mean that he was in prison?"

Mimi's face lost its passivity. "How did you know that?"

"He and Jamie—Kerry's dad—were cellmates."

"What?" She shook her head in disbelief. "How did you hear that?"

Why was she so resistant?

"Are these rumors already running through town? Juliet, you should know better than to trust the rumor mill around here. I love Ashland as much as the next person, but sometimes this town is way too small." She rolled her eyes.

"What do you mean?"

She paused as Rosa delivered her veggie panini with a side of our kettle chips and fruit salad. Once Rosa had returned inside, Mimi leaned across the table. "Listen, you can't trust everything you hear. That's all I'm at liberty to say."

The Professor was a reliable source in my opinion. I wanted to ask more, but I could tell from the way she clenched her jaw tight that she wasn't going to divulge anything else.

As she reached to pick up the sandwich with her bruised hand, she let out an audible sigh and winced.

"Are you okay?" I asked.

She tried to wiggle her fingers, but stopped in mid-motion, pain washing over face. "I had a little accident. My hand is sore and swollen, but nothing some ice and rest won't mend."

"What did you do?" My thoughts immediately went to what the Professor had said about a witness seeing her and Brett fighting.

"Excuse me?" She pointed to her left ear with her good hand. "A car went by, and I must not have heard you."

Or was she trying to buy time to come up with an excuse?

"I wondered what you did to your hand."

"The dangers of Pilates at my age. Things don't bend the way they used to." She flexed her fingers again. Another flash of pain showed on her face.

Her friend arrived, so I made my exit. I wasn't sure that I had learned anything that was going to be helpful to the Professor's case, but if my instincts were right, there was more that the judge wasn't saying. And I was certain that she wasn't telling the truth about her hand. The question was what was the likelihood that she could have overpowered Brett? Sure, she did Pilates and she was certainly spry for her age, but was it possible that she had the strength to take down Brett? Stab him and thrash his bass? I wasn't sure, but I wasn't about to rule her out as a potential suspect either.

Chapter Twelve

Lance sauntered across the plaza, waving with two fingers. "Juliet! Over here."

I motioned for him to hold on and went inside to return the coffee carafe before going to meet him.

He waited by the information kiosk. Its shiny copper A-frame roof sent specks of sunlight scattering around us like confetti. Posters announcing spring lavender farm tours, concerts at the Britt fest, rafting trips on the Rogue, and SOU's commencement had been tacked to one side of the information booth. Nearby a poet troubadour typed out spontaneous sonnets for passersby on a vintage Underwood typewriter.

Lance tapped the expensive gold watch on his wrist. "That took forever. I thought you'd never come back."

"Uh, that was like two seconds."

"Two seconds wasted, darling. Absolutely wasted."

"So sorry." I rolled my eyes. "Why didn't you just come over to the bakeshop?"

"I don't want to be seen," he said through clenched teeth.

I glanced around us. The kiosk was in the middle of the plaza, hardly out of sight from anyone. "We're literally standing in the middle of town."

"I know. I know, but it looks like we're merely passing each other with a casual greeting. It's not a formal meeting."

"Okay. I'm still confused. We're friends. Why would it matter if we're seen hanging out together? We're always hanging out together."

"Keep your voice low." He patted the air with both hands, as if I was having a fit of hysterics and needed calming down.

"Lance, I love you, but I have work to do, so can you get to the point?"

He cupped one hand over his cheek. No one was watching, so the gesture was futile. "There's been some developing news involving someone at Torte."

"What?" That wasn't what I thought he was going to say. "My team?"

He scoffed. "No, no. With them." He tilted his head to the side.

I turned to observe the bakeshop. Mimi and her friend were seated at one of the outdoor tables. I recognized some of our regular customers at the others. "You mean Judge Barbarelli?"

"No." He repeated the head tilt. "Look inside."

I took another look and spotted Randall, the third member of Heart Strings, sitting at one of the window booths alone.

"Randall?" I crinkled my brow.

"Finally." He threw his hands up in exasperation. "Thank you."

"I don't get it. Why can't Randall see us hanging out together?"

"Because I've just been speaking with his bandmate and learned something most revealing." He pressed his fingers together.

"What's that?"

"Apparently things weren't as pretty as they seemed in la-la land." He smoothed his designer dot-print short-sleeved shirt.

"Are you talking about Heart Strings?"

"Yes. Shocking, I know, but there was drama amongst the band."

"Yeah, that was obvious."

He cleared his throat. "According to my source, things were getting very heated, as in coming to a boiling point."

"You mean Dani?"

He brushed me off. "As I was saying, my source confirmed that there was infighting amongst the three of them, and she wasn't even sure if the band was going to stay together. It sounds like things got very nasty. Blood was about to be shed."

This wasn't exactly news to me, but I could tell that Lance wanted to share his new nugget. "Why?"

"She wouldn't spill all the tea, but she certainly hinted that there was serious animosity between Randall and Brett."

"What does this have to do with us?"

He blew air out of his lips like he was trying to explain physics to a kindergartner. "It means we need to divide and conquer. You should seize this opportunity to go get chummy with that skinny jeans hipster nursing a tea, and I'll continue to work my charm on our sassy blue-haired lead singer. We can't let them know that we're in cahoots.

It will ruin everything. Play it cool, and we can reconvene later. Say cocktail hour?"

"Sure."

"Excellent. Ta-ta." He waved and crossed the plaza toward the police station.

Lance was up to his usual antics. I would play along, but it was hardly a secret that he and I were close. I had a feeling that Dani and Randall probably already knew and likely didn't care. However, I didn't want to pass up the opportunity to learn more about the inner workings of Heart Strings, so I followed Lance's advice and returned to Torte so I could get a minute with Randall.

I stopped by his table. "Just checking to see if you need anything? More water for your tea?"

He slammed his sketchbook shut like I was about to get a glimpse of nuclear codes. Then he glanced at his empty plate and cup. "No, I'm good. Did you need the table?"

I felt bad that he took my check-in to mean I wanted him to leave. "No, not at all. Please stay as long as you like. In fact, do you mind if I sit for a minute?"

Randall's face flinched, but he motioned across the table. "Go ahead." He set his sketchbook on the seat next to him and eyed me with suspicion.

Whatever he was working on was clearly something he wanted to keep private.

He looked like he could use one of Andy's wedding hangover caffeine cures. His eyes were red and bloodshot. The retro '80s Nintendo T-shirt he was wearing made me wonder if he had grabbed it from the dirty clothes pile. It was wrinkled and stained.

"I wanted to check in and see how you're doing. It must have been awful to have your bandmate die and then have to perform. I'm surprised you went on with the show. I'm sure Lance could have found another group to step in."

There was a long pause before he answered. "Dani and I were pretty shaken, but we didn't want to let everyone down."

His words were expected, but his tone and his body posture said otherwise and made me doubt his sincerity. His arms hung limply at his sides, and his shoulders sagged like it was hard for him to hold them upright.

"Were you and Brett close?"

He twisted a linen napkin into a long cylinder and then rolled it up like a snail with a strange detachment, like he wasn't even aware he was doing it. "We've been in the band for a couple years."

That didn't exactly answer my question.

"It must be a shock."

He unwound the napkin. "Not really. The dude was always in trouble."

"What kind of trouble?" I didn't even care that I wasn't being more discreet. Randall wasn't holding back; I might as well dig deeper.

"He had some demons."

"You mean drugs?"

"Among other stuff, yeah." Randall picked up the napkin again. This time he folded it into a tight square. I was waiting for him to transform it into a swan or a shark like the housekeeping staff did on the *Amour of the Seas,* folding bathroom towels into sea creatures and leaving them on guests' pillows as a little surprise.

"Do you think he was on something yesterday?" A picture of Brett stumbling on the stage came to the front of my mind.

"Who knows. Maybe. I know he and Dani got into it before our warm-up session." He yanked at a thick black rubber band around his right wrist. Rubber bands covered each of his wrists like bracelets.

"About what?"

"I don't know. She's working on some LA angle. You'll have to talk to her, but she was pissed. I overheard her threaten to kick him out of the band if he couldn't pull it together." He flicked the band away from his wrist like he was playing an instrument.

That matched what I'd seen. Could Brett's self-destruction have been motive for Dani to kill him?

Randall answered the question for me. "Dani's been super focused the last six months. We're booked every night. Some days we're double-booked. She's been talking to these producers in LA and making connections to send some demos that way and shoot a video here. She wants to take Heart Strings to the next level, and she wasn't about to let Brett get in her way. We've put in thousands of hours trying to catch a break on our own, and she thinks this is our last shot. She warned Brett too many times to count."

"Warned him about cutting him from Heart Strings?" I asked.

Randall set the folded napkin on top of his empty plate. "Yep. He wouldn't listen. It probably got him killed."

I gulped. Was he hinting that he thought Dani had done it?

Before I could ask for clarification, his phone rang. "Look, I need to take this call." He answered as he exited the bakeshop.

My mind spun with new possibilities about the crime. If Dani was that serious about furthering her career and landing a record deal, it wasn't unrealistic to consider her as a suspect. Brett's behavior and criminal past could have put her goals in jeopardy. She had been at the scene of the crime. Maybe she took Brett behind the band shell to have it out with him. If he was really under the influence, she could have overwhelmed him with his bass.

Maybe she smashed it first and then used the shattered pieces to stab him.

I shuddered at the image.

But I couldn't rule her out. There were two things I needed to do next. The first was find out from the Professor whether the coroner had reported any substances in Brett's bloodstream. And the second was to reconvene with Lance later. Maybe he had been successful in getting more information out of Dani. Lance was a genius at getting people (even complete strangers on the street) to confide in him. What if Dani had confessed to him? It wasn't out of the realm of possibility. I would love nothing more than being able to text Kerry to tell her to enjoy her honeymoon because we'd confirmed that Jamie wasn't the killer.

Chapter Thirteen

The day passed quickly, probably because we'd opened late and there was so much post-wedding cleanup to do. Having extra work was a blessing in disguise. It kept me focused and stopped me from replaying the murder over and over again.

After I sent everyone home, I decided I needed to cook. Carlos had texted to let me know he was finishing a tasting at Uva and would stop by to pick me up as soon as the guests left. I didn't mind. I needed to clear my head, and I had an idea. Instead of going out for a drink with Lance, I called to invite him and Arlo to join us for dinner at Torte. We could talk more freely in the privacy of the bakeshop's cozy basement.

Lance loved the idea, so I got to work on dinner. I knew exactly what I wanted to make—vodka penne pasta with spicy sausage. My conversation with the Professor about Verona had inspired me to cook something Italian.

I started on the sauce by sautéing onions in olive oil

until they were translucent. One trick I teach every staff member is to refrigerate onions thirty minutes before chopping them, or if time is short, they can also be stored in the freezer for ten minutes. The cold stops the cells from exploding in the air when the onion is chopped, which means there's no need to cut an onion in misery or wear scuba goggles in order to avoid burning, stinging eyes while working with the root vegetable.

Next I added red pepper flakes and plump canned Italian tomatoes. While those simmered, I boiled spicy link sausages in a combination of water and chicken stock. Once the sauce had cooked for a few minutes, I poured in a cup of vodka and heavy cream. Then I stirred in a couple of heaping tablespoons of tomato paste. I turned up the heat and stirred the sauce for ten minutes. Then I reduced the heat and let it simmer for another thirty. I pan seared the cooked sausages and set them aside. Next I boiled penne pasta until it was slightly undercooked. Most of Torte's customers knew our process well enough to understand that we would never serve a soggy pasta. "Make pasta like the Italians," Carlos always said to new staffers on the *Amour of the Seas*. "Tender but firm," he would say. "Overcooked pasta is a crime."

Carlos and his fellow chefs claimed that even al dente was overdone if you were finishing pasta in a pan, like the professionals. "Molto al dente," Carlos repeated to his staff. It meant to undercook until the pasta was chewy with a chalky and gritty center, then after draining it, add the pasta to the sauce along with a splash of the pasta water for thickening, cook for another two to three minutes, and you were guaranteed a true Italian al dente pasta every time.

To accompany our pasta, I panfried fresh green beans with olive oil and garlic, and I warmed up a loaf of focaccia bread that Marty had made earlier in the day.

While I waited for Lance, Arlo, and Carlos to arrive, I set plates around the seating area in front of the atomic fire, which I turned to low. The basement stayed cool year-round, no matter what the temperature was outdoors. The fire would give us a touch of warmth and add ambiance to our impromptu dinner. I brought out a couple bottles of red wine, glasses, and a small vase of pink and yellow tulips left over from the wedding.

No dinner with friends would have been complete, especially at Torte, without dessert. Since I still had time before everyone was due, I decided to whip up a favorite—shortbread cups with dark chocolate and raspberries. They would bake fast and be a wonderful accompaniment to our Italian themed feast.

For the shortbread, I creamed together butter, sugar, vanilla extract, and vanilla bean paste. Then I incorporated salt and flour. The key to flaky, melt-in-your-mouth shortbread is using quality butter. There's no skimping on cheap or imitation butter in the popular cookie. Shortbread doesn't leave a baker anywhere to hide. The butter is the star of the show.

I loved the versatility of shortbread. It could work as a base for cookies, as an easy way to elevate a piecrust, or simply as a treat on its own.

I pressed two-inch round balls of the thick dough into miniature muffin tins and placed ceramic pie weights into each of them to ensure they would retain their shape while baking. I put them in the oven for eight to ten minutes, until they turned golden brown.

For the filling I melted semisweet chocolate with butter. Once the chocolate had developed a lovely glossy sheen, I added a splash of heavy cream. I filled the cups with the chocolate and whipped the remaining cream with sugar and more vanilla bean paste. The cups needed to cool for thirty minutes. Right before I served them, I would top each of the little chocolate shortbread cups with a single raspberry and a dollop of whipped cream.

I had to try one to make sure I had gotten the flavors right. That was another hard-and-fast rule I had learned in culinary school. It's a chef's responsibility to taste everything that goes on the plate. Nothing leaves the kitchen without being tasted first. I had taught my team the same lesson, and truth be told, it wasn't such a bad gig to *have to* sample a morsel of melty chocolate paired with buttery shortbread.

My culinary school pastry instructor had told us that a chef should always be slightly envious that they weren't eating the dish they were sending out to customers. I had shared that wisdom with my team. It was a good philosophy for every working kitchen.

Carlos showed up first. He looked handsome as always in a pair of khaki shorts and a crisp white button-down shirt. "How was your day, Julieta?" He greeted me with a kiss. "You have been working hard, I see."

"You know me, cooking alone helps center me."

"Si." He uncorked a bottle of red wine. "Should I fill your glass?"

"Sure." I pointed to the stove where dinner was waiting. "Everything is ready. I just need to plate it when Lance and Arlo get here."

"And this dinner, it is just for our friends, si? You have no hidden agenda, do you?" His eyes twinkled as he teased me.

"A hidden agenda? Me?" I could hear Lance's influence in my tone.

"Did you learn anything new about the murder today?" he asked, offering me a glass of the burgundy wine.

"I did." I filled him in on some of what I had discovered in my conversations with Mimi and Randall.

He shook his head as he took a long sip of the wine,

letting it linger on his palate for a moment. "It is still no excuse for murder, even if Brett was a criminal."

"I agree," I replied. "Before I forget, the Professor is planning a secret getaway for him and Mom. He wants to take her to Italy—Verona to be specific."

"Verona is one of my favorite cities."

"Mine, too. That's why I wanted to bring it up. What do you think of the idea of flying to Spain to pick up Ramiro? Then the three of us could spend a few days in Italy with Mom and the Professor before coming home."

"I love it." Carlos grinned. "How wonderful. I could show you my village in Spain, and you can meet the entire family. Si, this is such a good idea."

"You think?"

"Yes. When would this be?"

"It sounded like their dates are flexible. That's why I was thinking we could work it into a bigger trip, and it might be fun for Ramiro to get to travel with us instead of having to take such a long flight by himself. I don't know. Maybe I'm wrong about that. Maybe it's not cool to travel with your dad and his wife."

"No, no." Carlos waved off the thought. "I know he would be so happy to get to show you around Spain, and what kid wouldn't want to spend a few days in Italy before coming to America for the summer? I think it sounds perfect. Let's book it."

"Well, there are lots of details to work out first. Like who is going to run the bakeshop and winery while we're gone? Especially since Mom will be gone, too."

"This is easy. We have a strong team. They don't need us. The bakeshop and Scoops will be fine. We have more tasting room volunteers at Uva than I know what to do with. I can make a call, and we will have a line of people signed up to cover any extra shifts."

We had hired two additional staff at Uva to help with tastings and vineyard maintenance. One of our colleagues in the wine industry had suggested that we also use volunteer servers. Since the Rogue Valley had such an engaged and active retired community, it was a perfect fit. Our volunteers worked two- or four-hour shifts pouring at the tasting room. We offered them training and exclusive tasting sessions so that they would be well versed on each wine's profile and characteristics. In exchange we paid them for their time in wine.

It was a win-win. Our volunteer pool loved getting to spend time chatting up tourists in the tasting room, and they always left with bottles of wine for themselves and plenty more to share with friends. Additionally, we offered them free tastings when not volunteering and deep discounts on any extra bottles of wine.

Carlos was right. Every time we put out a call for volunteers, shifts were taken within the hour. Maybe we could do this.

"I see it in your eyes, Julieta, you want to go. Let's do it. We are young. We are healthy. What an opportunity to travel with your parents and for Ramiro to get to experience Italy with his grandparents."

When Carlos referred to Mom and the Professor as Ramiro's grandparents, it made my heart want to burst right out of my chest.

"It will be fun, and we can sneak off for a romantic moment, too. Perhaps before we venture into starting a family?" He raised one brow. "Yes?"

"I'm in."

"In for what?" Lance's voice interrupted us. He and Arlo came in holding hands.

"We are making plans to travel to Spain and Italy this summer," Carlos told them.

"Uh, and you haven't invited moi?" Lance dropped Arlo's hand so that he could clutch his stomach.

"Maybe they're hoping for a getaway alone," Arlo said, taking a seat on the couch.

"Ha, as if. Who wouldn't want to travel with yours truly?"

"Sorry, I can't take him anywhere," Arlo teased, patting the spot next to him. "Come sit, and let these two lovebirds make their travel plans without barging in."

Lance pretended to be hurt. "Barging in. Never." He sat, holding an envelope on his lap. "What's wrong with wanting to travel with your besties? We could do some serious damage in Seville."

Carlos poured them each a glass of wine. "You can certainly come meet us, but we will have Ramiro with us and then will go to Italy to meet Helen and Doug."

Lance gasped. "The plot thickens. Both Capshaw women together in the Italian countryside. That is an opportunity not to be missed. What do you say, Arlo, a mini break this summer?"

Arlo shook his head and caught my eye. "I think that we're here for dinner, not to harass our friends into letting us tag along on their vacation."

"Actually, I'd love it if you guys wanted to come," I said with sincerity. "An Ashland meetup in Verona. I mean, that is pretty fitting. But, just so you know, it's a secret for Mom, so we have to keep any plans under wraps."

"Good thing I'm here." Lance shot me a wide grin. "You all know that no one keeps a secret better than me."

The three of us cracked up.

"What's in the envelope?" I asked.

Lance handed it to me. The thick cream paper felt expensive, and the envelope had been sealed with a red wax stamp. "Consider this a token of my affection."

"You don't need to get us anything." I looked to Carlos to see if he had any idea what was inside. He shrugged.

"Just open it. You'll see."

I carefully peeled off the wax seal. Inside were two tickets. Two front-row seats for opening night at OSF's Elizabethan stage. I immediately started laughing.

"What is it?" Carlos looked perplexed.

I handed him the tickets as Lance and I shared a chuckle.

"Opening night tickets, how nice of you."

"You're most welcome." Lance gave him a half bow.

"Yes, thank you," I parroted. Then I pointed to the name of the show on the tickets. "It's kind of a joke, too."

"What? Perish the thought." Lance gave his lanky body a little shake. "I want Ashland's favorite celebrity couple sitting center stage for opening."

"Right, and it has nothing to do with the fact that you're debuting *Waitress*?"

"Noooooo." Lance stretched out the word.

He had tried to convince me to take the leading role in the musical a few months ago. I declined for a variety of reasons, mostly because I'm not a professional actress, nor can I sing. That hadn't dissuaded him from teasing me endlessly about missing out on the role of a lifetime.

"I can't wait to see it."

"You're going to love what the props department has done with the pastries. They might even fool your expert eye."

"Speaking of pastries, who's hungry?" I stood up.

Everyone raised a hand. "Let me go plate dinner." I left the three of them chatting about our potential European itinerary and scooted into the kitchen. It didn't take long to assemble dinner. I finished the vodka pasta with fresh shaved Parmesan and a sprinkling of basil. The plates were a show of color, with the creamy pasta, green beans, and rustic bread with small ramekins of olive oil and balsamic vinegar for dipping.

"Who needs to get on a plane?" Lance studied his plate. "You've brought Italy to us."

"I don't know if I'd go quite that far. The pasta we've had in Italy is next level, but this is a favorite recipe."

"Si, and it was made with love, which is all that counts." Carlos raised his glass in a toast to me.

Our conversation was light throughout dinner. Lance didn't bring up the murder. Nor did I. It felt wrong to ruin the night, but once we had consumed enough pasta to make me wish I had worn stretchy pants, Carlos and Arlo offered to do the dishes.

"You two sit," Carlos directed. "We will do the dishes."

"How lovely," Lance replied.

"It's not entirely altruistic," I said, nodding to Carlos's phone. He had pulled up a soccer match.

"What?" He winked. "We know you two want to talk, so what is wrong with catching a few minutes of the match?"

"Absolutely nothing. Go, go." Lance shooed them off. Then he moved to the far edge of the couch to be closer to me. "Okay, dish. What did you learn from Randall?"

I told him about the ongoing drama within Heart Strings and how Randall had confessed that Dani was planning to kick Brett out of the band. "What about you? Did you get anything more out of Dani?"

"Basically more of the same. She didn't hold back. It was obvious that there had been some deep animosity brewing for a while."

"Do you think she could have done it?"

He was pensive for a minute. "Arlo is encouraging me not to jump to conclusions, so I will say I don't know yet, but there was no love lost between them. That's for sure."

"I got that impression from Randall, too. He didn't

seem particularly emotional about Brett's death. He was more focused on what was going to happen to Heart Strings now. He also mentioned that Brett had had long-term issues with drugs and alcohol. Did Dani say anything about that?"

"Yes." Lance pressed his index finger to his chin. "As a matter of fact, she did. Although this twist might surprise you."

"How?"

"She told me *she* gave Brett something to calm him down."

"Wait, she gave Brett drugs?"

"Apparently, he was having a full-blown panic attack. Dani told me she's had some mental health struggles and carries anxiety medication in case she has an issue before a show. Brett was starting to freak out, so she offered him one of her pills."

"She must have known about his addiction issues."

Lance nodded. "Agreed. It does make one ponder just how committed she was to the performance. Was she willing to risk his health and well-being to ensure that the show went on?"

"And would anxiety medication make him appear drunk or like he was under the influence of something?" I asked.

"That is a question for the authorities."

"I'll be sure to bring it up when I talk to the Professor." I processed the information. "Could that also explain how the killer was able to overtake Brett? I've been struggling with that. He was a big guy. If Mimi or Dani, or even Jamie, for that matter, is the killer, it's hard to imagine how they could have done it. But if Brett was really relaxed from taking Dani's medication, that makes more sense, don't you think?"

"Agreed." Lance glanced to the kitchen where Carlos

and Arlo had finished the dishes and had their heads together at the island, watching soccer on the tiny phone screen. "The question is, what is our next move?"

"I'm not sure. I'm feeling kind of stuck."

"Then there's only one solution."

"What's that?"

"Let's start from the beginning. Tomorrow we shall divide and conquer. You take Judge Mimi and Dani. I'll have a chat with Randall, and perhaps saunter by the police station and see if I might be able to get a word with the prisoner. Tomorrow is a new day, and we need new eyes on this case. We made a promise to Kerry that I intend to keep."

He was right. We could enjoy dessert and the rest of the evening, and tomorrow start anew.

Chapter Fourteen

The next day I didn't have to go searching for an opportunity to have a face-to-face with one of our suspects.

I had offered to do our morning bread delivery route. It was a good way to stretch my legs and have face time with our wholesale customers. New banners had been installed along Main Street advertising the opening of *Waitress*. Latticed cherry pies, rolling pins, and music notes flapped in the breeze. I chuckled, trying to imagine myself in the role. It would have taken less than a minute of my off-key singing to have the audience shielding their ears and begging for mercy before there was a mass exodus out of the theater.

As I passed by the elegant lobby of the Ashland Springs Hotel, I spotted Dani's electric blue hair. She was warming up at the piano. I had finished my last stop on my route, so I tucked the empty delivery box under my arm and went inside.

"I didn't know you played the piano, too," I said.

She forced a smile and pushed a pair of blue-rimmed sunglasses higher on her head. "I play five different instruments."

"That's impressive."

"It's the business. You have to be versatile. My main role in Heart Strings is singing, but that doesn't preclude me from mastering other instruments, which has greatly improved my solo career."

"Are you doing a show here?" The lobby was empty except for a woman reading near the large fireplace, which wasn't lit, and a couple savoring coffee and watching people walk past the floor-to-ceiling windows.

"I come play for tips a couple times a week. It gives me practice and gets the name out." Almost as an afterthought, she reached into her leather and rhinestone bag, took out a folded note card with the Heart Strings logo and a stack of business cards. She placed them on the piano next to a tip jar.

"I heard that you have been getting some interest from music producers in LA. That's great news."

"It's a long game." She tapped a key with her pinky. "We'll see how it plays out, but yeah—that's the end goal."

"It must be competitive."

Her eyes hardened. "You have no idea. It's brutal. Over the years we've had a few breaks that I thought were going to get us our shot, but every time, things fizzle out. I can't let that happen this time. At some point you become a dinosaur. Gigging is a young person's game."

Dani wasn't old. I would have put her in her late twenties or early thirties at most. Her vibe was youthful with her cropped blue hair and funky style. Maybe I'd misjudged her age.

A line of questioning popped into my head, which I

decided to follow. "Is it easier to break out as a solo artist than as a band?"

She nodded. "Without a doubt. I do songwriting, too. The singer/songwriter angle is hot right now, so let's just say that I'm exploring *all* potential avenues."

The longer we talked, the more evident it appeared that she had a singular mindset on achieving stardom. If Brett stood in her way, it was seeming more likely that she would have done anything to make sure he wasn't holding her back.

"What about the rest of the band?"

"What about them?"

"I just wondered what they think—thought—of trying to break into the music scene?"

"Oh, they want it, too. They want the fame, the future, the perks. They want to finally get paid to go on tour versus lugging everything in our van and having to sleep on strangers' couches to make barely enough money to cover our gas and food, but here's the thing they don't want. They don't want to put in the work that it takes to make it big. If it weren't for me, Heart Strings would forever be a Rogue Valley wedding band."

"That must be a lot of pressure."

For a second I thought she was going to scream. Her face reminded me of a pressure cooker. I could almost see the steam building inside her. Instead she pounded her fist on the top of the piano. "Well, someone has to do it, and that's why I'm in this for me. If our Heart Strings demo gets traction, that's great, but if it doesn't, I'm not dragging around deadweight anymore."

Her words sent goose bumps up my arms. I knew it was an expression, but in light of Brett's murder, it was a poor choice of words at best.

"Was Brett deadweight?" I asked.

She glanced at me with a strange look in her eyes. "I didn't say that."

"I know, I just wondered if that was one of the issues in the band." I thought to our conversation at Torte before the wedding. Dani hadn't tried to hide the fact that she was charting the trio's course for the future.

She played a melody on the piano. "Every band has issues. You learn to deal."

I got the sense that she wasn't going to say more. "Where are you playing next?"

"I'm opening the Green Show tomorrow night. At least it's a paying gig."

"I'll try to stop over and listen," I said. The Green Show was OSF's opening act. A variety of performers—musicians, actors, spoken word poets, dance companies, and more—treated theatergoers and the community at large to a free show on the bricks before the main doors opened to the OSF stages. Often in the summer months, we would bring sandwiches and lemonade to the grassy area above the bricks and have dinner al fresco while listening to the pulsing Latin drumbeats of a salsa band or taking in the high-flying acrobatics of the Levity Circus.

Before I left, I wanted to ask one last question, and she had given me the perfect in. "Do you get nervous performing?"

She kept her eyes on the piano keys. "Depends on the venue. Depends on who's in the audience."

"That makes sense. As a chef, I get a bit jittery if I know I'm serving a VIP guest."

"Most creative types I know, regardless of our mediums, struggle with anxiety." She stole a glance at her purse. "They make medication for that now."

"How do you deal with it?"

"This." She pressed her middle fingers on the keys. "Music is my saving grace. That and anxiety medication, guided meditation, deep breathing, long walks, therapy."

Since she had brought up anxiety and medication, I decided to see if she might say more. "I heard a rumor that Brett had taken anxiety medication before he died."

The music stopped. Dani's eyes shot toward mine. "What? Where did you hear that?"

I hoped I sounded casual when I replied. "Um, I'm not sure. I think maybe one of the police officers at the scene."

She gulped and placed her hand on her throat, like she was having difficulty swallowing. "Crap. That's not good."

This was the kind of response I had been hoping for. "Why?"

She scooted to the side of the piano bench and motioned for me to sit next to her. Her voice was quivery and low as she whispered, "I think I might be in big trouble." She snuck a glance toward the lobby to make sure no one was listening. "If what you're saying is true, then I'm totally screwed."

"Do you want to talk about it?"

"I mean, this is going to look super bad to the police, but I swear I didn't kill Brett."

I waited for her to say more, trying to hold space for her to feel comfortable.

"The thing is he was totally wigging out during our sound check. It's not out of the ordinary for him to have freak out sessions. He struggled with anxiety, too. He had a long history of self-medicating with drugs and alcohol to try and deal with it. He'd actually been getting better. I'd sent him to my therapist, and he had even tried meditating. But the morning of the wedding, something set him off. I don't know what it was. He wouldn't tell me, but something triggered him. He had a full-blown panic attack. He told me he didn't think he could perform. I felt terrible for him, so I gave him one of my pills." She shook her head. "I know that sounds stupid. It was stupid, but I didn't know what else to do. I thought I was helping him."

"I'm sure you were."

She massaged her temples. "What do I do?"

"You should probably tell the police."

"I can't do that." She felt around on her hair for her sunglasses and took them off. She positioned them over her eyes like they were going to help conceal her identity, and lowered her voice. "The police are going to think that I killed him. The medication was just supposed to make him chill out. I didn't think it was going to kill him."

I froze. Did she not know that Brett had been stabbed? She was implying that she thought her medication had killed him. Or was she a good enough performer to know how to act?

"Dani, I really think you should talk to the Professor. You know him. He's the most trustworthy person in Ashland. He'll understand if you tell him the truth, but if you let this linger and he finds out another way, it's going to look even worse for you."

She considered that for a minute. "Oh no, you're right. I'm sure you're right, but now I feel like I'm going to throw up. I can't believe that my harmless anxiety medication killed him."

I wasn't sure what to do. She certainly seemed distraught. I decided the best course of action was to stay vague. "I don't know if it killed him. I just heard that he was on something."

"Really?" Her voice was breathless. "I hope you're right. I don't know how I'll live with myself if it ends up that my medication played a role in his death."

Her response seemed authentic, like she was genuinely upset, but I decided against saying more.

Dani began playing again. She hummed along to the light, airy sounds drifting from the piano. I took that as a sign that our conversation was over.

"I should head back to the bakeshop." I stood up.

She nodded. "Thanks for the talk. I'll go to the police station soon."

On my way to Torte, I ruminated on Dani's behavior. She was clearly driven to take her career to the next level, which lent weight to the idea that she could have killed Brett if he was threatening to hold her back. Then again, her reason for giving Brett anxiety medication and her reaction just now made me more inclined to believe her. I hoped that she would follow through on her promise to talk to the Professor. If she didn't—I would.

Chapter Fifteen

My phone buzzed when I was about a block away from the bakeshop. I glanced at the screen—Kerry was calling. I stopped in front of London Station and answered right away. "I hope you're calling to ask me about the best spot on the ship to watch for pods of dolphins and not calling about the murder investigation."

Kerry laughed. "Guilty as charged. Although Thomas and I did see dolphins from our deck this morning while we were enjoying coffee and croissants. Please pass our thanks to Carlos for arranging this—everything is perfect, better than I could have imagined. Part of me wonders how either of you ever left. It's like a dream."

"I'm so glad you're enjoying your honeymoon, and yes, it is dreamy as a guest. Working on the ship is another story, but that's not why you're calling." My gaze drifted to the shop window where staff members were constructing a graduation display with dozens of black caps and gowns. Party supplies in SOU's black and red along with Raiders

T-shirts and hoodies, and stuffed animals of the mascot Rocky the Raider were being put on display for parents and grandparents coming to town for commencement.

"No. Thomas went to sign us up for dance lessons tonight, so I decided to check in quickly."

"Okay, I'll give you the rundown, but only if you promise to go enjoy yourself and not worry about anything here in Ashland as soon as we hang up. This is your honeymoon. You should have a DO NOT DISTURB sign on your cabin door and your phone on airplane mode."

"I promise, I won't call again."

"Here's where things stand." I continued walking until I was in front of the pizza shop, then filled her in on everything I had discovered so far.

"Dani's reaction sounds authentic to me," Kerry offered. "Unless she's a pathological liar, it would be hard to fake that. You're right to have told her to go to Doug, and if she doesn't, definitely loop him in. What about Randall? What's your take on him?"

It was strange to be reviewing suspects with Kerry. In the past, I'd tried to avoid letting her know that Lance and I were doing anything related to a case.

"I don't know. This is where your professional training comes in," I told her. "He doesn't seem very upset about Brett's death, but maybe that's a coping mechanism, and there was obviously a lot of drama with the band. I think with all three of them, but he's not an easy guy to get a read on. I had to drag complete sentences from him. In terms of motive, I'm not sure on that either. He didn't sound thrilled with Dani's constant push to get them gigs, but wouldn't that make him more likely to have killed her, not Brett?"

"Noted."

I wondered if she was actually taking notes. Thomas wouldn't like that.

"Then there's Judge Barbarelli. It sounds like there was some history with her and the deceased," Kerry continued.

"I agree. I'm going to try to talk to her again today. In some ways, she's at the top of my list. I'm stuck on the physicality of her stabbing him. I can't figure out how she could have had the strength, even with Pilates. He was a big guy, and she's an eighty-year-old woman."

"You'd be surprised at what people can do under duress or extreme rage," Kerry replied. "What about Nat?"

"The park maintenance manager?" Nat hadn't been on my radar.

"Yes. He was on the scene. He had full access to the band shell and basement storage area. He would be a person of interest for me."

"Okay. I'll swing by the park and see if I can find him. Anything specific I should ask?"

"No. Do what comes naturally. Ask and listen."

"You got it."

"Thanks for doing this, Jules. It makes me feel better."

"Of course, but I'm serious about you soaking up the sun and enjoying your time away with Thomas. Here's a pro tip. If you're not in the mood for dressing up for dinner one night, order room service and then take it up to the pool deck as the sun sets. You'll likely have the space to yourself. There's nothing better than watching the sun sink on the horizon as you cut through aqua blue waters."

"That sounds wonderful," Kerry said.

"Don't forget to bring a bottle of wine or champagne, and order the Neapolitan éclairs for dessert—they are to die for."

She chuckled. "I'm on it."

"Happy travels! Don't worry about your dad or the case. It's going to work out."

"Thanks," she said with sincerity. "Give our love to everyone."

"I will." We hung up. I reflected on how much our relationship had grown and evolved. I was glad Kerry trusted me. I couldn't let her down.

Torte was bustling with Monday activity. Marty was scoring bread dough. Bethany had arranged our lunch special, meatloaf paninis with a side of herbed salad, in the center of the island so that she could stand on a stool and take an overhead shot of it for our social media.

Steph pulled one headphone from her ear when she spotted me. "Andy needs you upstairs when you have a sec." She steadied her right hand with her left as she piped sweeping loops around the edge of a single-tiered white cake.

Rosa passed by with a tray of grilled meatloaf paninis and bowls of corn chowder.

"Those smell amazing."

She smiled and nodded to Sterling. "Tell the chef."

He pressed his hands together in thanks.

I followed her upstairs, where the lunch rush was in full swing. Every table was packed with happy diners. The outdoor tables were taken, too.

"Did I hear you needed me?" I asked Andy, who was steaming milk.

"When did you sneak in, boss?" he asked over the sound of the steam.

"I came in downstairs. What's up? How can I help?"

"We're good. It's not that. I wanted to let you know that Nat stopped in and asked for you earlier."

"Nat, from Lithia Park?" That was fortuitous, given my conversation with Kerry.

"Yeah, the maintenance guy who comes in early sometimes for coffee before we open. He didn't elaborate. He asked if you were here. I told him you were out doing deliveries but should be back in an hour or so. He didn't want to wait. I offered to make him a latte, but he said he'd check later."

"Got it."

Andy finished foaming the milk and turned off the steamer. "I kind of got a weird vibe off him."

"Weird how?"

"It's hard to describe. He seemed almost desperate to talk to you."

That was odd. Nat and I didn't know each other well, short of him dropping in to grab a plain cup of coffee a few days a week. I couldn't imagine what he needed to talk to me about, unless it was connected to Brett's murder. But why me? Why wouldn't he go to the Professor?

"Thanks for letting me know," I said to Andy. "I'll wander over to the park and see if he's around."

I stuck a couple snickerdoodles in a bag and headed for the park. Nat was directing his crew near the entrance.

"Be sure you get the weeds, but leave the ground cover." He knelt down to show them the difference between an invasive weed and the delicate greenery filling in the park's borders. The same clipboard he'd used for the wedding was tucked underneath his left arm.

I waited for him to finish.

He checked notes off his clipboard and then grabbed a khaki backpack from his maintenance cart. Before shoving the clipboard inside, he gave it another look and nodded to himself like he was mentally checking off tasks.

He noticed me after a minute and looked toward the creek. "Care to take a stroll? I need to check the water."

"Sure." I handed him the cookies. "A little pick-me-up."

"Thanks. I never turn down Torte." He looked into the bag and pulled out one of the cookies dusted with cinnamon and sugar. "Snickerdoodles, my favorite."

"Andy, my barista, said you were looking for me earlier?"

Nat chomped on the cookie. "Yeah. Let's get down closer to the water."

I followed him across the wooden bridge over the creek, and then around a well-worn deer trail. The temperature dropped as we neared the gurgling water. Light filtered through the trees, illuminating the dense greenery on the forest floor—snowberries, leafy ferns, and western mock orange plants blended in with the packed bark trail. Signs warned visitors not to disturb the spawning steelhead.

Nat stopped at one of the picnic tables tucked alongside the creek. A cell phone had been left on one of the wooden benches. "Tourists," Nat muttered. "You wouldn't believe the things I find in the park."

"What do you do with them?"

He gave me an odd look before stuffing the abandoned cell phone into his bag. "Take them to lost and found. Where everything is lost and nothing gets found."

We continued on until we reached the creek's banks. Nat finished his cookie and then proceeded to remove a testing kit from his canvas backpack. He dipped the plastic tube into the water, added in a few drops of a chemical, and then shook the tester.

"Not bad." He held the sample to the sun.

"What are you testing for?"

"E. coli." He dumped the sample back into the creek. "Have to keep the waders safe. It's getting into the busy season at the park."

Nat was referring to the wading area up near the playground. It was a popular spot for little ones to splash in the water on a hot summer afternoon.

"We test it three times a day to make sure it's safe. Green is a go. Red shuts the area down."

"Right." I knew that the city posted notices about the creek for would-be swimmers so they could enjoy it with confidence. What I was curious about was why Nat had summoned me.

"You're probably wondering why I wanted to talk to you."

"I'm always happy for an excuse to come to the park." That was true. Just being in Lithia brought a calm to my body.

"It's about the murder investigation. I heard through the grapevine that you might have a direct line to Doug?"

"I mean, he is married to my mom." I wasn't sure what else to say, or why Nat wouldn't go to the Professor himself.

"That's why I was hoping to get in a word with you. I need the police to know what I'm about to tell you, but for reasons I'd prefer not to share, I don't want them to know this is coming from me."

"Okay." Now I was really intrigued.

"I think I might know who killed him."

Chapter Sixteen

I felt my throat tighten. Nat knew who killed Brett? From the harsh way he was clenching his jaw and his serious gaze, I had to guess he wasn't going to say Jamie.

"You see, I saw something that I wasn't supposed to." He put the testing supplies away while he spoke. "I got here early the morning of the wedding. I always do when we have an event of that magnitude in the park. My wife calls me a control freak, but I've been doing this long enough to know where everything goes and how to efficiently set up without extra hassle or work. The summer crew is a bunch of high school and college students who I can never keep in line. Half the time they flake and don't show up on time."

"Getting an early start makes sense." I wasn't sure I agreed with him on this point. I was the opposite. I trusted my young team, and was thankful that I didn't have to bear the load of running the bakeshop alone.

"Dani and Brett from Heart Strings were here at the crack of dawn."

"They were?" I interrupted. No one had mentioned that, at least not to me.

"Yep. It was odd. We deal with a lot of performers, and never do they show up early. Usually we're having to chase down band members or dancers to get their sound checks in. But not these two. They were on the stage shortly after seven."

That was early, not for me, but Dani had said herself that they were used to pulling late nights. "Do you think they were eager to practice?" Even as I said it, I doubted that was true. Heart Strings was a seasoned trio. Aside from making sure their mics worked, I couldn't imagine why they would need to warm up hours before the wedding.

"I got on Brett right away about his instrument. The guy was super disrespectful. He couldn't care less about my band shell. He was dragging his bass across my stage. Gutting my stage. Drag marks everywhere. I warned him that they were going to have to pay for any damage they did."

"Why would he drag his instrument?" That didn't sound like something a professional musician would do. I also found it interesting that Nat referred to the band shell and stage as "his." Lithia Park belonged to all of us.

"I don't have the foggiest idea, and frankly I don't care. I warned him to stop and went about my business."

Where was he going with this?

Nat fiddled with a Swiss Army knife clipped to his belt buckle. "I was running around the park for a good hour, doing our normal maintenance checks. When I got back to the band shell, they were still there. Only both of them had snuck into my storage area underground."

"Snuck in?" I repeated.

He nodded. "I caught them in there. I shouldn't have

left it unlocked. Usually I keep everything under lock and key, but with setup for the wedding and reception, I knew there were going to be people in and out of there all day. Don't know what those two were doing, though. Said they were looking for a mic stand, but I don't buy it. They were acting weird. I told them to get out. They had no right snooping around down there."

"How were they acting weird?"

"Uh, I'd call it cagey. They startled when I caught them, and Dani sputtered out a bunch of lies about needing the mic stand. There were already two on the stage. For professionals, they weren't acting professional."

"What do you think they were doing?" I wondered if he was trying to imply that they were having an affair. That would certainly change things.

"Snooping. They moved a bunch of my stuff around. I don't know what they were looking for, but I know that's why they were at the band shell early."

Nat's information could be helpful to the case, but I still had dozens of questions, and the most important one was why he couldn't share this himself.

"They knew they shouldn't have been snooping, and they knew they were in a restricted area." He gave a half nod to a trio of runners who sprinted past us on a pressed bark path that eventually connected with the White Rabbit and Red Queen trails that wound through the heavily forested upper hillside of the park that continued all the way to Mount A and deep into the Siskiyou National Forest.

"Restricted area" sounded like a bit of a stretch for a storage space beneath the band shell. "How do you think this connects to the murder?"

"I think she did it." His eyes darted from the creek to me.

"Dani?" I bit the inside of my cheek. Every time I thought I was getting closer to figuring out who had killed Brett, something new like this surfaced.

"Yeah. I think she was setting it up. I think she lured him down there early under false pretenses, then she got him back there to kill him later when no one was looking. It's convenient that the murder happened when everyone was busy setting up chairs and tables. We'd already transported everything from storage. That can't be a coincidence. The killer must have known that no one was going to be around back there." Nat had removed the knife from his belt and was flipping the blade open and shut over and over again.

I took a minute to process his theory. He was jumping to some pretty big conclusions, but I wanted to hear more. "That could be, but that seems like a lot of extra effort, doesn't it?"

"Not if she wanted to frame someone else," he countered. "After I ran them off, I saw her talking to the guy they arrested. It looked like she was paying him money."

"What?" This was getting more complicated by the minute.

"Yep. They were over by the bark path that leads to Bandersnatch." He motioned in that direction with his pocketknife. "She handed him an envelope."

Bandersnatch was a popular hiking and running trail in the watershed. "Why do you think there was money in it?"

"Isn't there always money in it? What else would it be?"

That I couldn't answer. Again, I wondered how reliable Nat's information was. He seemed to be quick to make judgments and assumptions.

His walkie-talkie crackled. He listened as a request came in for him to go to the upper duck pond. "I've got to get moving. You'll pass this on?"

"I will," I told him. "But it seems like you could easily share this with the police." Nothing that he'd said indicated that he was a suspect or even involved. It didn't make sense.

"Like I said, I'd rather not for personal reasons."

"Okay. I'll pass it on," I promised.

He left for the duck pond, and I retraced my steps to the bakeshop. I would definitely keep my promise to share the information, but I hadn't agreed to withholding who I had heard this piece of news from. Nat's story didn't add up. He definitely wasn't telling me the whole truth.

What was I missing?

There was nothing in his story that implicated him in Brett's murder. That is, if he was telling the truth about any of it. He had to be lying. But about what? And why involve me?

Chapter Seventeen

I tried to push my conversation with Nat away for the remainder of the afternoon, but I kept coming back to the question of what I had missed. Clearly there was something glaring that I wasn't seeing or hadn't picked up on.

Luckily, there was plenty to do at the bakeshop to keep my mind from spinning—lunch, weekly orders, custom cakes, and planning our next event, Torte's monthly Sunday Supper.

"Do you have a minute to chat about next Sunday?" Sterling asked, holding a notebook and pen.

"Sure." I motioned for everyone to join me at the island. Sunday Suppers were a way to gather friends and neighbors together to share a meal. We served everything family style around a long communal table. Our Suppers were themed around a particular dish or cuisine. They were a scaled-down version of elaborate thematic dinners that Carlos and I used to host on the *Amour of the Seas*. They blended our love for handcrafting beautiful food with encouraging guests to mingle and linger as long as they liked. The casual evenings had become such a hit that they usually sold out within minutes of being posted.

We had hosted some at Uva in order to open up more seats, which was something Carlos and I had talked about doing on a more recurring basis over the summer.

"What's everyone thinking?" I asked, making room on the island for my afternoon cold brew.

Sterling leafed through his notebook and landed on a page with a number of recipe sketches. "Steph gets credit for this idea. What do you think about a pasta and poetry night?"

"Tell me more." I rubbed my hands together. "Does this mean that you might finally grace us with your wise words?"

Sterling had dabbled in poetry for the last couple of years. He was fairly private about sharing his work. As much as I wanted him to take his writing to the next level, I understood that it had to be on his own terms and when he was ready. Baring your soul on the page took courage.

His blue eyes glinted with a mix of excitement and fear. "I think I might."

"That's so great." I smiled back at him.

"It doesn't have to be pasta and poetry. Alliteration, you know?"

Bethany munched on a strawberry and white chocolate chunk cookie. "Alliteration is the best. Second only to puns." She tapped her T-shirt, which featured a rolling pin and the saying LET'S DOUGH THIS.

"I want to see inside your closet," Andy said, pouring himself a refill of his cold brew. "How many T-shirts do you own?"

"So many." Bethany's tone was flirty. "So, so many. I'm just getting started."

I chuckled and shifted the conversation back to Sterling's idea. "I love the alliteration, too, and you had me at pasta."

Marty chimed in. "We had discussed perhaps doing a variety of pasta styles from different regions around the world. Greek pasta, Italian, maybe something spicy from South America, and a curry pasta. A cultural mash-up. I had a Thai curry fettuccini at a restaurant in San Francisco once that has stayed with me. I'd love to try and recreate it."

"Yes. Such a cool idea," I said. "Poetry is a pure reflection of the soul, so I like the idea of the pasta building on that concept."

Bethany reached for another cookie. "We could do the same thing with desserts, but maybe tasting bites, because that would be a lot of dessert. Like a chai spice pudding to go with your Thai curry, Marty, and something super Italian." She paused for a second.

"Tiramisu," Andy offered.

"Yes, yum!" Bethany caught his eye. "I'll have to come up with a pun for that. Maybe something like, 'Watch out—if you're not careful, I'm going to tiramisu you.'"

"Keep working on that." Sterling rolled his eyes. "I'm glad you guys like the idea. Maybe we do a simple green salad with a few different vinaigrette infusions—spicy cilantro, basil and balsamic, that sort of thing, for the starter."

"I love it." I raised my cold brew to him. "You are all such an amazing team. I think this one is going to be my new favorite Sunday Supper."

"Doesn't she say that every month?" Marty teased.

"Maybe, but this time it's true." I chuckled. "What about the poetry?" I asked Sterling.

"Steph said she could design a menu with a couple short poems on the back. I can put a call out if you want to turn it into a spoken word event. Or we can invite a few poets I know personally."

I glanced around the team. "What do you think? I have a feeling that our customers would appreciate getting to hear from a variety of voices."

Everyone agreed.

"What's better than pasta, hearty bread and desserts, and free entertainment?" Marty asked.

"Nothing, in my opinion." A Sunday Supper was just what we and the rest of the community needed, and adding in live poetry was a sweet touch. I had a feeling that if the evening went as I envisioned, poetry might become a recurring theme.

"Should I start promoting it?" Bethany asked. "Steph and I can work on some pictures for social, and I can send out an invite to our email list. We're doing it here, not at Uva, right?"

"Yeah, let's do it here," I replied. "Keeping it smaller and more intimate will be good for our first foray into poetry. Who knows, if it goes well, we may end up partnering with OSF on the big stage."

A look of terror washed across Sterling's face.

I patted his shoulder. "I'm kidding. Don't panic."

"More like, *don't* mention that idea to Lance, even if you're joking. That's dangerous territory, Jules."

"True." I grinned. Everyone scattered to focus on their own tasks. I was at a crossroads in terms of what to do next with the murder investigation. I had followed through on my promise to Kerry to talk to Nat, and since he had asked me directly to pass on his information to the Professor, I decided my best option was to do that while our discussion was still fresh in my head. What could his reason for not doing it himself be? There had to be more he hadn't told me, and his excuse about my connection to the

Professor was flimsy. Why had he come to me? It didn't make sense.

"I'll be back shortly," I said to Sterling, assessing the kitchen to make sure everything was running smoothly. No one so much as batted an eye when I left.

The police station was directly across Main Street from Torte. Its blue awnings, window boxes overflowing with bright red geraniums, and secret fairy door hidden in its stone foundation made it a welcoming spot for tourists to stop in and ask for directions, get a map of downtown, or even get recommendations for where to make dinner reservations. The focus of Ashland's small team was on building community. Cadets patrolled the park and plaza offering to take photos of visitors in front of OSF's stately Elizabethan theater and doing well-checks on the un-housed. I knew that we were fortunate to have someone as cerebral and as caring as the Professor at the helm of Ashland's peace officers.

I knocked on the door and let myself in. A young cadet I didn't recognize dressed in the standard uniform of blue shorts and a matching blue shirt greeted me with a formal salute. "Can I help you, miss?"

"Is the Professor in his office?" I nodded behind the desk where I could see the narrow hallway that led to his office and a small storage area and holding cell.

The cadet studied the phone on the reception desk. "He's on a call. Do you have an appointment?"

"No, I'm his stepdaughter." I didn't like the word "step" when it came to the Professor. It was one of the reasons I continued to call him by the term of endearment he'd been given years ago by the community. "Step" had a negative connotation. There was nothing negative about our relationship. He had become a second father to me. After I lost my dad when I was young, our connection had filled a hole in my heart, and in a strange way made me feel even more in touch with my dad's memory. That was probably because he and the Professor had been dear friends. Getting to know my dad through the Professor's lens had made him whole again. I loved hearing stories of their youthful escapades. Like, how one Halloween they'd decided to go reverse trick-or-treating after the annual parade down Main Street. They snagged a stack of Halloween sugar cookie cutouts from Torte, remained in their *Midsummer Night's Dream* Puck and Bottom costumes, and went door-to-door passing out sweet treats and cracking funny jokes.

Having the Professor in my life was an unexpected gift, but calling him Dad didn't feel right either, so he would always be the Professor to me.

"Sorry, I'm new," the cadet replied. "Can you wait? I'll let him know you're here when he's done with his call."

"Sure." I studied a wall that was covered with event posters. The Juneteenth parade was coming in a few weeks. I made a mental note to make sure to have Rosa decorate the front windows for the celebration and to create some special Juneteenth cookies and treats to give away to everyone who came out to mark the holiday. The Oregon state legislature had recently unanimously voted to make Juneteenth a state holiday. Ashland had been ahead of the curve, hosting commemorative ceremonies for the holiday for the last decade. The parade and post-parade festivities included food and cultural booths at Lithia Park, music, entertainment, poetry, and performances that had commemorated the historic day for as long as I'd been back home.

The cadet waved me over. "He's off the call. You can head in."

"Thanks."

The Professor stood when I entered his office. "Juliet, what a lovely surprise." He motioned for me to sit across from him. His office was a reflection of him, with framed posters from previous OSF productions, his own time on various stages throughout the Rogue Valley, quotes from Shakespeare, and a collection of photos of Mom and me on his weathered desk. Photos of him on the stage dotted his walls. His tweed jacket hung on a wooden coatrack near the window. Given that we were moving into June, the jacket might have a more permanent place on the rack for the next few months.

"I learned a few things that I wanted to follow up on while the details are crisp in my mind," I said, taking a seat across from him.

"Ah, yes, yet another reason I appreciate you." He sat and riffled through a stack of paperwork on the desk. Once he found what he was looking for, he held a pencil at the ready. "Do proceed."

I told him about my conversation with Nat. "Don't you think it's odd that he asked me to relay this instead of coming to you himself?"

"It raises more questions than it answers, for sure."

He didn't elaborate, so I proceeded to recap how I had bumped into Dani at Lithia Springs.

"Have you heard anything more from the coroner?" I asked. "Could Brett have already been dead when he was stabbed?" If Dani's medication had been the cause of death, then was this a possibility? Maybe stabbing him had been the killer's attempt at trying to cover up their crime.

"No," the Professor answered immediately. "Cause of death has been determined to be sharp force trauma to the chest. That is definitive."

Dani would be relieved to hear that, although that still

didn't mean she couldn't have been the one who stabbed him. I continued on, relaying everything else I had learned.

He took copious notes, pausing every so often to ask for clarification or further details. When I finished, he leaned back in his chair and ran his fingers along his graying beard that was flecked with red. "Most excellent. This is indeed quite helpful. As the Bard would say, 'Lord, Lord, how this world is given to lying.'"

"You think someone is lying?"

"I believe each of our suspects is lying. That is without a doubt. The question that must be pondered is which of the lies connect to this case."

"What do you think about Jamie at this point?"

"I'm still inclined to want to believe that his intentions for appearing in Ashland were altruistic. It seems that he intended to do right by Kerry, but I must leave it to time, and the evidence will out. For the time being, we have him on a tight leash. He's well aware that one misstep will land him in jail again."

I was glad to hear that the Professor was keeping an eye on Jamie. "Speaking of Kerry, she called me this morning."

"Did she?" He closed his notebook and sat up.

"She wanted to know if there were any updates yet."

"I fear that I may have been too harsh with her." The Professor sighed. "When they left for their honeymoon, I told her she was forbidden from calling the office. Only because I want her and Thomas to soak up this time together. In hindsight, I'm realizing that perhaps I went too far."

"No. Not at all," I assured him. "She knows how much you care about her. I think it was just easy for her to do a quick check-in with me. That way she wouldn't get looped into work."

"You are your mother's daughter, Juliet. You know

exactly the right thing to say. I appreciate the sentiment, and like you, I'm invested in bringing a killer to justice as quickly and efficiently as possible. If that can be accomplished before Thomas and Kerry return, all the better."

I agreed. And after we chatted briefly about a potential Italian getaway, I returned to work. There was only one problem. If everyone was lying, how was he going to solve the case before the newlyweds were home?

Chapter Eighteen

"Juliet Capshaw!" Richard Lord's voice pulled me from my thoughts as I crossed Main Street. Richard stood blocking the entrance to the bakeshop with his bulky frame. He thrust his grubby thumb on the shiny glass of the front window. "What is the meaning of this display?"

"What are you talking about, Richard?" I wanted to run inside to grab a rag to wipe the greasy smudge his thumb had left behind.

"Don't play dumb with me, young lady. You know exactly what I'm talking about."

I stared at our window display. In the time that I'd been at the police station, Rosa and Bethany had started the process of changing our front window to advertise our upcoming pasta and poetry Sunday Supper. They had set up a chalkboard easel in the center of the oversized bay windows. Steph must have also had a hand in the new artwork, because I recognized her exquisite calligraphy right away. The words PASTA AND POETRY were surrounded by her signature scroll and intricate filigree patterns. It was obvious the window was still a work in progress. There were boxes of twinkle lights in one corner waiting to be unpacked. And empty cake stands flanking the sides of the chalkboard.

"I haven't the faintest clue why you would be upset about our window display."

He heaved his shoulders backward and puffed out his chest. "Cut the little innocent act with me. You've stolen my idea for the last time. You're not going to get away with this."

"Your idea? What are you talking about?"

Richard swiveled his body in the direction of the Merry Windsor. "Are you blind?"

There were too many offensive things in that question to even warrant a response.

"Look," he commanded. "Bard slam! It says it right there on the banner hanging above the porch. We are hosting a Bard slam next weekend, and you've ripped off the idea." He puffed out his portly chest like a peacock.

"I don't even know what a Bard slam is, Richard."

He rolled his eyes with dramatics that even Lance would approve of. "A Bard slam is exactly what it sounds like. A Shakespeare poetry slam night. What a coincidence that the same day we put up our banner, Torte decides to have a pasta and poetry dinner. I smell a rat."

"You smell coffee," I retorted. "And I promise you that this is a coincidence. One of my staff suggested the idea this afternoon."

"Caught you!" He snapped his fingers above his head. "I knew it. Your staff has been snooping around my hotel trying to steal my ideas."

"Richard, you're acting paranoid. No one has been

snooping around the Merry Windsor. We've been busy catering a wedding and keeping up with orders. My staff doesn't have time to be hanging around the hotel." I didn't even get into the fact that if anyone had stolen ideas over the years, it was Richard.

"Please. What are the odds? I want you to admit it right now. Right here in the middle of the plaza in front of all of these witnesses." He raised his voice, I guessed in hopes that people passing by would pay attention. "Juliet Capshaw, you stole my idea, and if you move forward with your poetry and pasta dinner, I will sue you."

"Sue us for what?" I had to stifle a laugh. Bethany's bad tiramisu pun came to the top of my mind. I wanted to say, *What, are you going to tiramisu me?* Because even for Richard, the threat was over the top.

"Did I stutter?" He made a face. "For stealing my idea. There's only one Shakespeare slam that's happening in this town, and it's happening at the Windsor."

"Great. Go for it. We're not hosting a Shakespeare slam. We're having some local poets read their work at a pasta dinner. That's two totally different and unique events."

"Unique, my . . ." He stopped short of swearing as a mom with two toddlers squeezed past us to go inside.

I gave him my best mom look.

He scoffed. "This isn't the last you've heard from me, Capshaw. Do you have a permit for your event?"

"No. We don't need a permit. It's a Sunday Supper with some poetry. You're really overreacting, Richard. Ashland is big enough to support both of us." I believed that. My mantra had always been one of abundance. Richard's, on the other hand, was clearly one of scarcity.

"It will be interesting to see what City Hall has to say about your lack of permits for a public event." His attempt at sounding threatening made him more comical. "If I were you, I would take that display down now and cancel your event. Otherwise you're going to regret it."

"I appreciate your concern." I plastered on my broadest smile. "Good luck with the Bard slam."

I left him sputtering on the sidewalk and went inside.

"Do I want to ask?" Andy scowled. "Sequoia and I were watching that interaction. Richard looks like a volcano waiting to erupt."

"That sums him up." I scooted behind the espresso counter to wash my hands. "Apparently he's hosting a Shakespearean poetry night, and he's convinced that we stole the idea from him. He threatened to sue me." I chuckled.

Sequoia frowned. "How could he sue over that? That would be like every venue on the plaza suing each other for hosting live music. It doesn't make sense. Am I missing something?"

"Richard Lord rarely makes sense," I replied. "He likes to spout off. I'm not worried about him, but if he comes in and tries to engage either of you, or anyone else on staff, for that matter, don't respond. Just come get me. He thrives on getting a reaction out of people."

"No worries, boss. We know how to handle Richard." Andy winked. "What I really want to know is who would show up for a Shakespeare poetry slam at the Merry Windsor? Part of me kind of wants to sneak over there and check out that crowd. Yikes."

We all laughed.

"I'm sure that Richard has some devoted fans of the Merry Windsor, and I bet they'll have a great time." I tried to take the high road.

"Good luck to them. They're going to be stuck drinking that sludge he tries to pass off as coffee." Andy stuck out his tongue.

"Can you even imagine how bad the poetry is going to be?" Sequoia added. "I feel like it's going to be a lot of roses are red, violets are blue, it's sad that Shakespeare's dead, but I'm glad it's not you."

"Whoa!" Andy reached out to give her a fist bump. "Mad skills. You should throw your name in the hat."

She punched him in the shoulder. "The universe believes otherwise." She folded her hands in gratitude and gave him a half bow.

Rosa passed by with more supplies for the new window display. As much as I knew I was being petty, now I really wanted our pasta and poetry night to be a success. Richard Lord brought out the worst in me. I shouldn't have given him the satisfaction of taking up any space in my head. He wasn't worth it.

I tried to forget about Richard as the afternoon continued. Before I knew it, the day had faded in a blur of closing activities. I glanced at the clock as Sterling and Steph got ready to make their exit.

"How is it already after five?" I asked. "Where does the day go?"

"Tell me about it," Steph replied, tugging a backpack covered with a variety of pins and stickers over one shoulder. "My night class doesn't even start for another hour. At least it's staying light when I'm done. I hate winter term when you go to school in the dark."

"Speaking of school, we're going to have to start talking graduation parties soon. You've only got a few weeks left."

She shrugged. "I don't need a party."

"Try telling that to Mom."

Her stoic gaze broke into a smile. "She is persuasive."

"Is your family coming for the ceremony?" Graduation, wedding season, and the opening of the Elizabethan collided in early June in the Rogue Valley. Every restaurant in the plaza would be booked solid for graduation week-end. It was always a delight to watch graduates pose in their caps and gowns in front of the SOU sign on campus. If students were lucky, they might get photobombed by a family of tame deer nibbling on the grassy lawn.

She shared a brief look with Sterling that I couldn't decipher before answering. "I'm not sure yet. Maybe."

"We should get going." Sterling caught my eye to signal not to ask Steph more. "We're grabbing falafels before her class."

"Have a great night. Thanks for all your help, and I'll see you two tomorrow."

I wondered if there was a reason Stephanie's family wouldn't come to her graduation ceremony. When she and Sterling had decided to move in together, he had mentioned that her parents weren't thrilled with the idea. Neither of them had brought the subject up again, and it wasn't my place to interfere. I hoped that Steph's family would come to support her accomplishment. Regardless, we were not going to let her graduate without a celebratory bash.

Mom came in at that moment. She took off a thin cream cardigan and hung it on the coatrack. "How is every-thing?" she asked.

"Good timing, I was just about to make a note to talk to you about doing something special for Steph's gradu-ation."

"Yes. I meant to bring that up, but we've been so busy with the wedding. What do you think she would like? She's not one for being the center of attention."

"Agreed."

Mom came to look at our notes for the Sunday Sup-per. "She loves reality baking shows. I wonder if we could play off that."

"Oooohhh, fun." Ideas began to swirl in my head. "What

if we had our own mini bake-off, or maybe a cake decorating challenge, with her?"

"She would love that." Mom nodded with enthusiasm. "I'll have a heart-to-heart with Sterling and see if he has any other thoughts."

"Perfect." I showed her our menu sketch for the Sunday Supper. "How does this look? It's Sterling's baby. I loved the concept from the minute he pitched it, and then on my way back from the police station, I had a run-in with Richard, and now I love it even more." I filled her in on Richard's Bard slam.

"Richard would be so much happier if he would simply embrace what he already has at the Merry Windsor and how it's different than what we have here. We should celebrate our differences, not let them divide us." Her response was wiser than my tendency to want to beat Richard at his own game. "You know what they say, comparison is the thief of joy."

"True." I reached out to hug her. "Thanks for your wisdom. I always want to throttle him."

"Honey, trust me, there have been many days when I've wanted to throttle him, too." She squeezed my waist and then released me. "Are you working late tonight or waiting for Carlos to pick you up?"

"Honestly, I can't believe it's already dinnertime. The day vanished. I should go find my phone and check in with Carlos. I don't know what our evening has in store. What about you?"

"Doug is finishing up a few details with the case and then we are meeting friends for dinner."

"Good. You both need a break, and I'm sure he's exhausted from the investigation. I spoke with him earlier. Have there been any new developments?"

She shook her head. "Not that I'm aware of. He's been

in touch with the warden from the prison where Jamie served time, as well as with the coroner and forensics. Last I heard they were waiting on the final toxicology report."

That report would likely prove exactly what had been in Brett's system at the time of the murder.

"You should take a break, too." Mom's tone shifted. "I know how hard you've been working, and I also know that Brett's death must be taking a toll on you. Finding his body had to be disturbing." She locked her eyes on mine. "You don't have to carry the load for everyone."

"Thanks, Mom. It was awful finding him. I guess I just went into focus mode with the wedding, which was helpful in the moment, but you're right. I can't stop thinking about the case, and I keep replaying the events in my head."

She reached for my hand. "That's normal. It's a response to stress, which is why I want you and Carlos to go home and have a nice dinner together or go out and have a glass of wine, but staying here alone and spinning your wheels isn't going to help anyone, especially you."

"Yeah."

"I'm serious, Juliet. If I've learned anything from Doug in the last few years, it's that taking care of yourself has to be part of the equation when you're dealing with tragedy. If you don't, it's going to build up internally and come out in all kinds of ways that aren't helpful."

"True, true." I nodded. "How did I get so lucky to have you as a mom?"

She kissed my cheek. "The feeling is mutual. Now, call your husband and go home. That's a mom order."

"Will do." I took her advice. There was nothing more I could do for the night. A leisurely dinner and glass of wine with Carlos on the deck sounded like just the medicine I needed for the moment.

Chapter Nineteen

The next morning I woke up with new resolve and energy. I was glad to have taken Mom's advice and given the murder investigation a break for the night. Carlos had made us shrimp quesadillas and guacamole. We had lit a fire and enjoyed the warmth of the first day of June, staying up until the first stars made an appearance overhead. It was just the escape I had needed from the assault of questions I couldn't shake regarding Brett's murder.

I left Carlos blissfully sleeping and decided to walk to Torte after a quick shower and cup of coffee. There was nothing like fresh air and exercise to get the brain cells firing.

The walk turned out to be a good idea. Not only did my quick pace get my blood pumping, but Shakespeare would have made Ashland his muse had he seen her in the late spring. Every tree and front lawn looked as if it had been painted a lustrous shade of green. Northern flickers tapped the red-barked cedar trees as a morning wake-up call. Swaths of fragrant purple lavender stalks bloomed in window boxes on the houses that lined Siskiyou. Kids had chalked hopscotch, pictures of butterflies and balloons, and sweet sayings on the sidewalk. Rocking chairs and bench swings sat empty on front porches. It was hard to believe that in a few weeks this space would be filled in by parade-goers to watch the Juneteenth and Fourth of July celebrations.

For now the upper plaza sat in a dreamy slumber. Not even a car passed by as I proceeded toward Torte.

Rosa and Bethany had finished the window display. I stopped to admire it, sneaking a glance at the Merry Windsor. If Richard had been angry yesterday, he was going to be fuming when he saw this. It might have been my favorite display of all time.

Steph had taken creamy sheets of parchment and written snippets of sonnets in calligraphy on them. Bethany and Rosa had strung them from the top of the window with fishing wire so that it appeared as if the quotes were floating. The easel was still centered in the front of the window. They had added garlands of spring blossoms and greenery around it and at the base of the windowsill. Cake stands of varying heights surrounded the easel. They had placed baskets of our rustic bread, bottles of wine, and a pasta bowl with a beautiful container of olive oil and bundles of garlic. The last cake stand displayed a simple single-tiered vanilla cake draped in white fondant and decorated with more poetry calligraphy that Steph must have done with an edible pen.

They had outdone themselves with this impromptu display. Even if I had no idea what a Sunday Supper was, I would have immediately signed up for a spot at the table after one glimpse of our picture-perfect window.

"Take that, Richard Lord," I muttered under my breath

as I unlocked the bakeshop and went through the opening routine. I was surprised to hear knocking upstairs when I finished heating the ovens and had just started upstairs to brew a pot of coffee.

It felt like déjà vu as I went to see who could be pounding on the door at this early hour. Like his daughter a few days ago, Jamie stood in the door frame.

Had the Professor released him? And what was he doing at Torte?

I considered my options. The man was a known criminal. If I unlocked the door and let him inside, I was putting myself at risk. The rest of the team wouldn't be here for at least another twenty minutes. That was plenty of time for Jamie to hurt me—or worse.

But then again, why would he attack me? What motive could he have to involve me?

My gut told me that if anything, he had probably sought me out because he knew that Kerry and I were friends. If I were in his position, I would have done the same.

Before I unlocked the door, I made sure that my phone was in my pocket and ready for me to make an emergency call if necessary.

Plus it was early morning. As long as I kept him near the door, there were likely to be delivery drivers and other business owners out and about on the plaza. This was usually the time that Nat stopped in to grab a coffee and croissant before making his rounds through Lithia.

With slight trepidation, I twisted the lock and opened the door an inch. "Can I help you?"

Jamie's face was ashen. His body movements were twitchy. "I need to talk to you."

"We don't open for another hour or so. Can you come back then?"

"No, it's important. I gotta talk to you now," he snapped.

"Look, I can tell by your face that you're scared. I'm not gonna do anything to you, okay? I need your help." He scratched his short red hair.

I hoped that I wouldn't regret opening the door farther to allow him to come inside.

"How can I help?"

His pupils were wide. "Can I get a coffee?"

From the way his body jerked and he laced and unlaced his fingers, caffeine might not have been the best idea.

"I can get a brew started. The espresso machine isn't ready yet."

"Whatever. As long as it has caffeine, I'll take it."

That didn't sound like a statement from a guy intending to harm me. Nonetheless, I refrained from turning my back on him as I added beans to the grinder. I kept one eye on him while the beans pulsed.

"Did the police release you?"

"Huh?" He studied the chalkboard menu. "You've got some fancy stuff here."

I scooped the beans into the coffeepot and poured in cold filtered tap water. "I asked if the police had released you."

"Yeah. They couldn't hold me any longer. Not without more evidence. I read a lot in prison. I know my rights. Didn't even need a lawyer for that."

"Did that just happen?"

"What?" He had shifted from fidgeting his fingers to bouncing his left foot on the floor.

"Did they just let you out? It's pretty early."

"I got you. Yeah, yeah, they let me out, and I came straight here. I know you and my daughter are friends, and I need to get in touch with her."

Was that why he wanted my help?

"She's on a cruise. There's probably not cell service

if they're out in the middle of the Pacific Ocean." I hit the darkest setting for the brew and let the machine do the rest.

"That's got nothing to do with it. She blocked my number. She won't take my calls. I need to talk to her. I have important information about the case."

The coffee had finished brewing. I poured him a cup. "Do you take anything in your coffee? Cream? Sugar?"

"Black is fine. Fine." He sounded impatient.

"If you have information about the case, you should tell the police. There's not much Kerry can do if she's halfway around the world. Your best bet is to share what you know with the Professor and let Kerry enjoy her honeymoon." I handed him the cup, stepping back so that he didn't spill it on me as he took it with shaky hands.

"I did tell the police. You think they're gonna believe me?" Coffee sloshed near the top of the mug. "Who do you think they're gonna trust? Me, a former criminal, or some know-it-all judge?"

Judge? Was he talking about Mimi?

"You don't need to answer." He paused to take a drink of coffee, barely getting the rim of the mug to his lips. He had to use both hands to steady himself. "Tell me, who is gonna doubt that a judge is lying? But she is. She's lying through her fake white teeth."

"You mean Judge Barbarelli?"

"I don't mean Judge Judy. Yeah, that lady is crooked. She's the one who should be serving time, not doling out sentences."

"Why?" I had to admit that Jamie probably had a fair point about the police being less likely to put much stock into whatever he was going to say about the judge. As much as I wanted to stay open-minded, it was hard to trust him.

"She's done some shady dealing." He intentionally

gulped down his coffee, pausing between each drink to kill time. I got the sense he was enjoying this.

I played along, though. "Okay, why? What kind of dealing?"

"Start with Brett." He finished the drink and held up his empty mug to signal he wanted more. It was one of my biggest pet peeves and a recurring point of annoyance amongst my team. Customers who waved their glasses in our faces as a way of *not* asking for a refill were the absolute worst. The same went for customers who snapped or pointed to their cups for more.

My policy was not to respond, and I had encouraged my team to do the same. Respect was reciprocal. We treated everyone who came through the front door like they were family, and I expected our customers to do the same. The vast majority of them did, but there were always a handful of people who had manners worse than a toddler.

Jamie kept his mug in the air. "Can I get more?"

"Thanks for asking." I smiled wide and went to get him a refill. "What about Brett?"

"He made a deal with the judge. A shady deal. One that I'm sure she doesn't want anyone to hear about. What would you do to keep that quiet?"

I gulped. "You mean you think she killed him so that he couldn't tell anyone about their deal?"

He took the refreshed coffee from me. "I don't think that. I know that. I might have made some mistakes in my past, but I've learned a lot about people from sitting in a jail cell for years, and I can tell you that it's the higher-ups, the ones trying to pass themselves off as respectable and all high and mighty, that are usually the culprits. What's she trying to hide sitting behind the bench in those long black gowns? Parading around town like she's the queen? Nasty secrets. That's what."

"Wait, I don't understand. Brett served time with you, but you were in prison in California. Judge Barbarelli has been on the bench in Ashland for as long as I can remember."

"I never said I served time with Brett in Cali." He shook his head. "No. We were cellmates up here in Oregon, a long time ago."

That was news.

"She presided over his trial. He was supposed to serve a three-year sentence, but that got lightened to barely three months. Guess who fixed that?"

"Mimi?"

"Is that her first name?"

I nodded.

"Mimi Barbarelli—what a joke. Everyone knows if you make the right kind of deal with the right kind of judge, you get a free pass." His eyes narrowed.

"I'm confused. Are you implying that Brett somehow bribed Mimi to reduce his sentence?"

"Nope. I'm not implying anything. I'm telling you outright that's exactly what he did. How do I know? Because he told me. He paid her off. Gave her a wad of cash to keep her quiet, and not just to reduce his sentence, but to basically erase it. Happens more than you think. I'm telling you, there's some dirty judges on the bench, and she's one of them."

"And you told the police this?" I was confused. Why had he come to me?

"Yeah, but they don't believe me. That's why I need you to get in touch with Kerry for me. You've got to tell her this so she can talk to the Professor guy. He won't believe me, but maybe he'll listen to her."

"The Professor is extremely professional. I'm sure he's following up on every lead, regardless of the source. Plus

Brett's arrest and sentencing are public record. He should be able to easily corroborate your story."

"She's not dumb. She's a judge who abuses her power. You really think she would have left a paper trail? No, no way. She's too smart for that. So yeah, he can check the records, but I'd bet good money that there's no evidence of her shady dealings."

"Do you really think it's worth it to drag Kerry into this? She's already had enough stress. I think you care about her, and if you do, my advice is to let her enjoy her honeymoon."

"She's my honey girl. Of course I care about her, but that's why you have to drag her into this. If we don't do something soon, the judge might get away with murder."

Chapter Twenty

Jamie was so insistent that it was hard to doubt his sincerity. I believed that Brett had told him the story of paying off Judge Barbarelli. Whether or not it was actually true remained to be seen. After he finished another cup of coffee, I agreed to look into it. I didn't agree to getting in touch with Kerry. There were a few people I wanted to talk to on my own first. If those leads didn't pan out, then I would have to make a decision about interrupting their honeymoon.

By the time Andy arrived, Jamie had left and I had returned to the kitchen. While I considered everything he had shared, I kneaded bread dough. The act of physically manipulating the stretchy yeast dough allowed me to work out some of the tension I had been holding in my body.

"Are you battling bread this morning, boss?" Andy asked, peering over my shoulder at the ball of sourdough.

He was dressed for spring weather in a pair of khaki shorts and an SOU sweatshirt.

"It kind of looks that way, doesn't it?" I brushed more flour onto my hands. "You know what Mom says about kneading—there's no better way to work out your problems."

"Mrs. The Professor is one smart cookie." He grinned, but then his expression shifted. "What's your problem, though? Is it the murder? You can't get it out of your head, can you?"

I nodded.

"Someone gave me some pretty good advice when I was in the same position." His eyes were soft. "They told me the best thing I could do was to take care of myself."

"Did I say that? That is sage advice." I sighed. "You're right, I can't get it off my mind, and every time I feel like I've made a new discovery or a breakthrough, I end up being wrong."

"Isn't that how life in general works?" Andy made a face. "I mean, that's what my grandma says, and she and Mrs. The Professor are two of the wisest women I've ever met. She always says that you have to take a few steps forward and then a few steps back on any path, but every step forward takes you that much farther ahead."

"That pretty much sums up how I'm feeling right now."

Andy gave me a two-finger salute. "I'm your guy anytime you need a nugget of wisdom or a coffee. When in doubt, turn to coffee. Coffee is always the answer. Isn't that a Bethany T-shirt or something?"

"If not, it should be."

"I'll hook you up in a few. Be kind to the dough. Carlos wouldn't like seeing you beat it like that."

"Beat it is a bit of an exaggeration, Andy." I pretended to be hurt.

"Hey, I call them like I see them, boss. But before I dig a deeper hole, I'm off to soothe your soul with the sweet, sweet nectar of freshly roasted beans." He shook a container of roast he'd brought from home. "Be back in a flash with something hot and frothy."

I smiled after he left. My team never failed to keep my spirits up, and one of Andy's strong espressos wouldn't hurt either.

As was typical, the kitchen was soon humming with activity and delightful smells. Marty wanted to do a test run of a couple of the recipes for our upcoming Sunday Supper. He started with a Greek lemon pasta.

"Since we're going Greek on this one, I believe it demands orzo. Do you agree?"

"I wouldn't so much as consider anything else." I gave him a look of solidarity, from one chef to another. Orzo is pasta shaped like small grains of rice. We often used it in soups and as a side dish.

"Glad you agree." Marty set out cloves of garlic, olive oil, lemons, fresh herbs, chicken stock, and chicken breasts. "What do you say to almost like a risotto style for this dish? I'm intending to sauté the chicken in olive oil and douse it with plenty of lemon flavor—juice and zest— and then dice enough garlic to make a vampire weep. I'm imagining a bed of nicely cooked orzo with a lemony chicken sauce and then slicing chicken on the top with a touch of lemon zest and fresh herbs."

"That sounds like a dish that I would be tempted to finish off on my own."

"I can arrange that." Marty tied on an apron. "I'll serve this for staff lunch this afternoon, but not add it to the specials board. It's better to let our Sunday guests get first dibs, don't you agree?"

"Absolutely. Assuming that everything is a hit, we can

rotate the pastas for next week's daily specials, but our Sunday Supper guests should definitely be the first to taste your wonderful creations."

Marty waved a dish towel like a flag. "Stop, you'll make an old man blush. I do appreciate experimenting with new dishes. A reason I'm grateful to be part of the team."

"We are the lucky ones." I gave him a sincere smile.

He started on the Greek pasta, and I turned my attention to dessert. Seeing his lemons had given me inspiration for a lemon chiffon pie. First I needed to make a buttermilk piecrust. I gathered cold butter, sugar, flour, salt, and buttermilk. The tangy buttermilk would enhance the citrus flavor of the lemon chiffon. Traditionally I use a splash of vodka in piecrusts.

The secret to any piecrust is flaky, buttery layers. In order to achieve that, I grated the chilled butter and then carefully forked it together with flour, a tablespoon of sugar, and a sprinkling of salt. I slowly incorporated the buttermilk, a few tablespoons at a time, until a dough began to form. For a flaky crust, I kneaded it, wrapped it in plastic wrap, and set it in the walk-in to chill while I made the chiffon filling.

For the filling, I needed an armful of lemons, eggs, sugar, salt, and a touch of gelatin. I started by separating the eggs. First I needed to cook the egg yolks and lemon juice and zest. While they thickened on the stove, I dissolved gelatin in cool water. That would give the pie structure and stability. I combined the egg yolk and lemon mixture with the gelatin and set it in an ice bath to cool. Then I turned my attention to the egg whites. I whipped them on high with sugar until they formed silky, stiff peaks. Folding in the egg whites would give the chiffon pie a light and fluffy texture, like a soufflé.

Next I floured a cutting board and rolled out the pie dough until it formed a fourteen-inch circle. I pressed the crust into a pie tin, fluted the edges, and added pie weights to the center. It would blind bake for ten minutes. As soon as the crust was a light golden color, I poured the filling directly into the warm crust and set it back in the oven to bake for an hour, rotating it a few times so that each side was equally cooked through. Then I would let the pie cool completely and serve it with whipped cream and candied lemons.

Baking gave me space to consider everything I had discovered thus far. At this point, there wasn't anyone on my suspect list that I could eliminate. Mimi had worked her way to the top, but I still couldn't reconcile how an eighty-year-old woman could dominate someone Brett's size. Unless he was already passed out from the medication Dani had given him. How realistic was that? Dani was short and petite. I wasn't a doctor, but it didn't take an advanced degree to surmise that one or two anxiety pills probably wouldn't have been enough to knock him flat on his back.

Unless Dani was lying. Maybe she'd given him more medication. Or perhaps she'd offered him something stronger and more deadly under the guise of trying to help calm his nerves. The toxicology report the Professor was waiting on would answer that question.

That led me to Randall. He and Dani had the most obvious motive—Heart Strings. If Brett had interfered with their ability to launch the band into new markets, that didn't justify either of them killing him, but it might explain their motivation to kick him out of the band permanently. Of the two of them, Dani seemed to be the most invested in breaking into a larger music scene, but I couldn't rule out

Randall. I also struggled to get any sense of his personality. Talk about a closed book. The guy had been less than forthcoming in every interaction we'd had. Was he an introvert, or was he worried that if he engaged in conversation, he might let something slip?

My weird interaction with Nat left me unsettled as well. It didn't make sense that he wouldn't go directly to the Professor. There had to be more to his story. He was lying about something, I just couldn't figure out what.

Lastly, there was Jamie. Kerry's father being a killer was not what anyone wanted, but given his past and the uncanny coincidence of showing up right before Brett was killed, I was not about to cross him off my list.

I let out a long sigh. How was it that I was as confused now as I had been from the moment I'd stumbled upon Brett's body? Every new clue led to more questions.

Lance's voice interrupted my thoughts. "Darling, here you are. I've been looking everywhere for you."

"Everywhere?" I brushed flour from my hands onto my apron.

He nodded to the seating area and then pointed above us. "Everywhere in Torte."

I laughed. "It's pretty hard to hide in here. What's up?"

He cleared his throat. "I was hoping you might take a stroll to the Lizzie with me. I need a professional pastry opinion."

"This isn't some kind of a ploy to get me onstage, is it?"

"Ouch." He scrunched his face and stabbed himself in the heart. "That stings. That really stings. No, we're in dress rehearsals for *Waitress*, and I swear that my leading lady is not holding the rolling pin correctly. I want an expert's advice. We can't open with even the tiniest details being off. The audience won't buy in, and I've told the company time and time again that the second you lose the audience, the show is over."

"Okay." I glanced around the kitchen. Marty was putting the finishing touches on his lemon orzo chicken. Bethany and Steph were decorating dozens of sugar cookies, and Sterling was chopping cilantro and romaine lettuce for his lunch special of taco salad served with a cilantro lime dressing and house-made tortilla chips. "As long as I'm back in time for the lunch rush."

"Not to worry. We'll have you home before your coach turns back into a pumpkin." Lance bent down in an exaggerated bow and then extended his arm. "This way, my pastry princess."

Outside the sun was bright on the plaza. Birdsong and music from a busker playing guitar in front of the bubblers filled the air. The traveling musician had propped open her red-velvet-lined guitar case. A cardboard sign read MARKET RESEARCH. WHO IS MORE GENEROUS? Arrows pointed to a bowl labeled COFFEE LOVERS and another labeled TEA LOVERS. I dropped a few dollars in the coffee lovers bowl as we passed by in a show of solidarity toward my favorite beverage.

"You seem off," Lance noted. He furrowed his brow. "What's perplexing you?"

"Is it that obvious?"

"Only to me, darling. You can't hide secrets from yours truly." He drew his eyebrows together and cupped his hand on my back as we moved past the Merry Windsor.

We ascended the stairs that led to the OSF campus, passing the members' lounge and Tudor Guild gift shop. "It's the investigation. I can't get a handle on who the killer is. I keep thinking I've got it figured out and then I realize I'm completely wrong. I guess I feel more pressure because I really want to help Kerry. It would feel so good to have the case solved and wrapped up before they get back from their honeymoon, especially if we can clear Jamie, but the more time that passes, the more I think that's not going to happen. I'll feel terrible if the first thing they have to do when they get home is dive into a murder investigation involving her estranged father."

Lance let me speak. "Your heart is why we all adore you, Juliet, but remember, Kerry and Thomas signed up for this. They are consummate professionals and no strangers to the darker side of police work. It is unfortunate to say the least that Kerry might be tasked with sending her father back to prison upon her return. I can say without a shred of doubt that that is exactly as she would want it."

"Yeah, you're probably right."

"I'm always right," Lance scoffed. "Don't misunderstand, I'm one hundred percent with you on sleuthing out the killer ourselves, I just don't want to see you beating yourself up over where we're currently at with the case. We simply need one break, and we'll be able track down the villain and put them behind bars for good."

"Well, that might be problematic, given that neither of us can make an arrest."

"Details. Details." He flicked the idea away with his wrist. "I happen to have a large assortment of handcuffs in the props department."

"That's a terrible idea, Lance."

He huffed. "Oh, ye of little faith."

We made it to the entrance of the Elizabethan theater. Ancient ivy snaked up the sides of the dark wood doors and wrapped around the top of the historic outdoor venue. Lance unlocked them and pushed me inside.

Stepping into the Lizzie, as it was affectionately known to locals, was like stepping back into London circa 1600.

The theater had been designed to resemble the Globe, with half-timbered walls and seating in a bowl. Balcony canopies and four main acting levels allowed company members to seemingly appear out of thin air. There was nothing that matched the experience of taking in a performance outside under a canopy of twinkling stars.

At the moment, the actors on the stage weren't drenched in starlight, but they were drenched in sweat. The late morning sun beat down on them. I didn't envy their midday rehearsal time.

"This way." Lance led me down the aisle to the front row, where the technical and lighting directors were giving the cast final notes. "Can I get a minute?" Lance asked. He glided onto the stage with the grace of a lion. I watched as he whispered into the lead's ear. Her costume made me smile. It resembled a classic 1950s carhop uniform with pink and white stripes and a ruffled white apron. The look was completed with a pair of bobby socks. I thought she might break out into an upbeat rendition of a number from *Bye Bye Birdie* instead of the heartbreaking, soulful music of Sara Bareilles.

Thank goodness bakeries and coffee shops had evolved. I couldn't imagine baking or serving customers in that skimpy dress.

The actress nodded along as Lance gave her notes on her performance.

When he returned to me, he motioned for me to sit. "Watch with an eagle eye. I can't put my finger on what it is, but I'm convinced she's not believable as a pastry chef in this scene." With that, he clapped twice and the actors launched into their roles.

Not that I had doubted him, but Lance was right. The woman playing Jenna, the pie baker in *Waitress,* was using a handled rolling pin as she prepared the piecrust on the stage. She rolled the dough, which I suspected was made of something sturdier than butter and flour, with such force that I was shocked that she hadn't worn a hole in the center of the crust. Although a wooden rolling pin with two handles is the quintessential image of baking, most professional bakers I knew, myself included, used a pin without handles. A handleless rolling pin allows for better control and uniform pressure on the dough. It's a superior tool for feeling the dough and for long days in the kitchen.

"I hate to say this out loud," I said to Lance. "But you're right. She's using the wrong pin and she's killing the dough."

Lance blew me a kiss. "Thank you. I knew it."

"Putting that much pressure in the center of the crust would ruin it," I explained.

"Cut. Cut." He clapped again. "Don't tell me. Please, go show her how a real baker does it." He yanked me to standing and dragged me onto the stage.

I proceeded to give his actress a brief explanation of the physics of a flaky piecrust and showed her how to roll the dough evenly and gently. She took my input to heart, while a member of the prop's department scurried off in search of a rolling pin without handles. We waited for everyone to resume their marks so that they could run the scene one more time.

"That's brilliant. Absolutely brilliant," Lance commented after watching the scene again. "Thank you, Juliet. You've added believability to the stage. I owe you."

"You don't owe me anything. I'm happy to help, and I'm really happy you didn't try to coerce me into taking over the role."

He shook his finger in my face. "Oh, I wouldn't get too comfortable. It's not too late. I could certainly arrange that."

I stood. "That's my cue to take off."

"No, wait. I jest. You know that. Since you're already here, let's take a moment to review what we know. I just may have some information that will shock you." His eyes twinkled with devilish delight.

Chapter Twenty-one

"What information?"

Lance pressed a finger to his lips. "Not here. Too many listening ears. Let's take a stroll to my office."

I followed him out of the Lizzie to the Bowmer Theatre. His office was located inside the building that housed the intimate six-hundred-seat theater. There was no bad seat in the house at the Bowmer. So many talented actors and musicians had graced the stages over the years. Some had used OSF as a launching point for careers in Hollywood and on Broadway, and others opted to embrace Ashland and make the Rogue Valley their permanent home. I felt grateful every day to live in such a vibrant artistic community.

Lance's office was a gallery of accolades. Awards, magazine and newspaper features, and playbills signed by some of the greats lined the walls. The window behind his oversized desk offered a view of the bricks and the campus. I knew he had planned it that way, to have a bird's-eye view of all the action down below.

"Sit, sit." He motioned to the leather couch. "Can I pour you a drink? Water, tea, something a bit stronger, perhaps?"

"It's not even noon."

"And your point is?"

I shook my head and chuckled. "I'm fine, thanks. Tell me what information you have, though."

"Patience." He walked to the bar near his desk and poured himself a glass of water. He moved like molasses, which I knew was intentional.

"Lance, I have to get back for the lunch rush, remember?"

"Oh fine, you never let me have any fun." He sounded exasperated, but his angular cheeks broke out into a grin. He sat next to me on the couch. "I must be a gentleman, though. Ladies first, right?"

"What do you want to know?"

"Everything, darling. Everything." He licked his lips and watched me with rapt attention.

I filled him in on my conversation with Jamie and gave him a recap of what I had learned yesterday.

"Well done. I can't imagine why you were feeling gloomy earlier. You've unearthed a treasure trove of information. Color me impressed."

"Your turn." I crossed my arms and leaned against the couch.

"Fine. There's no need to take a tone." He tilted his head to one side. "Where should I start?"

I was inches away from swatting him. "To the point."

He strummed his fingers on his chin. "For starters, I heard a juicy piece of gossip about our dear Mimi."

"What gossip?" I couldn't take whatever Lance was about to reveal as gospel. Rumors had a way of spreading around town as fast as a mirror glaze pouring over a cake. We needed to deal in facts, not speculation, which was not always Lance's slant.

"You heard that Brett bribed Judge Babs to reduce his sentence, but did you know that this isn't the first time that she's accepted cash in exchange for doling out a more lenient sentence?"

"Babs?" I raised my eyebrows.

"It's my nickname for her." He pressed his long, narrow index finger to the side of his mouth.

"Let me guess, she doesn't know that."

"What she doesn't know won't hurt her," he bantered back.

"Where did you hear that about Brett?"

"Darling, you know I never reveal my sources, but let's just say that this information comes from someone who is highly trusted and respected. This isn't mere hearsay. This is legit."

"Okay." I wasn't so sure about that, but I wanted to hear what else he had to say.

"Apparently Ms. Barbarelli has racked up quite the impressive collection of cars, including a very high-end Mercedes RV, as well as property on the lake and at the coast, and partial ownership in multiple vineyards and farms throughout the valley."

"How does that prove that she's accepted bribes?"

Lance rolled his eyes. "Please. I know the social circles she runs in, and they aren't people who work as a community judge. It's hardly as if her role on the bench is a supreme court position. She hands out parking tickets and reviews citations for petty theft. Maybe the occasional loitering in Lithia. Don't get me wrong, I'm sure she makes a nice salary. Is it enough to afford her lavish lifestyle? Doubtful."

"That's a huge assumption, even for you. She could have invested wisely. Or maybe she had a large inheritance."

"Listen, I don't pretend to enjoy some of my family's history. My brother still says that he runs with the jet set. Gag." He stuck his finger in his mouth like he was going to throw up. "However there are things you just *know* within certain circles. This is one of them. Mimi has recently gone on a spending spree. I'm talking new money. Cash burning a hole in her pocket. I smell something fishy. Very fishy."

I considered his perspective for a minute. "Let's say that you're right."

"Of course I'm right," he interrupted. "I reminded you earlier that I'm *always* right, darling."

"Like I was saying, if you're right, I still don't understand how an eighty-year-old woman could have killed Brett, at least in the manner the murder occurred. How could she have wrestled him to the ground and stabbed him with his instrument? I know that she does Pilates and is in good shape, but I don't think I could have done it, and I'm half her age."

Lance clapped twice. His eyes were bright with mischief. "Aha! This is where my second tidbit of information comes in."

"What's that?"

"I believe that Judge Mimi Barbarelli had an accomplice. Strength to accompany her smarts."

"Who?"

He raised one brow in challenge. "Who do you think?"

"Randall? He's not exactly a body builder."

His lips pressed together in a half smile. "Ah, but he's young, and don't let his skinny jeans and hipster style fool you. He's spry and wiry. One could imagine it, couldn't they? Nibble on this. Imagine that Mimi gets approached by one of her more savvy criminals. They propose a deal in which both parties win. Our culprit receives a reduced sentence—or perhaps even having their criminal record expunged—and our dear, sweet judge gets a fat payday, under the table of course."

I could tell he was just warming up from the way he uncrossed his legs and leaned in closer. Whenever Lance thought he had insight into a case, or anything secret for that matter, his eyes took on an almost predatory delight, like a wild cat waiting to pounce.

"Here's what I think went down. Mimi developed a taste for money. She realized how much power she wielded and seized the opportunity. I highly doubt that this was her first foray into crime. In fact, I believe that the recent upswell in her business dealings is the direct result of her dirty work behind the bench. This one got the better of her. Things went too far, and she realized that more drastic steps were necessary."

"You mean murder?"

"I mean *muuuur—duuur,*" Lance agreed. "I can see by the befuddled look on your face that you think I might be on to something."

"It's a possibility." Could he be right? Could the soon-to-be-retired judge have been making side deals on the bench? Could she and Randall have worked out a deal where he helped her enforce her shady practices, as Jamie had called them? It was possible, but was it probable?

"Don't stress those pretty pastry cheeks." Lance reached out to tap the side of my face. "I can tell that your brain cells are working overtime. Trust me, darling, Mimi is up to something. Something no good."

"What do we do?"

"We do what we always do—investigate."

I didn't like the tone of his voice or the way he pressed his fingers together like he was mapping out a master plan in his head.

"How?"

"Leave that to me. Let's just say that I have a few ideas brewing. You stay the course, and I'll be in touch with our next steps soon." With that, he stood and offered me his hand. "There's no time to dally. It's off to the baking for you, and off to the plotting for moi."

I started to protest, but he blew me a kiss and pushed me to the door. "Chat soon. Ta-ta."

I knew it was futile to try and have a rational conversation with him once he was on the scent of what he thought was a real lead. It could be. Or it could also be one of his imaginary theories that ended up quickly being debunked by the Professor.

I couldn't argue that he might be on to something with the murderer having an accomplice. It would explain a lot. Could Mimi have directed Randall to kill his bandmate? If so, that meant we needed to be careful. We could be dealing with two killers.

Chapter Twenty-two

I couldn't stop playing out Lance's theory in my head as I returned to the kitchen and busied myself with baking. We had dozens of orders for specialty graduation cakes. "I'll do the chocolate cherry tortes," I said to Bethany, who had a stack of eight-inch vanilla rounds in front of her.

"Cool, I'm finishing two birthday cakes, and Steph is going to do the black and whites once she's done decorating the cookie order. Isn't it cute?"

I glanced to Steph's work station, where sugar cookies in the shape of graduation caps and diplomas had been flooded with royal icing and hand piped with SOU's mascot and signature red, black, and white. "Those look great."

"Is it weird to be decorating so much stuff for your own graduation?" Bethany asked.

Steph shrugged. "Nah. It's fine."

I caught Bethany's eye and mouthed, "Let's chat," while pointing to Steph.

She caught my meaning and nodded in agreement.

Visions of Mimi in her black judge's gown flashed in my head as I began gathering ingredients for the chocolate cherry tortes. It was one of the most popular cakes we offered. We sandwiched eight thin layers of chocolate sponge cake with whipped cream spiked with brandy and cherry juice. Each layer was then lined with slices of bing cherries. The entire cake was frosted with more whipped cream and finished with whole cherries and chocolate shavings. Graduation season never failed to bring in daily requests for the simple yet elegant cake.

Today there were five orders, so I decided to round up to six. We could take the last cake upstairs and sell slices. I had no doubt that the slices would go quickly.

In order to achieve a light and airy chocolate sponge, I began by whipping egg whites to soft peaks. Then I folded in sugar, sifted flour, cocoa powder, ground almonds, and a healthy splash of brandy. The cakes would bake in eight-inch round pans. Once they had cooled, I would use our cake slicer to cut two cakes into eight perfectly even layers.

While the cakes baked, it was time to make the whipping cream. I used whole cream, vanilla infused sugar, brandy, and a splash of bing cherry juice. The finished product had a lovely pale pink color and a subtle sweet flavor. The cherries were the star of this cake, and using whipping cream instead of buttercream allowed them to shine.

My fingers were stained red after slicing market-fresh cherries.

"Jules, it looks like a crime scene in here," Sterling commented as he passed my workstation carrying a tray of mini pizzas destined for the wood-fired oven.

I held up my fingers, dripping with cherry juice.

"Heads up, everyone. No one mess with Jules today," Sterling announced.

"If only I had a pastry knife nearby," I teased, wiping my hands on a towel, leaving it spotted with the dark red cherry juice.

The lightness of the moment evaporated when visions of Brett's body sailed to the front of my head.

Sterling must have noticed the change in my face because he stopped and whispered, "Hey, sorry. I wasn't thinking. I didn't mean that."

"It's okay. Don't worry about it. I guess the murder is still fresh, you know?"

"Yeah, sorry." He winced. "Really, I should have been more mindful."

The last thing I wanted was for my staff to feel like they had to walk on eggshells around me. "I promise, I'm fine. Please, keep up the joking. It's a nice relief from the stark reality of what happened to Brett."

Sterling didn't look convinced as he continued to the oven. I knew that I was living in the space between two worlds at the moment. I wanted to be fully present and grounded in the now, but even joking about bloody cherry hands sucked me back into the past. The sooner Brett's murder was resolved, the better for everyone.

I forced myself to concentrate on the fact that my feet were making contact with the distressed wood floors and on the fragrant aromas of bubbling pizzas and sweet bread. I wasn't going to be of help to anyone if I couldn't complete basic daily tasks without being overwhelmed by my thoughts.

Fortunately my chocolate sponges were done and ready to be sliced. I slid the cake leveler through the delicate sponges. Then I began stacking the cakes. I used a flat spatula to spread a thick layer of the spiked whipping cream on the first layer. Next I covered the cream completely with sliced cherries. I repeated the process for all eight layers. Once the cake was stacked, I covered it with the remaining whipped cream.

I had reserved enough whole cherries, stems and all, to decorate the top of each cake. For that step, I placed a ring of cherries around the exterior of the cake and piled chocolate shavings in the center.

"That is so pretty." Bethany ogled the final product. "No wonder it's a bestseller. It's simple, yet totally on point at the same time. Can I get a couple snaps for our social before you box those up?"

"Sure." I gave the cake stand a final spin so she could see it from every angle. "Does it have a best side?"

Bethany laughed. "Yeah, right. I can't wait to see the day that one of your cakes has a bad side."

"You never know. It could happen." I grinned.

She took a break from stacking vanilla layer cakes to set up my chocolate cherry torte in the center of the island. Bethany had an eye for photos. Instead of simply taking a picture of the cake on its stand, she set the scene with intentionally spilled cocoa powder, a dish towel, and a handful of fresh cherries in the shot.

Lance would be impressed, I thought as I watched her take pictures from the top of one of our footstools. That pulled me back into my conversation from earlier. If the rumors Lance heard about Mimi were true, was there any way to prove it? There had to be records of her time on the bench. I couldn't believe that the court system wouldn't have noticed if she had continually issued reduced sentences. That would be a red flag. Then again, like Lance had said, she was a smart woman. Maybe she'd been able to cover up her tracks.

I decided to bring a care package over to the police station and make sure that the Professor was aware of the rumors circulating about Mimi. I packaged a turkey and Havarti sandwich with our tomato, olive, and basil tapenade and a sugar cookie with vanilla frosting and sprinkles. The cookie was one of the Professor's weaknesses. No one deserved a little sweet reprieve more than him.

Before I went to deliver his lunch, I took the extra chocolate torte upstairs. "Here's a bonus afternoon special for you," I said to Rosa.

Her eyes lit up. "That is almost too pretty to eat. Should we sell this by the slice? Do we have any whole cakes? I know customers will ask."

"We do, but they're all spoken for."

"Not a surprise." She placed the cake in the center of the glass pastry case.

I held up the lunch sack. "I'm off to deliver lunch. Be back shortly."

Rosa tapped the top of the display case. "My guess is that every slice will be gone before you return.

I didn't doubt it. Cake slices did well. It was a way for our guests to enjoy a confectionary treat without having to commit to an entire cake. Usually the hardest decision was deciding what slice to try. We typically offered our black and white, carrot, vanilla butter, and red velvet cakes by the slice. Then, each day, we would rotate in a specialty cake like today's torte. Cake slices often led to sales of whole cakes, so it was a win-win for us and our faithful followers.

When I stepped into the police station, I was shocked to see Judge Barbarelli in the waiting area. She snapped her head in my direction. "What are you doing here?"

It was an odd question, and her voice was laced with irritation. "Delivering lunch." I showed her the bag.

"Torte does individual lunch deliveries now? Are you trying to be Ashland's version of DoorDash?"

"No. This is a personal delivery. The Professor is family."

"What you need to understand, Juliet, is that Doug and I go way back. Long before he married your mother."

I wasn't sure how to respond. This wasn't a competition in terms of who had known the Professor longer.

"It might be difficult for you to grasp the value of long-time connections."

She was speaking to me as if I were a toddler. Why was she suddenly so consumed with her relationship with the Professor?

He came out to greet us before I could ask what point she was trying to make.

"Ladies, good afternoon."

Mimi pressed a finger on a diamond-encrusted wrist-watch. "Is it a good afternoon? I've been waiting for nearly ten minutes, Douglas. I was told to be here at one o'clock sharp, and I expect that if you've summoned me here, you will do me the courtesy of being prompt and timely."

"Many apologies for the delay. I got held up on a call, but please, let me show you to my office now." He motioned to the hallway.

Mimi muttered under her breath. She didn't bother to say goodbye to me. Instead she arched her shoulders and stomped toward the Professor's office.

"I won't keep you. I brought you lunch." I offered him the bag.

"What good deed did I do to deserve a daughter like you?" He kissed the top of my head.

"I thought you might be hungry. You've been working the case nonstop since the wedding." I paused to make sure that the judge was out of earshot. "Also I wanted to fill you in on some gossip about Mimi, but since you called her in, I'm guessing you might have already heard?"

He tilted his head to the side. "Rumor doth double, like the voice and echo." He quoted the Bard as his answer.

"Good. I'm glad you're on it. Enjoy the sandwich. I tucked in a little something extra for you."

He snuck a peek into the bag. "Oh, don't tempt me with Torte's sugar cookies. You know they are my Achilles heel."

"You deserve a sweet every now and then."

"Thank you for looking out for me. You Capshaw women are a rare breed." He gave me another kiss and whispered, "I shall be in touch shortly."

I took that as my sign to leave. Why had Mimi had such a change in attitude? She had been short with me and was clearly irritated that she'd been called to the police station. It was a complete one-eighty from our conversation the other day, when she had been warm, welcoming, and invited me to sit down and chat. Could she be feeling defensive? If the Professor had asked Judge Barbarelli to come in for an interview, did that mean that he had uncovered evidence linking her to bribes? Or, worse—murder?

Chapter Twenty-three

As Rosa had predicted, in the short time I'd been at the police station, every slice of the chocolate cherry torte had vanished.

"Jules, I think you might need to bake a few more tortes tomorrow. We had some disappointed customers. Not to worry, we pacified them with black and white slices, but the cherry torte is such a favorite and perfect for spring right now."

"Great idea. I'll add it to tomorrow's list. In fact, maybe I'll make a few extra for our Sunday Supper, too. Bethany and Steph are going to make tasting bites. Surprising our guests with a slice of spring chocolate cherry torte couldn't hurt."

Rosa pointed to the Torte logo on the top of our chalkboard menu. TORTE NEVER HURTS HERE.

Steph had swapped out our rotating quote for a new one. Her choice was tongue-in-cheek, which I appreciated. It read LET THEM BEAT CAKE. She had drawn a silhouette of a baker getting ready to whack a cake with a rolling pin next to the quote.

I chuckled. "That's hilarious, and good point about having more tortes at Torte. Let's do it." That reminded me that I should probably check in with Marty and Sterling about the final menu for Sunday. Their pasta menu sounded like something we would have served on the cruise. It was truly a global tasting that I knew our guests were going to love.

"How's the poetry coming?" I asked Sterling.

He pulled out his phone to show me social media pages of the poets he'd invited to be part of the night. "We've got four solid yeses, plus me, and one maybe."

"That's great. Everyone will read one poem?"

"Right. Most readings should be under five minutes, so we're talking thirty minutes for the poetry portion of the evening. Marty and I were wondering if you want the readings to be after dinner and before we serve dessert, or if you want to pepper them in throughout the dinner."

"I'm open to whatever you think is best." I'd never hosted a poetry night, so Sterling's input was invaluable.

"I'm leaning toward after dinner. That way everyone can mingle and chat while they eat. Then we can take a break for the poetry readings and serve dessert and coffee afterward. I've found that poems lead to discussion, so that will allow time after the readings for everyone to dissect what they heard."

"That sounds perfect. What do you need from me?"

"Nothing. I'm asking everyone to send me a brief bio. I will introduce each poet before they read." He wiped his hands on a dish towel tucked into his apron, which like Carlos, he wore tied around his waist.

"What about you? Who's going to introduce you?"

"I don't need an introduction."

"Uh, yes, yes, you do. I'll take care of that. How about

if I open with an intro to you and then you can take it from there."

"I guess, but it's not a big deal, Jules."

"It is a big deal. This is your idea, and you're taking a huge step in sharing your work publicly. It's my prerogative as your employer to get to celebrate that, so *deal* with it."

He shook his head. "You're so bossy."

"That's right. Don't forget it. Tell Steph that, too. I'm coming for her with a graduation party." I glanced around the kitchen. Steph had left for her afternoon class while I was at the police station. "Hey, that reminds me, I want to get your input on some ideas for her."

"Sure."

"What do you think about a *Great British Baking Show* themed party?"

"Are you kidding me? She's obsessed. She would probably lose her mind."

"In good way, though?"

"Absolutely."

"Do you know anything about what's going on with her family? Are they coming for graduation? I got a weird vibe when I asked about it the other day."

Sterling tucked a dish towel into his apron. "It's complicated."

"How?"

"Because of me." He stared at his feet.

"What do you mean?"

"They don't like me. I mean, Steph tries to say it's not that, but what else could it be?" His ran his fingers through his hair, brushing a strand that constantly hid his right eye. "It's bad when your girlfriend's parents don't even want to try to get to know you. What if I'm the problem? What if they won't come to graduation because of me? That would be terrible and so unfair to Steph. If they don't want to meet me, I won't get in the way. Graduation is her day. It's about Steph. She's worked so hard for this, and I'm not about to be the person who ruins that for her. I can celebrate with her anytime."

"Oh, Sterling, I'm so sorry. Are you sure they don't want to meet you?" My hand went to my heart. Sterling was one of the kindest young souls I had ever met. He was a faithful friend and a steadfast worker. How could Steph's family make a judgment about him without giving him a chance? Or had they? Was he jumping to worst case scenarios?

"I mean what else could it be?" He flicked a crumb from his apron. "It's okay. I get it. I'm sure they think that I'm a bad influence on her."

"You? What?"

"Jules, admit it. You're like a fierce mama bear to all of us, which—don't get me wrong—we appreciate, but I told Steph that I don't want to come between her and her family. That's not a healthy way to start a relationship. I don't need to be at graduation. I know she won't admit it, but she wants her parents there. It's fine. I'll hang out somewhere else and celebrate with her later. Like, this idea of a *GBBS* party."

"Wait, Sterling, that's not fair either. You and Steph are in a committed relationship. There must be a compromise. A way to at least meet her family and give them a chance to get to know you. Once they know you, you'll have them eating out of the palm of your hand."

He flipped his palm toward the ceiling. "This? I hope not. It smells like onions and garlic."

"I'm serious."

"I know." His voice cracked. "Me, too. I don't want to be the source of problems with Steph and her family. I've had enough grief and family angst in my life."

My heart felt tender for him. Sterling had had a difficult

path. After his mom died, he had lost his way, eventually landing in Ashland, but not before years of grief, estrangement from his dad, and drug use to try and mask the pain. His hardships had brought him a deeper understanding of the importance of connection. Something most people his age didn't develop for years, if ever.

I fought back tears as I reached for his arm. "Trust me on this, running away from the issue will only make it worse. I'm proof of that."

He knew about my history with Carlos and the impact that leaving the ship in a blur of emotions had had on my life—for better and worse.

"What can I do, though?" He massaged the hummingbird tattoo on his forearm with his thumb. "I don't think they approved of us moving in together. I'm sure they don't like the fact that I don't have a degree and I work as a sous chef. They probably have grand visions of Steph's next steps and her future career, and they think I'm going to hold her back. You know, in some ways, I can't help wondering if they're right."

I wanted to wrap him in a hug. He suddenly looked much younger and much more fragile than normal.

"You and Steph are a great match. I don't know what that means for either of your futures, but anyone can clearly see that you two care deeply about one another. You would never hold her back. I can already envision the two of you opening your own restaurant one day. You're the chef. She's the pastry genius. But even if that doesn't happen, here's the thing. Stephanie is a strong, modern woman. There's not a sliver of a chance that she would let you hold her back. She makes her own choices and doesn't apologize for that. It's one of the things I admire most about her. I wish I had had her confidence in my early twenties."

"She's pretty rad," Sterling agreed.

"I'm not telling you this to make you feel better. I have learned the hard way that even when it's challenging, it's better to face issues like this head-on. Maybe you can reach out to Steph's parents directly. Could you ask if they would be willing to meet you for a coffee? You can bring them here and show them what you do. I'll explain to them what an integral part of the bakeshop you are and how I don't know if we could survive without you."

"It sounds like you've been spending too much time with Lance," Sterling teased.

"I'm serious. Torte could be neutral ground."

He hesitated for a minute. "I had thought about Sunday."

"What about it?"

"They get in that morning. I was going to see about inviting them to Sunday Supper. It's a lot of pressure, though, to meet your girlfriend's parents, who already don't like you, and then get up in front of them and read your poetry."

"Actually, that sounds like a perfect opportunity to me. Do you think they'd come?"

He shrugged. "I don't know. I'm sure they want to see where Steph works. And, like you said, at least we'd be surrounded by people. It's not a bad idea. If they won't come to our apartment, maybe Torte could be our mutually safe space."

"My philosophy is and always has been that everyone who walks through our front doors is welcome, no exceptions. Steph's parents included."

"Thanks for listening. It helps to talk it through."

"Anytime." I met his eyes. "I'm here whenever you need a listening ear."

"I appreciate it."

"Keep me posted, okay?"

He went to the sink to finish cleaning up. "Will do."

I added more chocolate cherry tortes to tomorrow's baking schedule. Hopefully Sterling would follow through and invite Steph's parents to Sunday Supper. Assuming they came, I intended to make it my mission to show them how lucky Steph was to have a guy like Sterling in her life and vice versa.

Chapter Twenty-four

The Professor showed up as I was taking the last tray of cookies and hand pies upstairs. He waited for me to finish arranging the tray in the display case. "Might I bother you for a minute?"

"Sure." There was an empty table outside. I nodded that way.

He followed me. After we sat, he scanned the area around us with a seasoned detachment. His causal glance might have made a passerby assume he was looking for a friend in the crowd, but I knew he was confirming there were no potential threats or eavesdroppers nearby.

"I wanted to follow up after my conversation with Judge Mimi Barbarelli."

"It was fortuitous that you had already called her in." I glanced over to the busking guitarist. The money in her case had multiplied since earlier, and it looked like her nonscientific marketing study was proving that coffee drinkers were more generous with their cash. The coffee bowl was overflowing with change and dollar bills.

"And here I thought your visit was simply a lunch delivery." His eyes held a hint of mischief.

"It was," I sputtered. "I mean, you know, lunch along with a piece of news." I could feel my cheeks begin to warm.

"Not to worry. I'll take a Torte sandwich and cookie any day, any way." He chuckled at his unintentional rhyme. "I requested one-on-one time with Mimi due to a variety of rumors that many reputable members of our community passed on."

So Lance wasn't the only one.

"Prior to our interview, I did my due diligence and reviewed cases she presided over in the last ten years. I discovered something quite interesting."

"What?" I tried to stop my knee from bouncing. Had the Professor solved the case? Lance was never going to let me live this down if his theory ended up being true.

"I was able to make connections between the murder victim and the judge."

"She sentenced Brett?"

He bobbed his head in agreement. "She did, and as you heard, the word around town is that she intentionally reduced his sentence in exchange for money and perhaps other bribes—property, etc."

"Is it true?"

"Part of it is." He stopped as a group of actors from OSF passed by us. They were dressed for rehearsal in sweats and yoga gear. "Mimi was the judge assigned to Brett's court case. She did indeed sentence him to jail time for assault and battery, as well as theft," he continued. "However, in reviewing every sentence that she administered in the last ten years, there is not a shred of evidence of wrongdoing or intentionally reducing prison time. Judge Mimi Barbarelli has operated by the book."

"Why did you call her in, then?" I was confused and admittedly disappointed. I had hoped that maybe this case was about to come to an end.

"Because there's also old CCTV footage of Brett and Mimi having a conversation outside of the courtroom prior to his sentencing. It's brief. Brett handed her something in passing. An eagle-eyed young officer caught it when reviewing the footage. I wanted to hear directly from Mimi."

"Did she remember it?"

"She did. In fact, she kept the note." He removed his sports jacket and rested it on the table. The afternoon sun was warm. Not hot yet, but warm enough that coats or sweatshirts weren't necessary. We had entered that time of year when layering was critical. "Brett attempted to bribe her. The note offered her cash for reducing his sentence."

"But she didn't take it?"

"No." He shook his head.

"What about her finances? Lance postulated that she wouldn't bring in enough to cover her lifestyle and investments in her role on the bench."

"True. I followed that line of inquiry, too. Mimi is not only a well-respected judge, but it turns out that she's an extremely savvy investor as well. She brought in financial records showing purchases of stocks. She invested in tech companies in the late nineties. She was well ahead of the curve, and those have paid off with incredible returns in the last decade or so."

"Does this mean she's not a suspect any longer?"

"I can't rule out anyone officially until we make a formal arrest. However, this information certainly brings new light to her circumstances."

"That's good." I sighed.

"Ah, but your face says otherwise."

"No, it is good news for Mimi. I've always liked her and had a hard time imagining how she could have pulled off killing Brett, especially in the manner he died, without help. I guess I was hoping that you might have made an arrest. It would be so great to have the case closed by the time Thomas and Kerry get home."

"Agreed. This doesn't mean that we're not closer. Every piece of information reveals a new layer. I'm sure it's like decorating a cake. Some information closes one door but opens a new path forward."

"What about Jamie?"

"We've released him for the time being with a strict understanding that if he leaves town, he will immediately be taken back into custody."

"Do you think there's anything to his connection with Brett?"

"Again, I can't rule it out." He didn't elaborate.

I wondered if there was any meaning in his lack of response. "Have you gotten the toxicology report back?"

A conspiratorial smile flashed across his face. "As I've said before, if pastry wasn't your calling, I would gladly hire you as a detective. I did receive the report. Brett had beta-blockers in his system, a mild anxiety medication. Not enough to have killed him."

"Right."

He stood and draped his jacket over one arm. "I should be on my way. Do continue to keep me abreast of any other rumors swirling, and thank you again for the delectable lunch. I may or may not have consumed half of the cookie." He winked.

I watched him cross the street in the direction of Lithia Park.

Basically he had admitted that Mimi wasn't at the top

of his suspect list. It was good to know that the judge hadn't accepted bribes. Yet I was back to square one. Maybe I was approaching it wrong. Instead of focusing on Jamie's and Brett's past prison experiences, it might be time to do a deeper dive into the now.

The now was Heart Strings. Perhaps his murder was connected to his future and not the mistakes he had made earlier in his life. Dani and Randall had motive for killing him, especially Dani. She had mentioned that they were playing the Green Show when I had seen her at Lithia Springs.

What better way than go direct to the source? I could pack a dinner, take in their set, and see if I could get some time alone with the duo. Band fallouts weren't uncommon. With the news that Judge Barbarelli was in the clear, I needed to shift my focus and hopefully home in on the real killer.

Chapter Twenty-five

I texted Carlos to tell him to meet me on the bricks and packed dinner for us. Marty had made batches of each of the pastas we would be serving for Sunday Supper. The containers were neatly labeled in the walk-in with a stickie note that read TRY ME.

I scooped helpings of Mexican pasta salad and his fettuccine Thai curry into to-go containers, along with bottled sparkling water, fruit salad, and two of Bethany's strawberry cream cheese brownies. The kitchen was spotless and prepped for the next day, so I locked the bakeshop and walked up Pioneer Street to the OSF campus.

Attending a performance at the Green Show was like a mini reunion. Thanks to the brilliant spring weather and the upcoming opening of the Lizzie, a huge crowd had gathered on the grassy area above the bricks. I found a shady spot next to the Bowmer Theatre and spread out a blanket and our dinner. Lance appeared onstage to introduce Heart Strings.

"Welcome, welcome, friends and lovers, to our Green Show. Raise your hands if this is your first time in our hamlet?"

A scattering of hands shot in the air.

"Delightful. A special welcome to our new guests." Lance clapped. "As many of you know, I'm the Artistic Director here at OSF, the largest repertory theater west of the Mississippi. Tonight we have a pre-show treat for you. Heart Strings is a jazz trio that has taken the Rogue Valley by storm. They've performed on some of the biggest stages with some of the biggest names in the business. Tonight they'll get you moving and grooving before we open the doors to the Bowmer and Thomas. For those of you who haven't heard, we're opening our season at the Elizabethan tomorrow night." He pointed in my direction to the historic theater behind me. "Our first show is *Waitress*. It is going to be a musical and confectionary delight. I hope you'll consider joining us. We'll also be premiering *King Lear* and two additional shows as the summer season starts to heat up. You don't want to miss out on any of these performances. The box office across the street is open, so if you haven't scored tickets for any of our shows, be sure to do that before you leave. Now, without further ado, I give you Heart Strings." He exited the stage.

Dani and Randall were joined by their temporary new member. I had to give them credit. They didn't miss a beat. Kids spun in circles and danced in front of the stage as they performed their first set. I watched them both, hoping I didn't look as intense as I felt.

What I was looking for was hard to articulate. A stolen glance. Any sort of sign that things were off.

Nothing appeared, at least not to my untrained eye.

Dani delivered a smooth, sultry performance, connecting with the crowd. She was clearly at home on the stage. I didn't see an ounce of nervousness. Randall was much the same. He made less eye contact with the audience, which I chalked up to his role in the band, not because he seemed uncomfortable or jumpy.

Carlos showed up halfway through their second set. "Sorry I am late." He sat down next to me and scooted close so that our knees were touching. "They have a nice turnout for this."

I plated up dinner and offered him a choice of pink grapefruit or mango raspberry sparkling water. We enjoyed the music while polishing off both pastas and the fruit salad. It was good to give my brain a bit of a break, but I still intended to try to talk to Randall and Dani once the concert was over.

"Dessert?" I asked, holding up a to-go container.

"Is this even a question?" Carlos peered into the box. "Chocolate and strawberries are one of the most perfect pairings. Do I have to share?"

"Um, yeah." I pretended to be offended. "Unless you want to sleep on the couch tonight."

He threw his head back and laughed. "No, no. I will share. I will share."

The brownies vanished as Dani and Randall wrapped their performance. The audience jumped to their feet to demand an encore. Heart Strings obliged, returning to the stage for three more songs. This time when they finished, the doors were opening to the theaters, so the crowd dispersed.

Carlos helped me pack away our leftovers and folded the blanket. "I parked the car at Torte. If you want to wait for a few minutes, I'll go put this away, get the car, and come pick you up shortly. I told Sterling and Marty that I would take a look at the menu for the Sunday Supper."

"What service. You're my personal ride share. Maybe we should add wine shuttle service to our menu at Uva."

He grinned. "That is not a bad idea."

Normally I would have walked with him, but he had provided me with a perfect opportunity to see if I could talk to Dani or Randall.

"Sure. I'll hang out. I want to sneak in and see the final set for *Waitress,* anyway. Plus I might happen to bump into Dani or Randall, which wouldn't be so bad. Take your time."

"Ah, there it is. Be careful. I know what you and Lance get up to." He gave me a quick kiss. "I'll be back in a while, then, mi querida."

I spotted Dani signing autographs on the side of the stage. Her loyal fan base waited patiently as she signed postcards and CD covers. Randall was tearing down the stage. He was surrounded by five other crew people, so I decided to wait in line for Dani first. The queue moved fast.

She peered at me from beneath the rim of her blue sunglasses. "Hey, did you want an autograph?"

I wished I had purchased one of her CDs. "Are you selling your music? I'd love to get your most current release to play at Torte."

Her eyes drifted over to Randall. "We were supposed to be selling them. However, someone forgot them."

Randall lurked near the piano. I couldn't tell if he had heard Dani's comment or not.

"No worries. If you're in the plaza, just drop one by the bakeshop, and I'll leave a note at the register to have my staff pay you out of petty cash."

"Great." Dani checked to see if any additional fans were waiting to get a moment with her. Since the crowd had scattered, she put her pen away and began gathering her things.

"Have you heard anything more about the murder?" I asked.

She frowned. "No, why would I?"

"I just wondered if the police were looping you and Randall in, since you knew Brett better than anyone else." I looked up to see Randall staring at us. He caught my eye and pretended to tune the piano.

She handed me a mic stand. "Can you help me take this inside? We're doing the Green Show tomorrow, too, so Lance said we could store our stuff in the basement of the Bowmer."

"Wow, two nights in a row. That's great. Usually the Green Show rotates through acts. Lance must be impressed."

"Maybe. I think it had more to do with another act canceling. I won't turn down a gig, though. We are always happy to fill in, especially if the gig comes with a nice paycheck."

I helped her with her gear. We walked to the Bowmer together. She showed the usher her Green Show pass. "We're taking this downstairs."

He let us through. Dani led the way past the concessions, where ticket holders waited to purchase drinks and snacks before going into the auditorium. "This way." She pointed to a door at the far end of the windowed lobby.

I was familiar with the layout of the Bowmer, having spent many hours traipsing around its long corridors in my youth. Since Dad had been a self-taught Shakespearean scholar, I had practically grown up in the theater. He and the Professor had been part of the Midnight Club, a group of Bard aficionados who gathered in the wee hours of the night to recite sonnets and share new works. Sterling's poetry night felt like an homage to him. He would have certainly approved of the idea.

We made it to a storage area in the bowels of the theater. The space was crowded and dark, with a faint aroma of must.

Dani kept her sunglasses on as she flipped a light switch. Fluorescent lights flickered and hummed. A dull yellow halo guided us through the maze of props and old equipment. "Just stick it over here." She squeezed past a mannequin.

A surge of fear pulsed through my body. It came out of nowhere. One thing that I had learned over the years was to trust my instincts. If something felt off, there was probably a good reason for it.

Had I made a mistake coming down here with Dani? I should have listened to Carlos's warning.

No one had seen us other than the usher, and it was hardly as if he would be on the lookout for us. There were throngs of ticket holders waiting to come inside for the show.

He did see you, though, Jules, I reminded myself, trying to also remember to breathe. If Dani tried anything, he was a witness. Plus, there were at least a thousand people in attendance for tonight's show. Dani wouldn't try to hurt me here, would she?

She stopped in place and stared at me. "What are you doing?"

"Huh?"

"You're just standing there." She spun her free hand in a circle to indicate that I should keep moving.

"Sorry. I got caught up in my thoughts."

"Can you bring that to me?" She sounded irritated.

I swallowed hard and stepped forward. The lights on her side of the storage room were barely as strong as a single flame on a birthday candle. It was hard to see her in the dim light. Had she grabbed a weapon? Was she planning to stab me, like she had stabbed Brett, and leave me in the damp basement to die?

Or are you imagining things, Jules? The rational part of my brain tried to take over. I could easily be jumping to conclusions. I had no proof that Dani had killed Brett. She wasn't even necessarily my top suspect.

Then why was my neck tingling and a chill spreading through my body?

I didn't like the way she was standing in the shadows, like a prey animal waiting to pounce.

"What's your problem?"

"Nothing."

"You're acting really skittish. Can you just bring me my stuff?"

I gulped and clutched the mic stand tighter. If nothing else, I could use it as a weapon if she tried to attack me.

I stepped forward with a grip on the stand so tight I had a feeling my fingers were going to go numb at any moment. Before they did, something worse happened.

The buzzing sound overhead grew louder.

It reminded me of a swarm of mosquitoes Carlos and I had encountered once on the shore of Cozumel. They had sounded like a jet engine taking off as they surrounded us on the white sandy beach.

The buzz was followed by a loud cracking sound and then a large pop as what little light was above us went out and we were plunged into complete darkness.

Chapter Twenty-six

My worst fears had come true. Had Dani arranged this? How?

Sweat pooled on my forehead. My heart thudded against my chest. I froze.

What should I do?

I could inch backward toward the exit door. The only question was whether Dani had already made a move. Was she about to hit me? Was she planning to sneak around behind me and whack me in the back of the head? Or was I being ridiculous? Had I spent too much time with Lance? His overly dramatic tendencies could be getting to me.

I kept my body as still as possible and tried to listen.

The only sound I heard was thudding above us. I assumed that was the crowd taking their seats.

"Jules!" Dani's voice cut through the panic building in my body. "Jules, where are you?"

Should I answer? Would that be a mistake? Could she follow the sound of my voice and make her attack, or was I spinning out of control?

"What happened to the lights?" Her voice sounded like it had a touch of panic as well. "Jules, are you still here?"

"I'm here." I kept a tight grip on the mic stand.

"What happened?"

"I don't know. The lights went out." I blinked hard, trying to force my eyes to adjust to the blackness. It didn't work.

A bell chimed.

It made me startle. My heart skipped a beat and then thudded in my chest.

"That's the five-minute warning," Dani said. Was she coming closer?

I took a step backward.

"Lance warned me that this might happen. He said the electrical system needs updating and that sometimes the lights in this section of the basement go out when they dim the lights upstairs."

Right on cue, the lights came back on.

My eyes revolted.

Spots clouded my vision. I blinked again, trying to make sure to keep Dani's fuzzy frame in my line of sight. She hadn't moved.

"What are you doing with that? Were you going to hit me?" The look of shock on her face was enough to make me lower the mic stand, which I was holding like a base-ball bat.

"I thought you were going to attack me." I wondered if my voice sounded as breathless as I felt.

"Why would I attack you?" She frowned and made a weird face, like I was speaking in a foreign language.

"Because of Brett."

She shook her head. "What am I missing? What about Brett?"

"I thought you killed him and dragged me down here to kill me, too."

Dani's mouth hung open. "Are you for real?"

"It was just a theory. I was going to ask you about it, and then the lights went out and I guess instinct kicked in." As I said it out loud, I felt slightly ridiculous. I was accusing her of killing her bandmate.

No wonder Dani gaped at me with a confused frown. "The light switch is behind you. How would I have managed to turn them off? And what makes you think that I killed Brett? Nothing could be further from the truth. I told you that at Ashland Springs. I was devastated when I thought my anxiety medication might have killed him. I went to the police. They assured me it wasn't that."

The final warning bell dinged above us, causing the lights to flicker again, but this time they remained on.

"You seem so intent on taking Heart Strings to the next level, and Brett was holding you back. I thought maybe you killed him because you knew you would never be able to break out of the Rogue Valley with him. I thought maybe it was an accident. That you guys got in a fight about the band's future and things got out of control."

"That's quite a theory." Dani shifted her head to the side to study me. She ran her fingers through her hair like she was trying to spike it. "Completely wrong, but I give you props for creativity. Why would you think that Brett was holding us back?"

"You said that."

"No I didn't."

"But you did, when we met at Torte and you were talking about Heart Strings. You made it pretty clear that Brett was going to get kicked out of the band."

Dani waved me off with both hands. "No. No, I didn't. You misunderstood. I wasn't talking about Brett. I was talking about Randall."

"Randall?"

"Yeah, Randall. Brett and I were planning to kick him out of the band. We talked about it the morning of the wedding and decided we were going to do it after the reception. We'd been discussing it for weeks. We'd given him ultimatums. He refused to change his behavior, so Brett and I agreed this was it. He'd had chances. He kept flaking on shows and wouldn't put in the effort it would take to work with the producers I had my eyes on. Brett had been the holdout. I've wanted Randall gone for months, but Brett had finally come around. And then he was killed. It's the worst. Now I'm stuck with Randall."

How had I gotten it so wrong?

"I'm so sorry, Dani. I was obviously mistaken. I can't believe it's Randall you wanted to kick out of the band. I assumed you were talking about Brett." That's what Randall had told me at Torte. Maybe he was the one lying.

"No. Brett and I were in total alignment on this. He wanted Randall gone as much as me. He was ready to fully commit to Heart Strings and whatever it took to get to the next level. That was part of getting sober for him. He was refocusing on his life and his career."

She sounded sad.

"Do you think that Randall could have killed him? Maybe he figured out that you and Brett were getting ready to kick him out of the band."

"Randall?" She let out a curt laugh. "He's a slug. Even if he was fuming about getting kicked out of Heart Strings, he would have had to muster up the energy to kill Brett. That was our biggest argument—moving at more than a snail's pace." She shook her head. "I can't see it. Not that he wouldn't have it in him. The guy is a loner. Even after playing with him for the last couple years, I'm still never exactly sure what's going on in his head. Maybe nothing."

She made space for her set list clipboard and portable speakers on one of the shelving units. "I told the police they should be looking into Nat."

"The park manager?"

"Yeah, he and Brett got into a wicked fight that day, and then I found him going through our stuff." She moved boxes to make room for the rest of her gear.

"You did? When?" Again, this was the exact of opposite of what Nat had told me. He had claimed that Dani and Brett were snooping through his stuff.

"The day after the murder. He claimed that Brett had stolen supplies and some of his tools. What would Brett have needed lawn tools for? I don't know what he was really up to, but the guy is weird. I don't trust him. If anyone killed Brett, my money's on him."

That triggered a memory. "Did you give Jamie, Detective Kerry's dad, an envelope the morning that Brett was killed?"

"No. I don't even know him. Who told you that?"

There was no need to throw Nat under the bus, not yet anyway. "It's just a rumor going around."

"I don't know who started that, but the only people I spoke with the morning of the murder were Brett, Randall, and the judge." She sounded adamant.

What a shift from the way our conversation had started. I felt guilty for accusing her of murder. "Let me put this away, and I'll walk out with you."

"Don't worry about it. I have to go find Lance. He's working on a connection for me. A producer he knows in LA who might be interested in hearing our demo. Keep your fingers crossed."

"I will," I promised. I put the mic stand next to her other gear and went to find Carlos, who was waiting for me on Pioneer Street. My conversation with Dani had been revealing in ways I couldn't imagine. I may have made a mistake in assuming that Dani wanted Brett out of the band, but now I had a new suspect to focus on, and if my hunch was right this time, I was closing in on a killer and just might solve the case before Thomas and Kerry got home.

Chapter Twenty-seven

The next morning I woke up wishing there was a way I could put an end to the barrage of questions running through my mind. I'd spent the night tossing and turning, dreaming about sharp instruments jabbed into wedding cakes.

There was only one way to stop the anxiety loop. I had to try and get some answers. Instead of starting my day at Torte, I bypassed the bakeshop and went to Lithia Park. Nat was one of the only people in town who worked hours earlier than me. He often stopped in for a coffee before we officially opened. Andy and Sequoia had come to know the sound of his cart. They would bring him a black coffee and a scone or muffin that he would take with him on his morning rounds through Lithia. At the end of each week, he would swing by to pay in advance for the following week.

I never minded serving any of our early-rising colleagues during unofficial Torte hours—Nat, delivery drivers, housekeeping staff on their way to Ashland's many

B and Bs and hotels. If we were at the bakeshop and the coffee was brewing, we enjoyed getting to be the first stop and keeping everyone fed and caffeinated.

As expected, Nat was in his cart near the park entrance. The cart was necessary to navigate the pathways of Lithia Park's ninety-three acres. One of Nat's responsibilities at this hour was to drive through the park and alert the police to any danger—illegal campfires were the greatest threat to the city. The forested park didn't have boundaries that Mother Nature would recognize. It backed up to untamed mountains that stretched as far as the eye could see. One spark or ember could ignite a wildfire that would quickly become impossible to control.

Dusky light made it hard to see Nat's facial features. I waved and called to him. "Morning, Nat."

He cut the engine and waited for me to approach the cart. "It's early, even for you."

"I know. I haven't had a single cup of coffee yet either, so you can anticipate that I'll get the shakes any minute." I wiggled my fingers, hoping to keep the tone casual. The last thing I wanted was for Nat to get spooked. I had a few specific questions I wanted to ask him. My only chance of having him answer honestly was to make sure he didn't think I was trying to interrogate him.

"What brings you to the park?"

"You, actually. I was hoping we could chat."

He patted the seat next to him. "Sure. Get in. I've got something I want to show you anyway."

"Show me?" I repeated, trying to buy myself time to decide what to do. Was it a huge mistake to get in Nat's maintenance cart? Hadn't I learned my lesson last night? Then again, last night had also taught me not to jump to conclusions without evidence.

Before I could make up my mind, Richard Lord lumbered toward us. I don't think until this very moment there had ever been a time in my life when I was happy to see Richard. I made sure to greet him. If he saw me leaving in the cart with Nat, there was no chance Nat would try to hurt me.

"Good morning, Richard. What brings you to town so early?"

He snarled at me. "Same as you Capshaw, work." He pointed to his canary yellow Hummer, which he had parked in a two-hour space across the street in front of the Green Goblin. "I'm surprised you're not baking yet. My kitchen staff have already been at it for an hour. Could it be that you've taken too much on and are finally going to fall flat on your face?"

"And to think all I said was 'good morning.'"

"Don't try your mind games with me. I know what you're doing." He looked to Nat.

Nat shrugged.

Normally I would have done anything to end a conversation with Richard as fast as possible, but the longer we spoke, the better I felt about getting into the cart with Nat.

"You're trying to snoop on our breakfast service." He nodded to the Merry Windsor, which sat to the left of the park entrance.

"Why would I want to spy on your breakfast service?" I couldn't contain my exasperation.

"Because you're going to steal our ideas." He shook a puffy finger in my face. "Just like you stole our ice cream cart concept and poetry night."

"Richard, you know that's not true."

"Ha! I know that you and your mother are Ashland's worst schemers, but you're not going to get your grubby hands on my new thing."

"What's your new thing?"

"Nice try, Capshaw. You'll have to work harder than that." Richard huffed off.

Nat pointed to the empty seat. "You coming?"

"Uh, sure. I just need to be at Torte within the next half hour."

"I wouldn't worry about that."

Did he mean because he would have me back in plenty of time or that he had no intention of bringing me back at all?

I got in despite my reservations.

Nat pressed his foot on the gas. The cart sped down the path like he was the getaway driver in a bank robbery. I grabbed the side and hung on tight.

"Richard's jealous, you know that, right?"

"Yeah."

"Don't let him get to you. That makes it worse." He flipped on the radio and found a classical station.

I appreciated that he agreed with the approach Mom and I had always taken with Richard. If he was trying to offer wisdom on how to deal with Ashland's one and only bully, that had to be a sign that he wasn't going to harm me. Or so I hoped.

We flew past the duck pond and play area. Nat steered the cart over the wooden slat bridge. Going across it was like off-roading on rocky sand dunes. I held on for dear life as he cracked the wheel and made a hairpin turn onto Winburn Way, the street that ran parallel to the park.

"Where are we going?" I asked.

"You'll see." His eyes were focused on a group of deer ahead. "Move!" he hollered to them. They paid no attention. "Such a menace. I've told the mayor I could take care of Ashland's deer population in a day if she'd let me bring my hunting rifle to work."

I let out a shudder. He owned a gun. Not that that was uncommon in southern Oregon. Outdoor sports, including hunting and fishing, were part of the lifestyle.

"But no, the tourists *love* the deer." He mimicked the mayor's voice. "They give the park and plaza a quaint charm."

Depending on the season, deer seemed to outnumber people. There were ongoing debates at city hall about how to manage the deer population, which to the mayor's point, did enhance Ashland's idyllic nature, but they also attracted larger prey animals into town—black bears and cougars. Janet often lamented that she could never leave roses out in front of her shop. If the deer caught whiff of their aroma, they would make quick work of them. Gardeners and hunters became unlikely allies in the great deer debate.

I wanted to believe Nat was simply in the "cull the herd" camp, but I was also on edge. His mention of his shotgun could be a veiled threat. I had to stay present.

"What did you want to talk to me about?" he asked as we headed for the end of the road, where Winburn turned to gravel and connected to the reservoir.

"I wanted to ask you about Brett's murder." I decided getting straight to the point was probably the best tactic with him.

"Shoot."

"I heard a rumor that you thought Brett had stolen from you."

"I didn't think that. I *knew* that. He went through the storage shed and cleaned me out."

"When?" Although the sun was slowly making its ascent over the mountains, as we drove farther into the forest, it was getting darker and darker.

Nat swerved to the left to avoid a large pothole in the

center of the gravel road. "No idea. Must have been the night before the wedding or early that morning. I caught him down there rummaging around through everything."

Why hadn't Nat mentioned this during our last conversation?

"He took a lot of stuff that didn't belong to him."

"You mean tools and stuff?" I couldn't imagine why he would want tools, unless he was desperate for cash and planned to sell them.

Nat didn't answer. He maneuvered around the reservoir and parked the cart. "I didn't say tools."

"What did he take, then?"

"Stuff he shouldn't have." He got out of the cart. "You coming?"

"To the res?" I looked to the dark water, where kids splashed and swam on hot summer afternoons. This morning the reservoir looked menacing, with shadows from the park's leafy oaks darting across its surface. Did Nat really want to show me something, or was he planning to knock me out and dump me in the water?

Chapter Twenty-eight

"You coming, or what?" Nat stood next to the cart waiting for me.

I could run. There weren't any houses on this side of the park for another half mile or so, but I had run cross-country in high school and figured I could beat Nat if it came to a footrace. Except for the cart. He could easily chase me down in four wheels. I would have to sprint to the upper Alice in Wonderland trails, where there weren't any houses or cell service.

"Why are you just standing there?"

"What do you want to show me?"

"I think it has to do with the murder, and I want another set of eyes." He pointed toward the restrooms up the hill. They were at least fifty feet from the water. Unless he had a weapon, odds were on my side. I didn't think he could manage killing me and dragging me down to the water.

There was always the chance that a mountain biker or morning hiker would happen by.

I inhaled through my nose and followed him toward the restrooms. Instead of stopping at the facilities, he continued past them on a bark path that wrapped behind the reservoir. We were still going away from the water, but we were also about to disappear out of sight of anyone who might pass by.

The circular cement water reserve had been graffitied. Remnants of garbage from an underage drinking party littered the pathway.

Nat came to an abrupt halt and pointed to the graffiti- and moss-covered wall. "There. Look."

I wasn't sure what I was looking at. Kids had etched their initials in the cement. Symbols and words in comic design had been spray-painted on the side.

Nat must have noticed me squinting, because he took his hand and placed it directly on the spot he wanted me to see.

"Here."

I gasped. The same pirate symbol that Jamie had tattooed had been painted on the reservoir in black and red paint. Beneath it were the words BRETT MUST DIE and a signature I couldn't decipher.

"Why are you showing this to me? Have you told the Professor about this?"

Nat shook his head. "I'm showing it to you so you can tell him."

"No. Stop. This is ridiculous. I'm not going to keep acting as your go-between." I could hear the frustration in my voice, and I didn't care. "Either tell me why you won't talk to the police yourself or I'm calling them now." I pulled out my phone to show that I was serious.

Nat held up his hands. "No, wait. Don't." He glanced around us and then took a key off a ring attached to his belt. "Come here, I'll show you." He proceeded to unlock an access door that I never knew existed on the side of the cylinder structure. Using his flashlight like a spotlight, he shone it around a tiny storage room stuffed with a variety of tools, equipment, cell phones, jewelry, wallets, and even bundles of cash.

"What is this?"

"It's my stash. I'm using it for leverage."

My stomach dropped. What kind of leverage did he mean?

"Listen, it's not a big deal. People drop things in the park, okay?"

"Is this lost and found?" I had a feeling I already knew the answer.

"You could say that, in a way." He shut the door behind him. "I make pennies at this job. The pension and benefits are the only reason I stay. The stash is a side gig. What do the kids call it these days? A side hustle?"

I wouldn't have defined a side hustle as stealing lost and found items. My mind flashed to seeing him pick up something from the grass when he and Brett had been arguing the morning of the wedding and then again to him grabbing the abandoned cell phone from the picnic table when I had accompanied him to test the creek water. How many items did he amass each day on the job?

"It's not like I'm stealing anything," Nat continued. "If anyone comes forward looking for a missing wallet or cell phone, I return the item to its owner, but that's a rarity. The park gets thousands of tourists every day. Are you going to remember that you left your wallet on the bench at the duck pond or in your B and B? I don't steal anyone's identities. I shred credit cards and driver's licenses. What's wrong with pocketing unclaimed cash or reselling a cell phone that some rich tourist has already upgraded?"

He was obviously trying to rationalize his crime.

"What does this have to do with Brett's murder?" I wasn't going to pass judgment on him. Not here. Not alone. That was for the professionals.

"Brett helped me out every now and then. He knew people. He was connected. If I needed to move inventory, he was my guy."

"Inventory" was one word for it. I could think of a few others, but I wanted Nat to keep talking.

"Brett knew Jamie. I guess they served time together a while ago, and I'd been sitting on some items I couldn't move. He wanted to bring Jamie in. I told him no way. We had to keep this operation tight. One thing about Brett was that I could trust him not to talk. He was smart, that one, which is why it was strange that he would even bring up the idea of using a third-party vendor."

"Vendor?"

"That's what I called him." Nat didn't sound the least bit apologetic. "He insisted that Jamie should get a cut and I could take this operation to the next level."

"And you didn't want that?"

Nat shook his head. "No. I'm ready to retire soon. I told Brett I would hire him on as a groundskeeper. He could take my job in a couple years and continue to have some extra cash."

"What did he say?"

"He refused. He told me he had had an epiphany. He was making some big changes and wanted out. That's why he wanted Jamie involved."

"Wait, you're saying Brett didn't want to be part of this?" I waved my hand toward the door to the storage area. Then I took a step backward. If Brett wanted out, that gave Nat even more motive. Maybe Brett had threatened to go to the police. Maybe his epiphany had made him have a change of heart. Had he decided to give up his thieving ways for good? That certainly could have forced Nat's hand.

Nat was oblivious to the fact that I was slowly inching away from him. "Jamie wasn't trustworthy. I told Brett that much, but he didn't agree. It didn't matter. I didn't need either of them. Without Brett, I could keep the whole cut."

"That would have been lucrative for you." I chose my words carefully.

"I guess." Nat wrinkled his brow. "No, I see what you're hinting at. I didn't kill him. Why would I be telling you this? Why would I show you this?"

I didn't answer.

He sighed and tapped the graffitied wall. "I brought you here because of this. I trust you. That's why I asked you to go to Doug. I know he's family, and I know you don't spread gossip like the rest of this town."

"I don't understand."

"I can't go to Doug, because then I'll have to confess about this side gig." He paused but didn't wait long enough for me to respond. "I'm not going to give it up, but I don't want to see a killer get away with murder either. I brought you here so you would understand where I'm coming from. Not to hurt you."

He sounded sincere, but I wasn't going to take any chances. I made sure my hand was on my phone, ready to make an emergency call.

His next words shocked me.

"I know who killed Brett, and I have tangible proof."

"Who? Jamie?"

"No." He shook his head and pressed his finger on the words spray-painted on the wall. "I didn't get it at first, but I put it all together last night. Brett's death didn't have anything to do with his past criminal record, or him moving merchandise for me."

I held my breath. What was he going to tell me?

"That was a convenient excuse for his killer to set up Jamie to take the fall. I should have figured it out earlier. I don't know what took me so long, but last night everything became clear. I had my own epiphany."

I wanted him to get to the point. I could feel nervous energy pulsing through my body. "What did you figure out?"

Nat again nodded to the graffiti. "This. I knew it was wrong."

"What's wrong with it?"

He shot me a triumphant look. "It wasn't here until last night."

"Sorry, I'm still lost."

"The killer came back and spray-painted this, probably sometime early evening when this area of the park isn't well traveled. They knew they needed to make sure that suspicion stayed on Jamie after the police released him, so they came here and spray-painted this. Only they got Brett's tattoo wrong." He picked up a broken branch from the trail and used it like a pointer. "See this?" He tapped the tip of the branch to the wall. "It's upside down."

I moved closer to get a better look. Nat was right. "How does this prove who killed Brett?"

"Because they messed up, and I saw them." He was about to continue when the sound of footsteps breaking branches on the trail behind the reservoir made him stop and press his finger to his lips. Nat's eyes widened in fear as someone rounded the corner and yelled, "Don't move!"

Chapter Twenty-nine

Randall rounded the corner holding a branch that was half my size. I had no idea how he had managed to lift it above his head. He wasn't a big guy to begin with, and the branch could have moonlighted as Sasquatch's baseball bat. Nat grabbed me and pushed me behind him.

"It's over, Randall." Nat's voice sounded authoritative.

"For you two," Randall snarled.

I made sure to keep my hand in my pocket as I began punching numbers on my phone. After an ordeal a few years ago, I had made it my mission to memorize the button to push for an emergency call without looking. Assuming the call went through. I couldn't exactly have a conversation with the operator given that Randall was threatening to smack both me and Nat with his tree branch weapon. My only hope was that the operator would pick up on my distress and send a squad car.

"You can't exactly leave two bodies here in the park," Nat said to Randall.

"Watch me." He jerked forward.

I let out an involuntary scream. Nat clutched me harder. "It's going to be okay."

I wished I had his resolve.

"Look, Randall. The police already know. Jules told them."

Why was Nat blaming me?

Randall's eyes narrowed. His beady stare made my stomach lurch.

"The police have no evidence."

"Are you sure about that?" Nat made his body bigger. I appreciated that he was using it to shield me, but if Randall decided to attack, I didn't think it would matter. The branch was enough to knock both of us out in one blow.

"What do they know? Tell me," Randall challenged.

"Everything." Nat tilted his head toward the reservoir. "You made some mistakes. Some big ones."

"Yeah, right. The police think Jamie did it. I made sure of that."

I couldn't be sure, but I thought I heard the sound of a muffled voice on my phone. *Please let the operator hear us,* I prayed silently.

I spoke up to give us a better chance. "Randall, the police have cleared Jamie of Brett's murder and are coming to arrest you. They're sending a car right now."

"You're in the wrong place at the wrong time, lady. It's a shame. You didn't need to die. Should have chosen your friends more carefully. My beef is with Nat, but since you're here, I guess it's a two-for-one special this morning."

"Why did you kill him?" I asked, loud enough for the operator to hear, but not so loud that Randall would catch on.

"He needed to die. He got clean. Had some ridiculous breakthrough and decided he was going to change his ways. Like that was ever really going to happen. But I couldn't let him cut me out of Heart Strings. Not now. Not with the contract that Dani's about to sign.'

"What contract?" This was good. If we could keep him talking, we could buy time for the police to arrive.

"Like you don't know. She's been bragging about it for weeks all over town. She told us to keep it under wraps, but she's been shooting her mouth off to anyone who will listen."

"No, I haven't heard," I replied. That was the truth. In all my conversations with Dani, nothing about a lucrative contract had come up.

"She's working with some hot music producer in LA. She and Brett went behind my back to cut me out of the deal. I heard them. They weren't even chill about it. They were so stupid. They think I'm dumb and that I don't listen because I'm quiet. Wasn't Brett surprised. I confronted him, and he tried to blame it all on Dani. Don't worry, I've got a plan for her, too, but he was too easy."

I shuddered.

Nat squeezed my waist. "How did you do it?"

Brett laughed. "It was easy. He was sauced. Took something of Dani's that knocked him out. I barely had to touch him and he was on the ground, flat as a pancake, begging for his life. He should have thought of that before he decided to screw me."

"And then you framed Jamie." Nat's question was more of a statement.

"Like taking candy from a baby. He and Brett were already into some nasty stuff. I overheard them arguing. I heard the whole story about your park operation." He glared at Nat with such intensity that I wanted to recoil.

Dani had called Randall a sloth. There was nothing sloth-like about his demeanor now. He was out for blood.

"I spent three years dragging around equipment and gigging day after day. Crashing on the floor of strangers' living rooms in a sleeping bag. Eating hot dogs and whatever free food we got in the green room, which was usually more like a janitor's closet with some water bottles and Cheetos, and what do they do as they're about to make a real break? Real money. Kick me out? No. I don't think so. Brett deserved what he got. Dani will, too, once I'm done with you."

I could tell we were running out of time. Where were the police?

"You're not going to get away with it," Nat cautioned. "If I figured it out, so will the police. Plus, what are you going to do with our bodies? One murder is bad enough. Three is impossible."

Randall's eyes darted toward the falls that spilled out on the far side of the res. "I'll dump you there. It will take them a while to figure out that you're missing, and then to find your bodies. By then I'll be long, long, gone. And thanks to you, I'll have a nice chunk of cash and items to hawk to get me started."

Nat pressed a key into my hand. "Take the cart. Run," he whispered.

"Hey! Stop talking," Randall yelled. "Get walking. That way." He motioned to the back of the res where a narrow pathway led to the falls.

"Run," Nat repeated through clenched teeth. "Get help."

I didn't want to leave him. What was he going to do?

Randall might have the upper hand, but two against one was better than nothing.

At that moment I heard the wail of sirens. Thank goodness.

Everything happened in a flash.

Randall lunged at us with the branch. He missed. It

smashed on the ground with a thud that made me want to throw up.

"Go!" Nat pushed me.

I sprinted toward the cart, looking over my shoulder to make sure Nat was behind me. He was, but so was Randall. The weight of the branch was slowing him down. My lungs burned as I raced through snarls of wild blackberry bushes, past the swimming hole, and up through the grass. Pain pierced my chest and spread to my stomach. I could feel a cramp coming on, but I couldn't stop.

The sirens were getting louder. I could see red and blue lights dancing off the tops of the trees.

Nat stumbled behind me. He had tripped on a snag.

I couldn't just leave him.

Without thinking, I turned around to help him. As I bent down to reach out my hand, Randall caught up with us. He didn't hesitate. Where had he gotten such strength? Was he on something? He drew the branch above his head and smashed it down on Nat.

Nat moved at the last minute, but the branch struck his leg. He yelped in pain.

His leg had to be broken.

Randall struggled to get the branch upright again. I yanked Nat by the shoulders and dragged him along the pathway.

He cried in agony, but I didn't have a choice. We had to get up to the road where the police could see us.

Kerry had said that in times of stress we tap into strength we didn't know we possessed. That must be true, because my muscles fired with power I wasn't aware of. I managed to get Nat to the park entrance just as a squad car pulled up.

"Help, Randall is after us." I pointed in the direction we had come, but there was no sign of him.

"Stay here," the police officer commanded. "More help is on the way."

I knelt down next to Nat. "Is it bad? It's broken, isn't it?"

He massaged the top of his thigh and rocked back and forth on the ground. "I think he shattered it."

I reached for my phone again. The 911 call was still live. "We need an ambulance," I said to the operator, who had me talk them through everything that had happened and assured me that the Professor and other teams were en route.

Time moved in a strange haze. I tried to keep Nat alert and talking. The operator had warned me that shock could easily set in. "I can't believe it was Randall."

Nat's face was strained from the pain. He rocked forward and backward like he was trying to soothe himself. "He shouldn't have graffitied the res."

"How did you know it was him from that?" I rubbed my shoulders. Cold was setting in, or maybe it was that my adrenaline had burned off.

"I caught him on the cameras I installed to make sure that no one got into my stuff."

And to think I'd been trying to piece together how an upside down pirate symbol had clued him in. A camera made much more sense. "I'm curious about Dani. You told me that you saw her give Jamie an envelope the day of the murder. Was that true? And why didn't you just say something about the camera?"

He winced. I wasn't sure if it was from his injury or if the truth hurt, too. "I don't know. I guess I was getting spooked that someone had seen me. I didn't want eyes on me. I thought if I could get people talking about something else, it would take pressure off."

So Dani had been telling the truth about everything.

The ambulance arrived in another piercing whirl of sirens and lights. The paramedics immediately began to attend to Nat's injuries.

The Professor showed up right after the EMS crew. He was breathless as he ran over to check on me. "Juliet, thank goodness you're safe. I was so concerned when the call came in. I was on the other side of town and couldn't get here fast enough. Are you hurt?"

I shook my head. "I'm fine. It's Nat." I pointed nearby. The EMS crew had set up a temporary field unit around Nat.

The Professor checked in with the paramedics. They had braced Nat's leg and were placing him on a stretcher. I watched them lift him and then carefully navigate the uneven terrain to get him into the ambulance.

More squad cars squealed up the gravel. *Everyone within a five-mile radius must be awake,* I thought as I watched officers dressed in tactical gear spill out of each vehicle. A manhunt was on for Randall. The Professor took charge. He directed teams to spread out in every direction.

Everything seemed to be happening in a weird dreamlike daze. My head felt fuzzy, as if I'd had too much champagne.

After a few minutes, the Professor came to talk to me. "No, you sit," he said, holding out a hand to stop me from standing. "I know you've had a shock, too." He sat next to me. "Are you in a position to be able to tell me what happened?"

I nodded. Everything spilled out. Confronting Dani last night. Nat. His cache of lost items from the park. Randall. Getting everything out of my body was like a purge. I hadn't realized how much stress I had been holding in.

When I finished, the Professor patted my knee. "Thank you. You've been through a lot. What can I do for you?"

"Nothing," I answered honestly. "I feel better telling you. I mean, I think I'm still in shock, but I'm relieved knowing that it wasn't Jamie and that the right person is going to serve time for the crime. That is assuming you catch him."

"We'll apprehend him. You can count on that," the Professor replied. "My team has him surrounded. There's nowhere to go. Now it's simply a matter of time, and we'll wait as long as it takes."

"That's good." I sighed. "What about Nat? What's going to happen to him?"

"I suppose that will be up to the city and the mayor. He'll have to answer to the powers that be for his crimes. I suspect that an early retirement will likely be in order. As to whether they press charges, my guess would be no. I suspect that they'll want to do everything in their power to return any lost items to their original owners and keep this quiet. Bad press isn't always good press, you know."

"Agreed." I glanced at the park, which had seemed so desolate only a short time ago. Police officers swept out in every direction, calling out orders. "Did you suspect Randall?"

The Professor's lips turned down. "I admit that he wasn't at the top of my list of persons of interest; however, Jamie continued to ask us to pursue that line of investigation."

"Do you think he knew all along?"

"I believe he suspected as much. With his past, he is likely skilled at spotting criminal behavior."

"That's such a relief for Kerry. She'll be so happy to hear that her father isn't a killer."

"I concur." He smiled. "Can I help you to your feet?"

"Yeah. I'm feeling calmer now." I took his hand.

"Shall I drive you home? To Torte? I know your mother is going to want to see you."

"Torte would be great." I wanted to see her, too. The ordeal of coming face-to-face with a killer had shaken me, and Torte was the best place to begin to heal.

Chapter Thirty

Mom, Carlos, Lance, and my entire team wouldn't let me live down my near brush with death. It was all I heard about for the next few days. At the opening of *Waitress,* in the kitchen, at home at night, and via multiple scoldings from Mom. It was fair. Everyone cared for me, and I shouldn't have taken an unnecessary risk.

Lance was the worst. Not because he was upset with me for venturing out into the park after a killer, but because I hadn't called him.

"Seriously, that is the last time you go sleuthing without me, understood?" His tone had been firm, but his eyes tender. "I don't know what this town would do if anything ever happened to you, Juliet Montague Capshaw. Myself included." He had wrapped me in a hug. "And yours truly *needs* to be in on the action, got it?"

"Got it." I held up my pinky. "I solemnly swear I will call you next time."

"Even at two o'clock in the morning."

"Especially at two o'clock in the morning," I teased.

Carlos didn't let me off so easy. "Julieta, you could have been killed."

"I know, I'm sorry. I wasn't thinking."

"You must be more careful. Think about our future. We are considering having a baby."

He was completely justified in his response. "I know. I just got caught up in the moment, and I did take precautions. I made sure that Richard Lord saw me getting in the cart with Nat."

"This is nothing." He scoffed. "I trust him less than I trust this killer."

I assured him that I wouldn't do anything so rash again, but the experience did make me think about motherhood. Putting my life in danger wasn't something I could do if Carlos and I decided to start a family.

As the week wore on, I kept thinking about what I could have done differently. The answer was simple—called the police. One call to the Professor could have ensured that I was never in harm's way. I made a promise to myself and my future self that I wouldn't make the same mistakes again.

Fortunately we had a Sunday Supper to put on, so I focused my attention on preparing for that. The kitchen was a frenzy of activity. Marty kneaded pasta dough. Sterling simmered sauces on the stove. Bethany decorated cookies, while Steph and Rosa transformed the dining room, pushing together tables to create one long shared table.

I went upstairs late in the afternoon to check on progress. The sight of the bakeshop ready for our shared meal took my breath away. They had hung swaths of pastel fabric from the ceiling and strung it with pink fairy lights. The dining room glowed like a blooming spring blossom. Janet arrived with actual spring blooms. She came in carrying a box of vases filled with pink and white roses and tulips, accented with sprigs of eucalyptus and lavender.

"Everything looks wonderful in here," she said, setting the box on the espresso counter. "I heard from Thomas. They land a little after six. He said they might make a surprise appearance, as long as their flight isn't delayed."

"That would be great. I can't wait to hear about the honeymoon." I picked up one of the bouquets and inhaled the sweet aroma.

"I spoke with Doug, and he already informed Kerry that he's cleared Jamie. She must be so relieved. Thank you for helping to make sure that happened." Janet met my gaze.

"Of course. I didn't do much, other than put myself smack in the middle of it."

Janet smiled with her kind eyes. "That's why I appreciate you." She unpacked the vases and left with the empty box.

I set the flowers in the center of the table, where Rosa had already placed white candles that we would light right before the guests arrived.

"Jules, can I talk to you for a minute?" Steph asked, after getting down from the step stool.

"Sure, what's going on?"

"It's about my parents." She chomped on a purple nail striped with vertical black lines.

"Are they coming tonight?"

She scrunched her face. "They're here."

I glanced around us. The dining room was empty. We always waited to decorate and set up for Sunday Suppers until after the last customers had left. "Where?"

"Outside." She pointed to the bubblers in the center of the plaza.

"Invite them in. What are you waiting for?"

"They want to meet you first." She looked at her feet.

"Okay. They can come in and meet me."

"I know. I told them. Don't ask." She gnawed on another nail. "They're weird, like, really weird, okay?"

"No problem. I love weird. Ashland is the epicenter of quirky. Don't sweat it. I'll go introduce myself. It will be fine, trust me."

She made her body small by crumpling her shoulders. "You don't know them. You don't get it."

"Is there anything you want me to say? Should I talk Sterling up?"

"No." She shook her head with force. "Don't bring him up."

"Okay. I won't." I gave her an encouraging smile and went outside.

I was in for a shock that nearly rivaled learning that Randall had killed Brett.

Steph's parents weren't anything like I expected. The way she and Sterling had described them, I was picturing them as professional and polished, buttoned up and serious, but the opposite was true.

They stood in front of a van painted like the traveler vans that hung out in the park during the summer. Steph's mom was dressed in a flowing pumpkin orange dress with layers and layers of fluffy rainbow tulle. She had a fascinator with yellow feathers propped on the side of her head. Her dad wore Shakespearean pantaloons, a white puffy pirate shirt, and a top hat.

I tried to mask my surprise. "You must be Steph's parents. I'm Jules. I own Torte."

They greeted me with bear hugs.

"We are so happy to finally meet you," Steph's mom gushed. "We can't believe our goth girl is about to graduate from college. All she talks about is Torte. Torte this. Torte that. Torte. Torte. Torte."

"That's so great. We're thrilled to have her. She's become invaluable to our team, and I'm sure you've seen her incredible cake designs and calligraphy." I pointed toward the window display.

Her dad shook his head, causing the top hat to slip precariously to one side. "No. She won't let us see anything she draws. She hasn't since she was a kid."

"Really? But she's so talented."

"We know," her mom interjected. "She's always been so private about her art and of course embarrassed by her quirky parents. Do you have kids?"

I shook my head. "No. Not yet."

"Just wait." She did a little shimmy. "Parents become the most mortifying people on the planet sometime around the teen years. For our Steph, that has never changed."

"We're still waiting for that phase to end," her dad added, winking at his wife.

"Steph will never forgive us for her childhood years. She thinks our lifestyle is too 'out there.'" Her mom adjusted her fascinator.

"How so?" I was so curious about the real story behind Steph's past.

"Didn't she tell you?" her dad asked. "We're traveling performers." He directed my attention to their converted VW van taking up two parking spaces. Funky paint swirls snaked around the side of the van, with the words CIRQUE DE SOUL. A picture of a man walking a tightrope and a woman taming a lion were drawn in a style I had seen many times before.

"Did Steph paint that?" I asked.

Her mom nodded. "You recognize her brushstrokes, don't you? She painted the van when she was twelve."

"What's Cirque De Soul?"

"That's our traveling show," Steph's dad answered. "She didn't tell you that either?"

I shook my head.

Her mom fiddled with her feather. "She's embarrassed by us. I told you we shouldn't have come."

"Not at all," I answered, and reached out my hand. "We're thrilled to have you here, and Steph's been talking about your visit for weeks."

"She has?" Her mom's face brightened. "That's great news. We thought she didn't want us to meet any of her friends. She won't let us meet Sterling. She told us the dinner tonight was full."

I tried to reconcile the story Steph had told me about her parents with the couple standing in front of me.

"We're free spirits. Steph grew up in the van, traveling from show to show. She's the first person in our entire extended family to go to college. We're so proud of her, but we don't want to embarrass her either. If you think it would be better, we can leave."

"You should definitely stay. Ashland is a place of free spirits. I know Steph wants you here."

They shared a brief smile.

"Come on, let's give you a firsthand look at your daughter's pastry talent." I walked them back to the bakeshop. Suddenly Steph's tendency to be tight-lipped about her past made so much sense. It wasn't that her parents didn't approve of her choices. It was that she didn't approve of theirs.

Chapter Thirty-one

I braced myself for impact as I showed Steph's parents inside. The dining room was empty. Everyone was probably downstairs putting the final touches on dinner.

"Why don't you two pick a seat here at the table. I'll run downstairs and check on dinner progress and find Steph. Can I get you a glass of wine? Red or white?"

"Red please," Steph's mom answered with a flourish of her wrist.

Bottles of both had already been placed on the table. I reached for our cabernet and filled each of their glasses. "Enjoy. I'll be back in a minute."

I hurried downstairs to find Steph sitting on the couch.

"You met them?" She didn't look up.

"I did. They're lovely."

She sighed. "They're circus performers."

I sat down next to her. "So?"

She rolled her eyes. "You wouldn't understand."

"Try me."

"I love them, I do," she said, brushing a tear from her heavily lined eyes. "It was a hard life as a kid. We were always moving. We never stayed in one place. I never had a chance to make friends. I was always the new kid at school. When I went to school, which wasn't very often. I got teased because I was the weird circus kid. That's why I got into baking shows. YouTube was free. I used to watch in the van while they were doing their shows, unless I was busking or working the tent."

"I had no idea."

When I first met Stephanie, I had found her to be a bit bristly. Now her steely exterior made sense. It was a coping strategy she had learned as a kid. If she acted aloof, like she couldn't care less about you, it was easier to deal with being excluded and an outsider.

"I taught myself. I got my diploma and then a big scholarship. It helps when your parents are traveling circus people. It's not like they had a lot of money."

"They're so proud of you, Steph. They're beaming with delight. I got that out of only talking to them for five minutes."

"Yeah. I know." She chomped on her nail again. At this rate, she wasn't going to have any nails left.

"You didn't want them to come, did you? Not the other way around. The whole story about them not wanting to meet Sterling, that's not it, is it?"

"It's not like I don't want them here. I do, but it's complicated."

"Can I tell you something from the deepest part of my heart?" I leaned closer and fought back my own tears. "After losing a parent, I can tell you that the ache never heals. It changes with time, but I carry that loss, that lingering grief with me. Sterling does, too. I'm not trying to take away the fact that your childhood must have been hard. I can't even imagine what it must have been like to never have roots, to move around like you did, and I hear you on your relationship being complicated. But please don't let other people's perceptions or influences keep you from letting your parents in. That is, if you want to let them in."

"I do." She nodded. "I guess it's just hard when everyone else had a normal childhood."

"Normal is overrated." I tried to wink, intentionally contorting my face.

She laughed.

Sterling came out of the kitchen balancing a tray of salads. "Hey, what's up?"

"Now seems like a good time to rip off the Band-Aid," I said to Steph, raising my eyebrows.

"Thanks." She gave me a genuine smile. "My parents are upstairs. You want to meet them?"

"Yeah." He shifted the tray to his other arm. "Definitely."

I gave them space. If anyone could handle Steph's unconventional background, it was Sterling. I was also glad that the tables had turned. I hadn't been sure what approach to take with parents who didn't approve of her life choices, but quirky parents who loved and adored her—that was a problem we could tackle together.

Soon it was time to open the doors and let in our guests.

Mimi Barbarelli was one of the first people in line. I greeted her with a glass of wine. "How's the hand?" I asked, noting that her injured wrist had been wrapped in a gauze bandage and splinted.

"It turns out that I have a hairline fracture." She took the wine from me with her opposite hand. "I suppose having to use my left hand for the time being is good for my dexterity."

"So it was a Pilates accident?"

She squinted from underneath a pair of reading glasses resting on the edge of her nose. "My broken wrist? What else would it have been from?"

I gave her a sheepish smile. "I don't know. My mind has been spinning since Brett was killed. Someone mentioned that they had seen you fighting with him, and I guess my imagination took it from there."

She threw her head back and laughed hard. "Juliet, you are too much. I have to say, thank you for considering the possibility. My Pilates instructor is going to get a good chuckle out of this, but no, my injury occurred in class. Brett and I did have a brief exchange the morning of the murder. However, our exchange was perfectly amicable. Brett sought me out to pass on his gratitude."

"Gratitude?"

"He attempted to bribe me during his sentencing a few years ago. Of course I refused. I would never have considered it. He shared that at the time he was furious with me, yet he credited his incarceration with his success. He had made revolutionary changes. Frankly, the system doesn't typically produce the kind of results that Brett experienced. He'd been sober for eleven months, was looking forward to a lucrative music contract with his bandmates, and was considering putting in an offer on a property in Talent. I don't know who has been stirring up such ludicrous tales. It would certainly behoove you to consider your sources in the future." Mimi gave me her best disapproving judge face before getting caught up in another conversation.

Dani tapped me on the shoulder.

"Oh hi, I didn't see your name on the guest list," I said.

"My boyfriend is doing one of the poetry readings, so he got me a ticket." She pointed out a guy who was chatting with Sterling near the pastry counter.

"I'm so glad you came. I still feel terrible about being so jumpy with you."

"No worries." She reached for a glass of pinot gris as Rosa passed by us with a tray of wine. "At least you were trying to help get closure on what happened to Brett." She knocked back the wine like it was a strong shot of whiskey. "I can't believe Randall did it. The police told me they found some pretty scary stuff in his apartment."

"Like what?"

"Sketches of my house. Photos of me coming and going at different times of the day, the alleyway behind my place, a cache of weapons—hunting knives, nunchucks, and a spiked bat. Randall was doodling in his sketchbook all the time. Brett and I used to joke that he was going to end up being a breakout songwriter. I thought he was working on lyrics, but no. The police think he was planning to kill me, too." She chugged the rest of her wine.

"That's terrible."

"I should have done it sooner—kicked him out. I should have listened to my instincts. Brett kept telling me that everything was cool with Randall and not to sweat it. I always got a bad vibe off him, though. I should have listened to my gut."

"You couldn't have known that he was a killer." I tried to console her.

Bethany came by with a platter of appetizers. Dani helped herself to a piece of bruschetta. "I don't know how I'm ever going to trust a future bandmate. I put in a call to the producer who signed up today to see if he'll take me as a solo act."

"What did he say?"

"It sounds like he's going to give me a shot. I fly to LA next week for my first studio session."

"Congratulations, I'll take any good news right now."

Her boyfriend came over. Dani introduced us before they went to find their seats. I circulated through the room, greeting friends and making sure the wine flowed.

Soon it was time for everyone to be seated. Music played on the overhead speakers. We passed around baskets of bread with Marty's herbed butter and salads and hearty bowls of pastas. The conversation naturally drifted to Randall's arrest. Carlos and I were seated next to Lance and Arlo. Mom and the Professor sat across from them, giving Lance the perfect opportunity to bombard the Professor with questions.

"How did you manage to capture him?" Lance asked, slathering garlic and rosemary compound butter onto a slice of sourdough.

"My team is well versed at tactical maneuvers." The Professor sipped a glass of buttery chardonnay. "We train for this very thing. To be honest, the suspect had exhausted himself and his options by the time we caught him. I'd like to claim that it was a struggle. The truth is that Randall had collapsed down near Ashland Creek when we found him."

"When is the trial?" I asked.

The Professor took another sip of wine. "He'll go in front of a jury, so likely in a few weeks, give or take."

"What about Nat? How is he healing from his injuries?" Lance sounded like he was interrogating a suspect with the way he kept following one question with another.

"He had surgery on the leg two days ago. He'll be in the hospital for at least a week and then will have many weeks of rehabilitation. I was able to have a meeting with the mayor and city council. Everyone is in agreement that Nat will be asked to turn in his resignation letter. They don't want to press charges. My team will be working to connect missing items found at Lithia with their original owners."

Lance started to ask another question, but Arlo stopped him. "The entertainment is about to begin. We wouldn't want to compete with these young budding poets. They could be future stars of the stage."

That shut him up.

Sterling stood at the head of the table nearest the espresso machine. He dinged a spoon on an empty wineglass. "If I could get everyone's attention, I want to introduce you to our poets." A row of wordsmiths waiting for their chance to share snaked down to the pastry case. "I'm the sous chef here at Torte," Sterling began.

Steph's parents cheered and applauded.

I caught her eye. She shrugged and grinned.

Sterling smiled. "Thanks for that warm welcome. The idea tonight is to pair the pastas we've made with poetry. I hope you'll enjoy food for the body and for the soul."

Everyone clapped.

I made sure to stop him before he began to share his work. "Not so fast, Mr. Sous Chef." I held up my wineglass. "I'd like to offer a toast to Steph and Sterling, who came up with this brilliant concept, and to our talented crew here at Torte for creating such a magnificent feast."

I raised my glass, and everyone followed suit.

At that moment, the doors opened and Thomas and Kerry walked in. They were greeted by more whoops and hollers, and a lot of hugs. Their sun-kissed skin and dewy smiles showed that they had enjoyed their honeymoon.

We made room at our end of the table for them to squeeze in. "Can I get you a plate?" I asked.

"We ate on the plane," Thomas replied. "It was shockingly good."

Kerry agreed. She had her hand locked in his. "I see the looks of horror on your faces, but he's right. Airplane food has come a long way."

Lance gasped. "Certainly not superior to Torte."

"Never." Kerry laughed. She looked lighter than maybe I had ever seen her.

Sterling was setting up a mic and stand for the poets.

"Thanks for everything, Jules," Kerry said to me while Thomas showed Carlos, Lance, and Arlo photos of the two of them swimming with dolphins. "I had a long chat with Doug about the case, and he told me you were instrumental in making sure Randall was arrested."

"That was kind of him, but I fumbled my way through as usual."

"Regardless, it's a relief to know that my dad wasn't involved. I appreciate that you put yourself out there and took a risk for me. You're a good friend."

"Is your dad sticking around?"

"I don't know. I'm not sure what I'm ready for with him, but it's nice to know that at least he's not going to be behind bars again."

The readings were about to start. We dropped the conversation for now. I looked around the table at so many faces I loved and adored. The first word that came to my mind was "family." This was my family. Family had been a theme the last few weeks. Weddings, babies, old conflicts, reconciliations. Since returning home to Ashland, I had learned that family is what you make of it. Some families are born from bloodlines, and some families we create on our own. Either way, it was these connections, these grinning faces breaking bread and sharing a meal together, who were my people. If expanding our family was part of the future for Carlos and me, I knew that we would be surrounded and supported in every possible way. That wouldn't shield us from future struggles, but it would ensure that whatever was next, we wouldn't have to face it on our own, and that was a gift that I would hold on to forever.

Recipes

Fruit Salsa with Cinnamon Chips

Ingredients:
For the cinnamon chips
1 10-ounce package of flour tortillas
½ cup butter, melted
Juice and zest of one small orange and lemon
1 tablespoon cinnamon
¼ cup sugar
½ teaspoon cardamom

For the salsa: *Note—Jules uses whatever fruit is fresh and in season.
2 pears, peeled and chopped
2 apples, peeled and chopped
1 small container raspberries, washed and drained
1 cup cherries, washed, pitted, and halved
2 kiwis, peeled and chopped
1 cup grapes, washed and halved
1 cup pineapple, peeled and chopped
Juice and zest of one orange, one lime, and one lemon

1 11-ounce jar of apricot marmalade
2 tablespoons coconut extract

Directions:
Make the cinnamon chips. Preheat the oven to 350 degrees Fahrenheit. Mix the melted butter with the juice and zest of the orange and lemon. Place the tortillas on a baking sheet and brush with the mixture. Then combine the sugar, cinnamon, and cardamom and sprinkle over each of the tortillas. Bake for 10 minutes or until tortillas crisp and turn golden brown. Remove from the oven and set aside to cool. Next, make the fruit salsa. Add the pears, apples, raspberries, cherries, kiwis, grapes, and pineapple to a large mixing bowl. Combine the zest and juice of lemon, orange, and lime in a separate bowl. Whisk in the marmalade and coconut extract. Pour the dressing over the top of the fruit salsa and gently toss. Break the tortillas into chips and serve with salsa.

Vodka Penne

Ingredients:
2 tablespoons olive oil
1 onion, diced
2 cloves garlic, minced
1 6-ounce jar of tomato paste
¼ cup vodka
1 cup heavy cream
1 teaspoon pepper
1 teaspoon salt
16 ounces of penne pasta, cooked until al dente
2 cooked Italian sausages, diced
Parmesan cheese (optional)

Directions:
Add the olive oil to a sauté pan and turn the heat to medium. Toss in the diced onion and cook the onion until it is caramelized: soft and deeply golden brown. Add in the diced garlic and tomato paste. Mix together and then stir in the vodka to deglaze the pan. Bring to a slow boil, then reduce heat to a simmer. Once a thick sauce has formed, add the heavy cream, salt and pepper and whisk until the sauce is smooth. Cover and reduce the heat to low. Allow the sauce to simmer for 5 to 10 minutes. Serve hot over penne pasta with diced Italian sausage. If desired, finish with a sprinkling of Parmesan cheese.

Shortbread Chocolate Raspberry Cups

Ingredients:
For the shortbread:
1 cup butter
½ cup sugar
1 teaspoon vanilla
1 teaspoon vanilla bean paste
2 cups flour

For the filling:
2 cups mini chocolate chips
¼ cup butter

For the topping:
Fresh raspberries
Whipped cream

Directions:
First, make the shortbread. Preheat the oven to 325 degrees

Fahrenheit. Cream the butter and sugar together in an electric mixer (or by hand) until light and fluffy. Then add in the vanilla extract and vanilla bean paste. Either by hand with a wooden spoon or with a mixer, slowly incorporate the flour ½ cup at a time until you've added all the flour and a batter forms. (It should be crumbly, but if not, add a tablespoon of extra flour until the right consistency is reached.) Grease mini-muffin tins with baking spray. Roll batter into one-inch balls and press into muffin tins to form cups. Use fingers to press the dough gently into the tins. Poke holes in the bottom with a fork and bake for 10–12 minutes or until the shortbread is golden brown. Remove the muffin tin from the oven and use the back of a wooden spoon to press the center of the cups down. Allow to cool completely. While the shortbread cups are cooling, make the filling. Combine the butter and mini chocolate chips in a saucepan over medium heat, stirring constantly until the chocolate is melted and shiny. Fill the cooled cups with chocolate and top with a fresh raspberry and a dollop of whipped cream.

Mom's Potato Salad

Ingredients:
10–12 Yukon gold potatoes
6 hardboiled eggs
1 cup chopped bread-and-butter pickles
¼ cup pickle juice
1 cup mayonnaise
½ cup Miracle Whip
2 teaspoons celery seed
2 teaspoons salt
2 teaspoons pepper

Directions:

Scrub, rinse, and dry the potatoes. Poke them with a fork and place them on a microwave-safe plate. Microwave for 8–10 minutes, then flip them and repeat until the potatoes are tender. Remove them from the microwave and allow them to cool completely. Once the potatoes have cooled, chop them into 1-inch squares and place them in a large mixing bowl. Chop the hardboiled eggs and pickles and add them to the bowl. Finally, add the pickle juice, mayonnaise, Miracle Whip, and spices. Stir gently until creamy. Serve immediately or cover and chill in the refrigerator until you're ready to serve.

Lemon Chiffon Pie

Ingredients:

1 fully baked buttermilk pie crust at room temperature or cooled (or crust of your preference)

4 eggs, yolks and whites separated

⅔ cup sugar

¼ cup fresh lemon juice

Zest of one lemon

2 teaspoons gelatin

⅓ cup cool water

For the topping:

Candied lemons

Whipped cream

Directions:

Whisk the egg yolks and ⅓ cup sugar together in an electric mixer (using the whisk attachment). Once the mixture is light and fluffy, transfer to a saucepan and add the lemon zest and juice. Heat over medium low for 10 minutes, continually whisking until the mixture thickens. Remove from heat and set aside. Dissolve the gelatin in the water, using a measuring cup or small bowl. Then combine the egg yolk mixture with the dissolved gelatin. Whisk and set in an ice bath or the refrigerator to cool. Next whip egg whites in a large mixing bowl with an electric mixer until they begin to foam. Slowly add in remaining ⅓ cup of sugar and whip until the egg whites are stiff and glossy. Gently fold egg whites in with the egg yolks and lemon and spread into pie crust. Chill for two hours. Serve cold with candied lemons and whipped cream.

Andy's Champagne Latte

Andy's new twist on a brunch latte. This would be perfect for a leisurely Sunday morning or to serve at any celebration.

Ingredients:
2 shots of strong espresso
1 tablespoon semi-sweet cocoa powder
¾ cup milk
¼ cup champagne
Dark chocolate curls for garnish

Directions:
Add espresso and semi-sweet cocoa powder to a warmed coffee mug. Whisk together. Froth the milk in a stainless steel pitcher, then add to the espresso mixture, reserving froth for the top. Add the champagne to the mug and stir to combine. Top with froth and dark chocolate curls.

Read on for a look ahead to
MUFFIN BUT THE TRUTH—the next Bakeshop
mystery by Ellie Alexander, coming soon
from St. Martin's Paperbacks!

Chapter One

They say that family can be more than our family of origin—that family can also be found. I had found my family in the foothills of the Siskiyou Mountains where I'd spent the last few years carving out a new home and a new future in my childhood town of Ashland, Oregon. My small family of Mom and me had expanded dramatically. Carlos, my husband, had recently joined me in the Rogue Valley, and his son Ramiro was taking a year away from his studies in Spain to do an exchange program here in Ashland.

It felt like an abundance of riches to have Ramiro with us for an entire year. And as if my heart wasn't already overflowing, my circle had expanded to include so many more people who I adored. Like Mom's husband Doug, aka The Professor, who had become a second father to me. There was my best friend Lance and my childhood friend Thomas and his wife, Kerry. Plus, there was my entire team at the bakeshop. Sometimes it was hard to remember how small I'd made myself on the *Amour of the Seas*, the cruise ship that had taken me from one far-off port of call to the next. Ironically, even though Ashland could hardly be considered a major city, my network of friends and family continued to grow, like a rising yeasty bread dough spilling over the top of a metal bowl.

Bread had been on my mind as of late. After a full summer of baking and traveling, we were settling into the shifting seasons. Carlos and I had flown to Spain to pick up Ramiro for the start of his summer holidays. From there, we ventured to Italy for two weeks with Mom and the Professor and Lance and his paramour Arlo. It had been the stuff of dreams and the vacation I hadn't realized I had desperately needed. Carlos surprised me at the Trevi Fountain with a new ring to symbolize our recommitment to each other. Our travels took us to the lapis waters of Lake Como, wine tasting at old-world vineyards in Tuscany, and to all of the historical sites in Rome. Seeing Italy through Ramiro's eyes had been an utter delight. We ate way too much gelato, devoured pasta, and drank copious amounts of espresso. For fourteen days, my mind wasn't filled with recipes or staff schedules. I checked out in the best possible way, savoring the time together with the people I loved.

On the flight home, as my head had fallen on Carlos's shoulder, he had whispered in my ear. "Julieta, you are more relaxed than I have ever seen you. Let's make a pact to get away more often, si?"

"Yes," I had replied as my eyes fought to stay open. "You'll get no argument from me on that." It was true. Since I had returned home to Ashland, I hadn't had much of a break. I'd been so focused on Torte, our family bakeshop, my staff, and managing our other endeavors—our boutique winery, Uva and summer pop-up ice cream shop, Scoops—that I hadn't taken time for myself. Italy had changed that. It had served as a reminder that I needed to take my own advice. I was constantly checking in with my team to make sure that they were practicing good self-care, but I didn't afford myself the same grace. When we returned to Ashland, I made a pact to change that. Even if it was a quick getaway to the coast or a weekend trip to San Francisco, Carlos and I needed to preserve time for ourselves. Time to recharge in order to be fully present for our customers and staff.

Don't forget that promise, Jules, I told myself on an early September morning as I arranged yeast, sugar, flour, and salt on Torte's expansive kitchen island.

We had been home from our vacation for just under a month, and Ramiro was starting school tomorrow. I couldn't believe how fast summer had flown by. It was probably because we had soaked up the time together, taking Ramiro on day trips to the Oregon Coast, Crater Lake, and the mountains.

Now it was time for routines again. School for Ramiro and baking for me. Torte had been hired to cater a corporate event that was quickly turning into much more work than I had originally anticipated. It had begun with a call from Miller Redding, a personal assistant, or as he called himself, a PA, for Bamboo, a tech company from Silicon Valley. He had reached out to me before we left for Spain and Italy about the potential of hosting an event in Ashland in September. His boss had tasked him with finding a venue and caterer for Bamboo's annual corporate leadership retreat. Ashland and Torte were at the top of his list, thanks to Arlo.

Arlo was the Oregon Shakespeare Festival's (OSF) interim managing director and Lance's boyfriend. Apparently, Bamboo had been a corporate sponsor at the last theater company Arlo had managed in LA. Miller hadn't taken much convincing. He flew up for a long weekend in early August and signed a contract on the spot for Torte to cater a "lit" (his word, not mine) corporate retreat.

The leadership team would arrive on Friday. We were hosting a dinner here at the bakeshop for them that evening. Then we would head to the Rogue River where we would prepare meals while the team went on a rafting trip. Miller had arranged for glamping yurts and a full kitchen to be set up at the campsite on the banks of the Rogue River. We would be responsible for breakfast, lunch, dinner, and snacks for the weekend rafting trip. I had catered plenty of off-site events over the years, but this was going to be a new challenge: creating high-quality, artisan fare over open flames and camp stoves.

My team had helped sketch out menus. The goal was to prep as much as we could at Torte, like breads that could be sliced for decadent raft sandwiches and breakfast French toast, as well as cookies, pies, and brownies that we could bake ahead and pack into camp. It was a bummer that the event was coinciding with Ramiro's first week of American high school. He had promised me that it was no big deal.

"Jules, I will come for the weekend when school is out and go tubing in the river. The Professor says he will teach me how to raft. It will still be warm, yeah?"

"It should be. September is my favorite month for weather," I had told him. "Warm days and cool evenings with a touch of a breeze and the first hints of changing leaves. Yes, it will be perfect for floating the river."

The Rogue River had been deemed a Wild & Scenic River in the 1960s. The vast wilderness canyon was known for its breathtakingly rugged scenery, wild salmon runs, and whitewater rafting. Adventure seekers like the group from Bamboo could raft the upper sections of the river and get their adrenaline pumping with some class III and IV rapids. But there were also plenty of lazy spots on the river for floating in inner tubes, swimming, and fly-fishing. It was the perfect opportunity for both solitude and team bonding.

Having Ramiro come with us for the weekend sounded like an ideal compromise.

With that thought in mind, I turned my attention to bread. I had been the first to arrive at the bakeshop this morning and had already gone through the opening checklist—lighting the bundles of applewood in the wood-fired oven, setting the other ovens to proofing temps, and most importantly, starting a strong pot of our Torte signature fall roast.

I tied on one of our custom fire-engine red aprons with blue stitching and a chocolate torte in the center. Not only did I want to get a head start on our bread orders for the day, but I intended to use a few loaves to test sandwich recipes for the weekend and for Ramiro's first day of school lunch. Okay, I was probably going a little overboard with packing a lunch for a high schooler, but this was my first time being a stepmom (a term I was not a fan of, by the way) and I wanted to do everything in my power to make sure that Ramiro knew this was his home, too.

Once the kitchen had hummed to life, I started the bread dough by pitching yeast and adding a touch of sugar and warm water, but not too warm. If the water temp is too high the yeast starts to die off. And no one wants a dead yeast.

While the yeast began to bubble, I measured flour. One tip that I always taught new staff members was to measure flour with a spoon. Most home bakers tend to scoop flour with a measuring cup, which doesn't give a precise measurement and can lead to packing too much flour in the cup. Instead, I would demonstrate how to spoon flour into our large measuring cups and then level the top with the edge of a knife. This would ensure a proper reading and not alter the recipe with too little or too much flour.

Once my yeast had doubled in size, I added flour and a touch of sea salt and set the mixture to knead in our industrial mixer with a dough hook. Trust me, I love to knead dough with my hands. I've found that one of the best ways to work out life's stresses—literally and figuratively—is by getting your hands deep in the dough. But sometimes on busy days, like today, letting the mixer do the heavy lifting had its advantages.

My first batch of bread was our classic white bread. I would form the dough into loaves and brush them with a generous amount of melted butter and a dusting of sea salt before they baked in the pizza oven.

Andy, our resident barista-turned-expert coffee roaster, arrived as I shifted my attention to sourdough and honey wheat bread.

"Morning, boss." He took off his puffy vest and hung it on the coatrack near the basement door. His youthful face was bright with energy. Andy was an anomaly. Most of his peers would be in bed until noon. I knew that like me he'd probably already been up for an hour tinkering with his latest coffee roast. "You can tell that fall is on the horizon. It's getting chilly out there in the morning."

"I know, I love it." I shot him a grin.

"Same." He lifted a canister of beans he had brought from home. "You're really going to love my new roast."

"What is it?" I strummed my fingers together in anticipation.

"I haven't landed on the name yet, but think of it as an ode to September." He swept his muscular arms toward the basement door. "If September could be a coffee, this is it."

"Ohhh, I can't wait to try it."

"Give me ten minutes and I'll have a taste ready for you." Andy motioned above us. He had finally grown into his height. When I had first met him, he used to walk around in a permanent slump, but as he had matured his posture had, too. It was nice to see him transforming and becoming a more confident version of himself.

He went upstairs to fire up the espresso machine and prep the coffee bar. I brushed flour from my hands and adjusted my ponytail. As I placed racks of bread in the oven to proof, I reflected on how much Andy had grown since I'd known him. He'd gone from being a slightly goofy college student to a mature young man who had a pulse on the latest trends in the coffee industry and an innate ability to create delicate and intricately flavored roasts.

The rest of the team trickled in slowly over the next hour. Marty, our resident bread expert, ambled over to my workstation after he had washed his hands and tied on a fire-engine red Torte apron.

"Uh oh, is there something you need to tell me, Jules?" His bright cheeks matched the apron. Marty was in his sixties with silver hair, a gray well-trimmed beard, and eyes that had experienced plenty of sorrow yet still held a bright spark of joy.

"No, why?" I wrinkled my forehead and looked up from the next batch of dough I had started.

"I was worried I was going to be out of a job." He pointed to the loaves resting on the island. "After all, you're baking my bread."

I let my mouth hang open and shook my head. "Never. No way. This place would crumble without you. I was just trying to get a head start and help you out because I'm going to use some extra loaves for testing recipes for this weekend's Rogue event."

"Phew." He wiped his brow. Some of the heat faded from his face.

"Marty, seriously, you know how much I appreciate you, don't you?" I met his eyes.

He smiled and winked. "I do."

Marty had come to us after his wife died. He had been a bread baker in San Francisco and moved to the Rogue Valley to be closer to family. A fortuitous ad placed at the right time had brought him out of semi-retirement and to us. I'd never been more grateful. Marty was such an asset to the team, for his bread making skills, but also for his wisdom.

Our staff swayed younger, which was a good thing in my opinion, but Marty and Rosa, our front-of-house manager, had balanced that. I liked the mixing of ages on our team. Bethany, our social media superstar, was constantly trying to convince Marty to set up an online dating profile, and he was teaching everyone how to play bocce.

"Good, because I would be lost without you, like lost-out-in-the-dense-Siskiyou-Forest without you." I poked my finger in the bouncy sourdough. "I will also gladly hand this dough off to you and get a batch of breakfast pastries going."

He tipped an imaginary cap. "Many thanks, my lady."

I chuckled and brushed flour from my hands.

Andy appeared from upstairs carrying a tray of coffee tasters. "All right, who's ready for some morning Joe?"

"Me." I raised my hand. "Always me."

Andy passed samples around to Marty, Steph, Bethany, Sterling, Rosa, and me. Then he stood back and appraised us like a zoologist studying animals in the wild. "Okay, be honest. It's a brand-new roast, so don't hold back. Give me the truth."

"What are we drinking?" Sterling held his taster beneath his nose.

"It's a bourbon, pecan Torte blend with touches of caramel and low acidity. It should be sweet with a full body." He motioned for us to try it. "That's why I want your honest opinions, though. I'm not sure if I need to tweak it a bit. Maybe add more nuttiness? Spike up the dark notes?"

I took a sip of the roast. As promised, it tasted like September in a cup. The pecan flavor came through first, followed by a hint of the sweet, buttery caramel. Rich bourbon undertones finished off the coffee. "This is incredible. I think you nailed it," I said to Andy.

He blew me off with a wave. "Come on, boss, I want the dirt. Give me the gritty feedback, too. Don't hold back. I can take it."

"I am." I looked to everyone else. "I swear, it's delicious. It tastes like fall. There's nothing I would change. The sweetness is balanced by the bourbon and the pecans give it a nice earthiness."

"Agreed," Bethany chimed in. "It's my new favorite."

"Everything is your favorite." Andy gave her a fake scowl.

"That's not true," she protested. "Remember your pepper coffee? I wasn't a fan of that, and I told you that it was a bit too much." She stuck out her tongue and grimaced. "So much pepper."

Andy gave her a sheepish look. "Yeah, okay. That's fair. I guess I just want this one to be a winner."

"Are you going to use it in a latte?" Steph asked. She had neatly arranged a stack of custom cake orders at her decorating station.

"I'm not sure yet. I'm going to play around with a couple ideas," Andy replied. "I feel like this roast stands alone.

It's an ode to September, and I'm not sure I want to dilute it, you know?"

Steph stared at her taster like she was examining a crime scene. "I actually saw a recipe last night for a cake with almost these exact flavors. It might be cool to try to pair this roast on its own with a slice of cake."

Bethany clapped. "Now you're speaking my language. That's the kind of stuff that goes viral on social. Let's do it."

"I'm intrigued by your recipe," I said. "I'm still wanting one more dessert option for the event this weekend."

"I'll find the recipe for you," Steph said as she tucked her violet hair behind her ears. "You bake it. I'll decorate it."

"Oh, yeah, we could do something super cute for fall," Bethany agreed. "Like a luscious beige buttercream with sweet bright red and green apples and fall leaves. What do you think?"

Steph nodded. "Yep. I'm with you."

Marty had moved next to the speaker system. "Since you mentioned the possible name Ode to September, how about if we kickoff the morning with some Ode to Joy?"

The swelling sounds of the melody reverberated through the kitchen.

"It's settled." I finished my coffee. "We'll collaborate on a dessert to pair with your blend."

Andy grinned. "I better get brewing then."

He went upstairs and the rest of us gathered to go over the morning schedule. September brought a slight reprieve from the crush of summer tourists. The Elizabethan stayed open through the end of October when OSF would go dark for the winter, so Ashland still saw its fair share of out-of-town visitors, but not to the same level that we experienced during the peak of summer.

"What are you thinking for today's special?" I asked Sterling. He had taken on the role of sous chef over the last couple of years and was thriving in the position. Like Andy with coffee, Sterling had a discerning palate. Food combinations came naturally to him. The only thing he lacked was professional training. Carlos, Marty, Mom, and me had all helped mentor him in that area. He was a sponge when it came to taking in knife techniques or how to embrace mise en place. I knew that soon he was going to be ready to strike out in his own. I was equally excited for him and dreading the day he would come to tell me he had landed a position running his own kitchen. It was inevitable in the business. If I did my job correctly, then there was a high likelihood that some of my staff would eventually grow their own wings and fly away from Torte's nest.

I sighed.

Don't think about that now, Jules.

"I was thinking of a creamy tomato parm soup with cheese tortellini," Sterling said. He had rolled up the sleeves on his hoodie, revealing a collection of tattoos that stretched across his forearm. "We can serve it with Marty's roasted garlic and herb flatbread."

"Count me in for that." I gave him a thumbs-up.

Bethany went through the list of custom cake orders, which she and Steph divided up. Rosa offered to make her grandmother's cinnamon sweet potato pastries as one of our breakfast specials. I took on our daily cookie and muffin offerings as well as the bourbon pecan torte, and Marty would be responsible for finishing each of our signature breads.

Within a few minutes the kitchen was alive with the aromas of fall and the sound of happy chatter amongst our team. I quickly fell into a calming rhythm as I whipped vanilla cake batter until it was light and fluffy. After a summer of adventure, I was lucky to be home and in the place I loved with people I adored. What could be better?

I added a healthy splash of bourbon and toasted pecans to the cake batter. Then I spread the batter into greased cake pans and placed them in the ovens to bake. While they baked to golden perfection, I started on a filling. Since Andy's roast had caramel undertones, I decided on a caramel buttercream.

For that, I would use our classic buttercream base. We made vats of French buttercream daily. I wanted to fold in caramel sauce to give it a richness. I melted butter in a saucepan and added in sugar, whisking the mixture until it turned golden brown. Then I removed it from the heat and stirred in sea salt and heavy cream by hand. The caramel thickened to the point that it stuck to the back of a spoon—a telltale sign it was ready.

I folded half of it into the buttercream, turning the frosting into a glossy beige color. I reserved the rest to use between the cake layers.

When the cakes had cooled, I spread on a thin layer of the caramel, followed by chopped toasted pecans and the caramel buttercream. I repeated the steps for all four layers. Then I frosted the entire cake with the remaining buttercream and placed it in the walk-in to firm up before Steph and Bethany put the finishing touches on it.

"Bread is ready for you, Jules," Marty said, as I returned from the fridge. "How many loaves do you want before I stock the upstairs and start packaging up our wholesale orders?"

"Can you spare four or five?" I asked. "I want to try a few different sandwiches and see which ones hold up the best."

"Consider these yours." Marty ran his hand over a row of bread fresh from the oven. The loaves' buttery tops glistened under the overhead lights.

"Where to start?"

"I'll leave that to you." Marty reached for a stack of our Torte paper bags and began placing loaves inside.

I went over the notes I had taken from my last call with Miller. He had been adamant that the lunches needed to be "worthy of executives." I had asked him for clarification, but he had just repeated the statement twice and reminded me that the leadership retreat was for Bamboo's top executive team who were used to the finer things in life. "It cannot be bougie enough, understood?" He had repeated it at least a dozen times.

I had to ask Steph for an official definition of bougie.

Last year their retreat had taken place at a private island in the Bahamas. "Think luxury. We need this to be top of the line," Miller had said on our last phone call.

I had tried to reiterate that rafting and camping on the Rogue wasn't exactly the textbook definition of luxury. "You realize the Rogue River is pretty rustic, right?" The river was one the most gorgeous places on the planet in my humble opinion, but it was hardly glamorous. A haven for backpackers and adventure seekers, yes. But a luxurious escape, not so much.

He had scoffed. "Listen, what I'm trying to tell you is that I need you to impress this executive team. They're used to the very best. Soggy tuna sandwiches or basic peanut butter and jelly aren't going to cut it. I hired you because I was assured that you can elevate food. I saw the photos of the park wedding you catered, and Arlo has been telling me that you're the best in town, but I cannot stress enough that no detail or expense can be spared. Got it?"

We could definitely elevate food. That was my mission in life, but the problem was that Miller would be arriving with the team. There wasn't time to do a traditional tasting and get his feedback and make any adjustments. I had been emailing him sample menus with photos, but it wasn't the same as having a client sit down and actually taste the dishes we were preparing.

After a lot of back-and-forth, we had settled on dinner for the first night. We would be serving a distinctly Northwest spread—a pear and gorgonzola salad, grilled salmon served with hazelnut rice, and marionberry cobbler for dessert. Dinner the second day would be prepared at the campsite. For that we had landed on a cowboy cookout with an assortment of sausages on handmade sourdough buns, rosemary and bacon baked beans, herb and butter grilled corn on the cob, pasta salad, and chocolate chip skillet cookies with scoops of our vanilla bean concrete on top. Breakfast would be French toast over the campfire with late summer berries, spicy egg and black bean burritos, and a fruit salad.

It was just lunch on the river that we were still trying to finalize. The main challenge was that the lunches needed to be packed because they would be taken on the rafts in coolers. At some point the river guides would steer the boats to shore and let everyone stretch their legs and take a lunch break before continuing down river to the campsite. I wanted to make sure the lunch fare was hearty but also up to Miller's high standards.

Today I was trying a third attempt at a chicken hazelnut salad sandwich with dried cranberries, tart apples, and celery. I wanted to serve it on our grain wheat bread. Then for a simpler, yet elegant option we would do a French ham and cheese on sourdough, and finally a chickpea and sweet pepper sandwich on our honey wheat. Along with the sandwiches, we were going to pack oranges, bags of kettle chips, mini carrots, and our giant cookies and brownies.

"It's like grown-up lunch boxes, Jules," Bethany said, as she peered over my shoulder.

"Good, because I'm going to send one of these to school with Ramiro tomorrow," I replied with a grin. "I need him to report back on whether or not the bread gets soggy from the chicken salad."

"Oh, that's adorable." Her dimples creased as she smiled. Bethany was our in-house cheerleader. Her upbeat attitude made it nearly impossible to be in a bad mood around her. I appreciated her authenticity. It was never a forced joy with her; it was simply her easygoing style that rubbed off on everyone. Additionally, she was an incredible baker in her own right. Mom and I had brought her on after discovering her Unbeatable Brownies at a chocolate fest. She continued to bake daily brownies for Torte, along with teaming up with Steph for custom cake design.

"As long as he doesn't get stuffed in a locker for bringing a packed lunch," I teased.

Bethany laughed. "I highly doubt that. I'm pretty sure that's an 80s movie thing. I don't think that happens anymore."

"Whew." I pretended to wipe my bow. To help protect the slices, I placed romaine lettuce between the bread and the chicken salad mixture. I also made sure to let the chicken salad chill completely before scooping it on the sandwiches.

I had Bethany take some shots of our school-box lunches for social media and for me to email to Miller. They would go on today's special board, too. As always, I was sure our faithful customers would give us constructive feedback on their favorites.

"I'll head upstairs and add these to the chalkboard," I said to her. After I'd done a quick check on how things were going in the main dining area, I went to my office to send a final email to Miller. Assuming the chicken salad held up well, I was feeling confident we had finally landed on a menu. It might not be Michelin-star worthy, but it was going to taste delicious and fit the brief for a picnic on the banks of the upper Rogue.

Miller responded right away, but not through email. My phone rang mere minutes after I had hit "send."

I recognized his number. "Hey, great minds think alike. I just sent you an email."

"I know. I read it." His voice sounded like he was on the brink of a panic attack.

"Is everything okay? How does the lunch menu sound? Like I mentioned, we're going to do a less-than-scientific poll today with our customers."

"It's fine. It's fine." His tone was dismissive.

"Okay." *What was his deal?*

"That's not why I'm calling."

My stomach dropped. I hoped he wasn't calling to tell me that the event had been cancelled. We had spent two weeks preparing for this weekend, and I had already four filets of salmon on order.

"Some stuff is going down here, if you know what I mean."

"No, I don't know what you mean."

He sighed, then lowered his voice. "Look, I can't talk right now, but let's just say that there is a lot of drama at the moment, and I need you to assure me that everything is going to be perfect when we arrive on Friday. I'm going to be tied up with other business and can't afford to have to worry about any catering details."

Miller was probably in his late twenties. I'm not always the best judge of age, but when he'd come to Ashland for our initial meeting, I guessed him to be mid- to late twenties.

He was talking as if I were a child, or this was the first time I had ever catered an event.

I tried to keep my tone calm and professional. "Understood. I wouldn't expect anything otherwise."

"Good. I'm glad we're on the same page. I don't have the bandwidth to worry about cookies and sandwiches. Bamboo is imploding and right now I'm the only person attempting to keep it together."

I wanted to ask more, but he ended our conversation abruptly.

"Look, I have to go. I'll be there at four sharp on Friday. You'll have exactly thirty minutes of my time."

I stared at the phone after he hung up. I wanted to give him the benefit of the doubt. He was working in a high-stress environment after all. Hopefully once he arrived in Ashland, he would be able to relax and soak in some of the Rogue Valley's lowkey vibe.

But what did he mean that Bamboo was imploding?

I wasn't looking forward to spending a long weekend on the river with a dysfunctional team, and I didn't like the sound of a company imploding. What had I gotten us into?